THE
NAKED
TYPIST

ALSO BY J. P. HAILEY

The Baxter Trust
The Anonymous Client
The Underground Man

THE NAKED TYPIST

BY

J. P. HAILEY

DONALD I. FINE, INC.
New York

Library of Congress Cataloging-in-Publication Data

Hailey, J. P.
　　The naked typist / by J. P. Hailey.
　　　　p.　　cm.
　　ISBN 1-55611-175-4
　　I. Title.
　　PS3558.A3275N35　1990
　　813'.54—dc20　　　　　　　　90-55022
　　　　　　　　　　　　　　　　　CIP

Manufactured in the United States of America

10 9 8 7 6 5 4 3 2 1

Designed by Irving Perkins Associates

For Lynn,
Justin and Toby

1

TRACY GARVIN FOLDED UP HER GLASSES, put her hand on her hip and said, "There's a young woman here to see you."

Steve Winslow looked up from his desk and frowned. When Tracy took off her glasses and folded them up, it usually meant she was annoyed at him. In this instance, Steve couldn't imagine why. An unexpected client showing up and wanting to see him could hardly be considered his fault. Unless it was Judy Meyers, the actress who was Steve Winslow's off-again, on-again girlfriend. That would explain it. Tracy Garvin's attitude toward her was catty at best. But Tracy knew Judy. If it were her, she'd have said so.

So what was it?

Steve put down the paper he'd been reading. "What does she want?"

Tracy shook her head. "She wouldn't say. Only that it's urgent and she wants to talk to you personally."

"All right. Show her in."

Tracy didn't move.

"What's the matter?"

Tracy took a breath. "I didn't point out to her how lucky she was that she happened to come by this afternoon."

"What do you mean?"

"If she'd come by any other afternoon this week you wouldn't have been here."

"I know. I have a new passion. I'm learning to play golf."

1

"I'm happy for you."

"Tracy, what's the problem?"

Tracy took another breath. "The problem is you haven't had a client in months. And not that there haven't been any. You've just turned them all down."

"I have a client."

"Who?"

"Sheila Benton. Her annual retainer pays for this office, pays your salary and gives me enough to get by. Basically, that *is* my law practice. Anything else is just gravy."

"That's not the point."

"What's the point?"

"The point is, there's no gravy. The Jeremy Dawson case has been over for months. You haven't had a client since."

"Is that my fault?"

"As I said, it's not that there haven't been any. You've just turned them all down."

"I don't defend drug dealers."

"They weren't all drug dealers."

"No, there was that vehicular homicide. The boy did it. You think I should have got him off just cause his old man's rich?"

"No, but—"

"Then there was the guy shot his wife because she was sleeping around. You think I should have gone to court and plead the unwritten law? Boom, boom, kill the harlot?"

"No, but—"

"Tracy, I haven't been turning down clients just to give you a hard time. The problem is, there's no work, so you sit in the office and read murder mysteries all day and it clouds your thinking. Real life isn't like that. A case like Jeremy Dawson doesn't come along every day."

"I know that."

"I know you know that. What I don't know is why you're bringing this up now."

"Oh."

"Well?"

Tracy ran her hand over her head, pushed the long blonde hair out of her eyes. "Well, this woman—her name's Kelly Blaine—I just know you're going to turn her down."

Steve's eyes narrowed. "Why?"

"Well," Tracy said, "she did tell me a little about the case. I mean, generally."

"And?"

Tracy bit her lip. "Well," she said, "she's a typist, and she was fired from her job."

Steve shook his head. "I don't do management/labor disputes."

"I know that, I know that," Tracy said quickly. "But there's more to it than that. I gather she was also subjected to unwanted attentions."

"I don't do sexual harassment either."

"I know that."

Steve looked at her, smiled, shook his head. "Tracy, we're not communicating. I know you. You're not really interested in sexual discrimination cases, either. You'll pardon me, but you have a storybook mentality. For some reason this woman interests you. What is it?"

"Well," Tracy said, "for one thing, she's barefoot."

Steve frowned. That was something. In New York City, no one goes barefoot. "Are you sure?" Steve said. "She couldn't be walking the streets barefoot. Maybe she has her shoes in her purse."

"She hasn't got a purse."

"No?"

"No. And she's wearing an overcoat."

Steve frowned. "An overcoat? In this weather?"

"Yes."

"She didn't take it off when she came in?"

"No. And it's too big for her, too. It's a man's overcoat."

Steve looked at Tracy sideways. "You set me up for this, didn't you? All that preamble about there being no work and me turning clients down. That's why you want me to take her case. There's a punch line to all this, isn't there?"

Tracy grinned, nodded. "Yes, there is."

"Well, what is it?"

"I think she's naked."

2

TRACY GARVIN HELD THE DOOR OPEN as Kelly Blaine padded bare-foot into the office and settled into the clients' chair. She started to cross her legs, thought better of it, pulled the overcoat around her and smoothed it down over her knees.

Steve Winslow had stood up to introduce himself when she came in, but so far she had avoided his eyes. Steve sat back down and sized her up.

Kelly Blaine was an attractive woman, somewhere in her early twenties. She wasn't at all what Steve had imagined. But that, he realized, was wholly based on Tracy's statement that the woman might be nude. Steve's mind had immediately leaped to topless dancers, nude models, hookers. He'd unconsciously been expect-ing a woman with exaggerated makeup, false eyelashes, heavy eye shadow, red lipstick, too much blush. A woman exuding bla-tant sexuality.

Kelly Blaine was none of that. Her makeup, if any, was light and natural. Her brown hair was cut short and stylish, conser-vatively so. But looks, Steve knew, could be deceiving. His own secretary, with sweater and blue jeans and long blonde hair fall-ing in her face, looked more like a college student than a legal secretary. And he, in T-shirt, corduroy jacket and blue jeans, with shoulder-length dark hair, looked more like a refuge from the sixties than a lawyer.

Kelly Blaine looked up at him and their eyes met. He could see

4

doubt in hers. Steve was used to that. He was *not* used to women sitting in his office barefoot in an overcoat.

"Miss Blaine, is it?" Steve said.

"Yes."

He motioned to Tracy Garvin, who drew up a chair and sat down. "My secretary tells me you were fired."

"That's right."

"Is that what you want to see me about?"

"Partly."

"That's good, because I don't do management/labor disputes."

"This isn't a dispute."

Steve smiled. "It was an amicable firing?"

"Hardly."

"Would you care to explain?"

Kelly Blaine took a breath. "All right. I was working for Milton Castleton."

"Who is that?"

She frowned. "You're an attorney and you've never heard of Milton Castleton?"

"I haven't been an attorney long. And I have an unusual practice. Basically, I handle one client."

She frowned. "But aren't you the one? The one who got the Dawson boy off?"

"Occasionally I make exceptions. Jeremy Dawson was one of them."

"Fine. Then I'm asking you to make one in my case."

"I'm not promising anything, but I'm willing to listen. Now," Steve said, "I'm who you thought I was—whatever that means. I've never heard of Milton Castleton—whoever he is. If that makes a difference to you, you should go see someone else. I don't do corporate work. I don't do management/labor. I don't do domestic hassles. If I take on a case, it's generally murder. If this case is the result of you being fired, it probably won't interest me, and I tell you that in advance. If you want to tell me about it, I'm here and I'm willing to listen. But if you just want to get me on the defensive by making me feel inadequate for not knowing who Milton Castleton is, frankly you're wasting your time and mine."

Kelly Blaine drew herself up, stuck out her chin. "That's not it. You're who I want. You fight for the little guy. The rest doesn't matter. I couldn't go to another law office anyway. They'd laugh me out of there."

"Why?"

She ran her hand over her face. "Because it's bizarre. The whole situation's bizarre."

Steve shifted impatiently in his chair.

She held up her hand. "Okay, okay. But first off, you don't know who Milton Castleton is. Well, he's rich. Stinking rich. He's a wealthy industrialist. Castleton Industries. That's how you would have heard of him. Anyway, he's retired now—he's close to eighty—and his son runs the business."

"Who's his son?"

She waved it away. "Stanley Castleton. But that's not important. Anyway, Milton's an old man. He's retired and he's writing his memoirs."

"His memoirs?"

"Yeah. Apparently in his day he was quite a character. Aside from being a cutthroat businessman—and he was certainly that— he was something of a rake hell. Women, booze, gambling. Lots of messy affairs involving court actions—paternity suits, breach of promise, named correspondent in half a dozen divorces."

"And you worked for him," Steve said, gently urging her to the point.

"That's right. As I said, he was writing his memoirs. I was hired as a secretary to type them."

"Oh, so you were working with him on the memoirs?"

"No. Actually, I never met the man."

Steve frowned. "What?"

"I never met him. I was hired by his business associate. Or business manager, or personal manager, or whatever. That was never quite clear."

"You're saying you transcribed his notes but you never actually met him?"

"Not his notes. His dictation. He dictated onto microcassettes. I typed them up."

"Where? At your apartment?"

"No. At his."

Steve took a breath. "I'm sorry, but this is really not making any sense."

"I know, I know," she said. "That's 'cause it *is* so bizarre. That's why I couldn't go to another lawyer. I worked in his apartment. That was the arrangement. But I never met the man. I had my own office. His business associate let me in and let me out. I never even knew if Milton Castleton was actually there."

"And you were fired," Steve prompted.

"Yes."

"When?"

"Today. This afternoon. Just now."

"And you came straight here."

"Yes. Well, I have to explain the situation. And it's not easy. As I said, I never met Castleton, never knew when he was there. But I assume he was, because that was the whole idea." She took a breath. "I had my own office. There, in his apartment. It was right next door to his office. But there was no connecting door. There were separate entrances—which is why I never saw him. His business associate, Phil Danby his name is, let me in in the morning. I'd go into my office. I'd close and lock the door. I'd be alone. The notes to be transcribed would already be on my desk. I'd take them and type them up. All straightforward and professional."

She bit her lip, lowered her eyes. "Except for one thing."

"What's that?"

"I typed them nude."

Steve blinked. "I beg your pardon?"

"I was nude. When I came in to work, I'd take off my clothes, hang them in the closet, sit down and start typing."

Steve found himself at a loss as to what to say next. He took a breath. "I see," he said. Which was hopelessly inadequate on the one hand and not true on the other. "No, actually I don't. What was the point? I mean, if you were alone, locked in this room . . . why were you supposed to do that?"

"There was a window. Between the two offices. You know, one-way glass. On my side it was a mirror. The other side, from his office, you could see through."

"You mean—"

"Yes. He could sit at his desk and watch me type."

"As well as anyone else who was in his office."

"No. That was specified. There would not be business meet-ings with him saying, 'Oh, have you seen my secretary,' if that's what you're thinking. That was made very clear. It would be just him."

"And you agreed to this arrangement?"

"Yes."

"Had you done anything of the kind before? Posed as a nude model, for instance?"

"No."

"Then why did you agree to this?"

"I resent the question."

"What?"

Kelly Blaine stuck out her chin. "I resent that. You sit there taking a high moral tone. What do you make—two, three hun-dred bucks an hour? You know what I make as a typist? Ten to fifteen. For this job I got paid a hundred bucks an hour. It was work and I took it. If you want to sit there being high and mighty, making moral judgments, well, I know whose side you're on, I might as well leave. The fact is, I took the job. You really want me to justify why?"

Steve held up his hand. "I'm sorry. I didn't mean to offend you. But you must admit, this whole thing is very unusual. I'm a human being. I'm naturally curious and I'm trying to understand the situation. Which, frankly, isn't easy." Steve smiled. "We have a peculiar situation here. You're touchy, embarrassed and defen-sive on the one hand. I'm intrigued, embarrassed and tentative on the other. We're both of us walking on eggshells. As a result, we're getting absolutely nowhere. So, let's try to set that aside and discuss this as if it were a normal, ordinary business deal, okay?"

"Fine."

"At any rate, you agreed to this employment?"

"Yes."

"When did you start work?"

"Two weeks ago."

"You've been working there for two weeks?"

"Yes."

"Same routine every day?"

"Yes."

"And you never saw your boss, this Castleton fellow?"

"No."

"How did you get the job?"

"I answered an ad."

"What ad?"

"In the *New York Times*."

"They advertised this in the *Times?*"

"Yes."

"As what?"

"Under 'Help wanted, female.' "

It was with an effort that Steve suppressed a grin. "Did the ad specify the requirements of the job?"

"No."

"Or the rate of pay?"

"No. It just said, 'salary negotiable.' "

"So you answered the ad and what happened?"

"I went for an interview."

"Who was the interview with?"

"Phil Danby."

"Where was it?"

"There. At the apartment."

"You didn't see Castleton then?"

"No. As I said, I've never seen him."

"So what happened?"

"Danby explained the requirements of the job."

"And you took it?"

"Yes."

"Fine," Steve said. "That was two weeks ago?"

"Yes."

"You started work immediately?"

"The next day."

"Did you have a contract?"

"Contract?"

"Yes. A written contract. With the terms of your employment."

"No."

"How were you paid?"

"In cash."

"You trusted him to pay cash?"

She shook her head. "No. It was in advance."

"Paid how?"

"On a daily basis. When I'd get to work in the morning there'd be an envelope on my desk with my name on it. In it would be my wages for the day."

"Which was?"

"Eight hundred dollars. A hundred bucks an hour for eight hours."

"Then you were fired?"

"Yes."

"When?"

"I told you. Today. Just before I came here."

"Were you paid for today?"

"Yes, of course. Or I wouldn't have started typing. I came in this morning as usual. The envelope was on my desk. I took the money, put it in my purse. Then I went to work."

"And what happened?"

"I was sitting at my desk, typing. Out of the corner of my eye I saw the door opening."

"I thought it was locked."

"It was. But of course they had the key. Stupid, but I never thought of that. I mean, I'd locked the door, no one had ever tried to open it—I thought, fine, the door's locked. But of course you can open it from the outside with a key."

"And someone did?"

"Yes."

"Who?"

"Phil Danby."

"This ever happen before?"

"No. Never."

"So what happened?"

"I looked up and the door was opening. I hadn't heard it. I hadn't heard the click of the lock because I had my ear phones on, transcribing."

"What did you do?"

"I was shocked. Terrified. I ripped the headset off, scrunched down at the desk behind my typewriter. Tried to cover myself. This wasn't supposed to be happening."

"Go on."

"The door opened and Phil Danby came in. I couldn't believe it. I screamed at him, 'Hey, get out of here!' "

"What did he do?"

"He acted like he hadn't heard me. He just stood there a moment, then he turned and closed the door."

"Then what?"

"I screamed at him again. But he just stood there. Then he smiled. The most smug, horrible smile. Then he walked over toward the desk."

"What did you do?"

"I felt helpless. I couldn't just sit there, but I didn't want to get up either. I was horrified, embarrassed. I was covering myself as best I could. I got up from the chair, crouched behind the desk. I started screaming. Screaming for Mr. Castleton.

"Then he reached out and grabbed me. Grabbed me by the wrist. He said, 'The boss ain't here today. It's just you and me.' "

"What did you do?"

"I slapped him. Slugged him hard. That startled him and he let go. I ran to the closet to get my clothes. I just got the door open when he came up behind me, slammed it shut, tried to grab me again."

"Then what?"

"I slapped him again. Tried to knee him in the balls. I missed, but he got the idea. His face changed. Before it was gloating. Now it was angry. He said, 'You little bitch.' He grabbed me by the arms and dragged me. I was screaming, crying. Before I knew what was happening, he'd jerked open the door and pushed me out of the office."

"You're kidding."

"No. There I was in the hallway of the apartment. With this maniac grabbing me. I screamed for help, but there was no one there. I knew he had servants, a cook, a maid, what have you, but nobody came.

"I broke free, ran down the hall. He caught me in the foyer, right by the front door. He said, 'Uppity bitch,' and slammed me against the wall. Then he jerked the door open and pushed me out."

Steve stared at her. "What?"

"That's right."

"He threw you out into the hall?"

"Yes."

"Naked?"

"Yes."

"And locked the door?"

"That's right."

Steve ran his hand over his head. "Good god."

Kelly Blaine took a breath, calmed herself down. "Yes. So there I was in the hallway of this apartment building, and I couldn't get back in and I couldn't go out and I thought I was gonna die."

"So what did you do?"

"I couldn't just stand there. I had to hide somewhere. I went down the hallway, looking for help. I found the door to the stairs. So I went in there. The door closed behind me. It's the type of door that's locked from the inside. So there I was, trapped in the stairwell. I didn't know what to do. I was almost hysterical. I went down the stairwell, trying all the doors. They were all locked. Even the one to the lobby. Not that I wanted to get out into the lobby, if you know what I mean.

"Anyway, there was another flight down. I took it. The door there was unlocked. It led into the basement. Thank god there wasn't anyone around.

"I searched the place, found a storage closet." She touched the fabric of the overcoat. "This coat was hanging in it. What a relief that was. I put this on, looked around for a way out. I found a back stairs that was unlocked. And I got out of there.

"So there I was, out on the street with no clothes, no money, nothing. I walked home. Twenty blocks. I didn't have my keys, but the super would let me in. Only he wasn't home. I didn't know what to do. I was getting hysterical. I needed help.

"Then I thought of you. I remembered reading about you in the papers. A lawyer, yes, but not what you think of as a lawyer. I'm sorry, I don't mean to be insulting. I'm saying it badly. What I mean is, you're not just concerned with legalities. You help people. I need help."

She paused, took a breath, looked up at him with pleading eyes. "Can you help me?"

Out of the corner of his eye, Steve Winslow could see Tracy Garvin looking at him. From the look on her face, he knew that if he said no he would be in serious trouble.

Not that he had any intention of saying no.

"What is it you want?" he said.

She stared at him. What a stupid question. "Are you kidding? I want my clothes. I want my purse. With my keys in it, so I can get into my apartment."

"I understand," Steve said. "But it goes a little deeper than that. There are several legal ramifications here. On the one hand, you've been unjustly terminated from your job. You've been fired without cause and without notice. And you've been humiliated and forced out in the street with no wherewithal. All of which gives you a cause of action against your employer.

"On the other hand, you've been the victim of a sexual assault. Which means you could file criminal charges as well. When I say What do you want, I mean there are various avenues we could take on this, and we have to explore the possibilities."

"I don't give a damn about the legal ramifications. I'm sitting here in a goddamn overcoat. I want my clothes and I want my purse."

"I understand. The question is how do we go about getting them back. Are we threatening to file criminal charges, a civil suit—"

"File?" she said. "What are you talking about, file? I don't care about long legal procedures. I want my clothes back now."

"And I'm going to try to get them," Steve said. "But we have to consider possibilities. First off, I'm going to get your clothes back this afternoon. In the event that I don't, the gentlemen in question will find they've bought themselves a great deal of trouble. If they do, we have to prepare for that contingency.

"Tracy, can you see about getting Miss Blaine some clothes?"

"Of course."

"I want my own clothes."

"I understand. But if they won't give them up, we can't have you running around naked. We'll get you clothes. We'll contact the super in your building and get you a new key. That's just if worse comes to worst. Meanwhile, I'm going to put some pressure on these guys and see what I can do for you now. Before I do, I wanna know how you want to play this. Do you want to file criminal charges against this Phil Danby?"

"No."

"That's fine, but I don't have to tell 'em that. I may have to threaten them with it to get your clothes. Now, with regard to the civil suit—"

"I don't want to file a civil suit either."

"Neither do I, but that's not the point. This man is a millionaire. He's done you irreparable harm. If I go in, talking civil suit, he's apt to offer a compromise to avoid litigation. Particularly considering the circumstances of the case. It's not the sort of thing he'd like to have made public. If he offers a settlement, how much would you be willing to take?"

"I don't want a settlement."

"Right," Steve said, somewhat impatiently. "You want your clothes. You're gonna get 'em, but in addition they're gonna compensate you for the humiliation you went through. From your point of view, how much would be enough?"

"I don't care."

"Maybe not, but I do. I'm a lawyer, not an errand boy. If I do this for you, I have to be paid."

"I have money."

"I wouldn't touch it. If anybody pays me, it's gonna be them. I'll take your case, but only on a contingency basis. If they give us a settlement, I get a third. The rest goes to you."

"Fine. Whatever."

"There's one thing I want you to understand. To settle this, we have to release them from all damages. That's why you should think about this. To accomplish anything, you'll have to sign a release. That release will be legal and binding. Once you've signed it and they've accepted it, if you change your mind and want to sue them for damages, you can't do it. You can't go after them again. You understand that?"

"Of course. That's fine. I don't mind."

Steve looked at her a few moments. "All right," he said. "Tracy. I want you to type up a release for me. Have it release Milton Castleton and Phil Danby from all claims of damages resulting from the employment and termination of said employment of Miss Kelly Blaine."

"Certainly," Tracy said. She stood up.

"One minute. First get me Milton Castleton on the phone." Steve looked at Kelly Blaine. "What's his number?"

"I don't know."

"You don't know?"

"It's not like I éver had to call there. I have his number. It's in my purse."

"Right," Steve said. "All right. Call information. See if they have a Milton Castleton listed."

Tracy called information, asked for the listing. She frowned and hung up the phone. "It's unlisted," she said.

"That figures," Steve said. "Get me Mark Taylor."

Tracy called the Taylor Detective Agency, said, "Steve Winslow for Mark Taylor." She listened a moment, then handed Steve the phone.

"Mark, Steve."

"Yeah, Steve. What's up?"

"Milton Castleton."

"What about him?"

"You know him?"

"I know who he is."

"Fine. He's got an unlisted phone number. I want it."

"No sweat. Hang on."

There was a pause and Steve could hear Taylor shouting at someone. A minute later he was back on the line with the number.

"Anything else?" Taylor asked.

"That's it," Steve said, and hung up the phone. He turned to Tracy Garvin. "Okay. Get going on that release. Take her with you. Check the details with her."

Tracy nodded. There was no reason she needed Kelly Blaine to make up the release. She realized Steve just wanted her out of the room while he made the call.

Kelly Blaine got up to go. Steve picked up the phone. Kelly Blaine turned back in the doorway. "I have to warn you," she said. "He's going to give you a hard time."

Steve smiled grimly. "That's where you're wrong."

3

THE MAN WHO OPENED THE DOOR was plump, bald, wore horn-rimmed glasses and a three-piece suit. "Yes?" he said.

"Phil Danby?" Steve asked.

"Yes. And who are you?"

Steve gave him a look. "I spoke to you on the phone. The doorman downstairs just called you to ask if he could send me up. Who the hell do you think I am?"

"You're Steve Winslow?"

"Yes."

"You don't look like a lawyer."

"You don't look like a rapist, either."

Danby frowned. "If that's the tack you're going to take—"

"No, it isn't," Steve said. "I don't feel like sparring in the hallway. Where's your boss?"

"Mr. Castleton is in his office."

"Let's see him."

Phil Danby stood glaring at Steve for a moment. His problem was clear. Since Castleton had agreed to see Winslow, it was his job to bring Steve in. But with Steve ordering him to do so, he didn't want to do it.

Danby took a breath. He stepped aside, let Steve in and closed the door. Without a word, he turned and walked down the hallway. Steve followed.

Danby stopped before a closed doorway, knocked twice, pushed it open. Steve followed him in.

It was a large office. At first glance it appeared to be a stage set, a period piece set somewhere in the thirties or forties. It was wood-paneled, with Persian rugs on the floor. There was a large marble fireplace. Solid oak furniture. It occurred to Steve that Bogart could have walked into such an office and found a body lying on the floor.

Or gotten sapped. In spite of himself, Steve glanced over his shoulder. But there were no unseen henchmen behind the door. Danby was it. Steve turned back to the room.

Dominating the office was a massive oak desk. Seated behind it in a high-backed desk chair was a frail wisp of a man. He was completely bald. His face was incredibly thin. His cheeks and eyes were sunken. His skin was stretched tight and was almost translucent, giving him the appearance of a skeleton.

That was Steve Winslow's first thought. That the man was dead. That Milton Castleton had been dead for years, that his body had been propped up at this desk here and that Phil Danby, the loyal and trusted associate, was nothing more than a fat Tony Perkins, psychotically maintaining the fiction that his boss was still alive.

Then the eyes in the skeleton moved. The lips moved, and a reedy voice said, "Come in."

Steve walked up to the desk.

The lips moved again. "Sit down."

Steve sat. As he did, he noticed Phil Danby had moved in and was standing to the left of the desk.

Castleton's eyes flicked to Danby, then back to Steve. "Talk."

"I'm Steve Winslow. I'm representing Kelly Blaine."

Castleton looked Steve up and down. "Are you with Legal Aid?"

"No."

"No?"

"I have a private practice."

Castleton frowned. "That's bad."

"Why?"

"If you have a private practice, you must be good. You look like a jerk. If you can dress like that and still get clients, you must be pretty sharp. Which means you're going to give me a hard time."

Castleton smiled. "I don't like sharp lawyers who give me a hard time."

"My client's the one who had the hard time."

"So you say." Castleton sighed. "All right. Let's have it."

"Miss Blaine worked for you."

There was a pause. Castleton said nothing.

"Do you concede Kelly Blaine worked for you?"

Milton Castleton smiled. "Concede?" he said. He shook his head. "I was right. You lawyers. Always want to sound like you're winning. Concede. I don't concede anything. Kelly Blaine worked for me. If that's a concession, I'll eat it."

"Miss Blaine left your employment today."

"So I understand."

"You weren't here?"

"No, I was not."

"The circumstances of her leaving were unfortunate."

"They always are."

"Some more than others. In this case, Miss Blaine was frightened into leaving. So much so that she left some of her possessions behind."

"Is that right?"

"Yeah, that's right."

Milton Castleton nodded. "I will have to look into the matter. Thank you for bringing it to my attention."

Steve Winslow stared at Castleton a moment. The emaciated face was bland, composed. There was an innocent serenity about him, like some elderly relative who had been propped up in the drawing room to have tea with the family but who had no idea what was really going on.

Which was disconcerting. Steve Winslow had come prepared to fight. But Milton Castleton's indifference left him with nothing to push against. Steve knew it was a charade, an act, a business tactic on Castleton's part. Still, it was hard to deal with.

Steve pulled himself together. Never mind the guy looks half-dead. This is not a kindly old relative. This is a dirty old man.

Steve glanced around. On one side wall there was a huge computer system that seemed anachronistic in that office. On the other side wall there was a rectangular curtain. It was shut. Steve got up, walked over to it, yanked it open.

Behind it was a picture window overlooking the adjoining office. The room was dark, but still Steve could make out the desk and chair lined up directly in front of the curtained window.

Steve was surprised. He realized that in hearing Kelly Blaine's story he had envisioned a desk with a typewriter. Instead, a CRT screen with a keyboard sat on the desk. Kelly Blaine naturally had worked on a word processor.

Steve Winslow turned back to Castleton. "Let's cut the charade." He jerked his thumb at the window. "Kelly Blaine told me the details of her employment. And the details of her leaving it. They are not pleasant. You have her clothes and you have her purse. I want those and I want compensation."

"Oh?" Castleton said. "Compensation for what? She wasn't fired, she quit."

"I'm not talking about severance pay."

"Oh? Then what are you talking about?"

Steve took a breath. "Let's cut the shit, Mr. Castleton. Let's talk about the window in the wall and the fact the woman was working nude."

Castleton's eyebrows raised. "Is that your angle? Is that your idea—blackmail? Mr. Winslow, there's nothing you can say about me that's not already been said. You wanna make a stink about the manner in which my secretary dressed, you'll only hurt her, not me. Frankly, I don't give a damn."

"Oh yeah?" Steve said. He jerked his thumb at Phil Danby. "What about him?"

"What *about* him?"

"He's your employee?"

"I'm sure he prefers the term business associate, but yes, if you want to call him that."

"As his employer, you're responsible for his actions."

"So?"

"In this instance we have a case of sexual harassment, sexual assault, attempted rape. My client was subjected to violence and the threat of bodily harm. She was humiliated and ejected from your premises with no wherewithal whatsoever—in fact, stark naked. Her cause of action against you for emotional and mental stress alone could run in the millions of dollars."

Castleton frowned. "Phil, what is this man talking about?"

Danby shrugged. "I have no idea."

"Oh really?" Steve said. "Are you denying you threw my client out of this apartment earlier today?"

Castleton held up his hand. "Now, Phil, you don't have to answer his questions. You are responsible only to me. So for my benefit, rather than his, would you please tell me what happened this afternoon."

"It's just as I told you before."

"Tell me again."

"Very well. I was in your office going over some documents when the buzzer rang."

"Buzzer?" Steve said.

"Yes," Danby said. He shot a look at Castleton. "I suppose I should explain." He turned to Steve. "There is no phone in the secretary's office, no intercom, no means of communication. Which is fine, because there's no need for any communication.

"Unless, of course, something goes wrong. A technical problem with the computer. Or the cassette recorder. Something like that. In that event, the typist needs to contact us. And she is under instructions not to leave the room and wander the apartment. So, in the event that she needs something, she can buzz us to open the door."

Danby shrugged. "And that's what happened. The buzzer went off. I figured it was a computer glitch, or something, I needed to fix. There's no connecting door. Only one door to the secretary's office. So I went out in the hallway, took my key and unlocked the door."

"And what happened then?" Castleton asked.

"I opened the door and Miss Blaine was standing there naked. Well, that was a shock. The typists have strict instructions. In the event something was wrong and they needed help they were to be fully dressed before they buzzed. Kelly Blaine had not done that. I was, of course, shocked and embarrassed, and I didn't know what she was doing.

"But I found out. She came on to me. I'd told her Mr. Castleton was going to be away for the day. And she said since he wasn't here there was no reason we shouldn't take a break together."

"Bullshit," Steve said.

Castleton held up his hand. "Let's hear the rest."

"Well," Danby said. "That was it. Mr. Castleton has strict rules. And that was one of them. A man in his position, it's only natural people would try to take advantage of him. Put him in a compromising situation.

"She'd been told this. She knew at the slightest bit of an indiscretion she'd be out. I guess she figured I wouldn't tell.

"She figured wrong. I told her so. Mr. Castleton would know of this and she was through.

"And she went crazy. Screaming, kicking, crying, hysterical. I tried to calm her down, but there was nothing I could do. The woman had lost it. She pushed by me, actually knocked me down, and ran out of the office. I got up and ran out in the hall just in time to see the front door close. By the time I got to the door, she was gone.

"And that's it," he said. "I suppose you being a lawyer, in some way you figure all that's Mr. Castleton's fault."

Steve paid no attention. He stared straight at Castleton. "Is he finished?"

"Are you finished?" Castleton asked.

"Yes, I am."

"He's finished."

"Fine," Steve said. "Are you going to let me cross-examine?"

"Certainly not."

"My client's story is that she never sounded the bell for assistance. Suddenly the door opened, this man appeared in the room, made sexual advances at her, abused her physically and forced her to flee the apartment."

Castleton nodded. "Naturally she would say something like that."

"Since you won't let me cross-examine Mr. Danby, my only alternative is to file suit and get you into court so I *can* cross-examine Mr. Danby."

Steve Winslow got up and started for the door.

"Stop." The word was like a whiplash, even from that reedy voice.

Steve Winslow stopped, turned around, "Yes?"

"Come back."

Steve walked back to the desk.

Castleton looked up at him. "Your suit has no merit. However, I'm an old man and I have no wish to be dragged into court. I also feel sorry for the girl, misguided though she may be. What will it take to make this thing go away?"

"Immediate possession of her clothes and purse, plus a sizable cash settlement."

"I'm willing,to be reasonable if you are," Castleton said. "The woman walked off her job and is entitled to nothing. However, I'm willing to consider she was terminated and give her two weeks severance pay. At a hundred bucks an hour, that comes to eight thousand dollars."

Steve Winslow shook his head. "You're not even in the ballpark. We're talking about a million-dollar suit here."

"A million dollars?" Castleton said. "No, no. I'm not talking about what you'd file for. I'm talking about what you'd settle for."

"You mean right now? Cash in hand?"

"That's right."

"A hundred thousand dollars."

"Dream on. My offer is eight thousand dollars. Take it or leave it."

"Fine. I'll leave it."

Steve turned to go.

"Without consulting your client?"

Steve stopped. "My client won't take eight thousand dollars."

"So you say. Why not let her make that decision?"

Steve frowned. He didn't want to make any concessions to Castleton, but if he walked out now it would be without her clothes and purse. "May I use your phone?"

"Certainly."

Steve walked to the desk, picked up the phone, punched in the number.

Tracy answered.

"It's me," Steve said. "Put Kelly on." There was a moment, then her voice came on the line. "This is Steve Winslow," he said. "I'm in Castleton's office. He's offered us a settlement. Two weeks salary—eight thousand dollars."

"And my clothes and purse?"

"Yes."

"Take it."

"That's what I thought you'd say," Steve said. He hung up the phone and turned to Castleton. "Your offer is rejected. See you in court."

Steve turned and headed for the door.

"Hold on, hold on," Castleton said impatiently.

Steve stopped. Turned back.

Castleton glared at him. "Can't we negotiate without these theatrics?"

"I wasn't aware we were negotiating," Steve said.

"Of course we are," Castleton said. "I have no desire to go to court, and neither have you. Let's settle the damn thing."

"Fine," Steve said. "Write me a check for a hundred thousand dollars."

"Don't be silly," Castleton said, irritably. "I'm willing to pay for the nuisance value, but within reason. Twenty-five thousand for a full release."

"You're talking about the civil suit," Steve said. "There are criminal charges here as well."

"You can't negotiate criminal charges. That would be unethical."

"Not to mention illegal," Steve said. "I'm not negotiating them. I'm just mentioning them to show you that the situation is somewhat complicated."

"Not for me," Castleton said. "If your client has some problem with Phil Danby, that's between him and her."

"Yes and no," Steve said. "Considering the requirements of the employment, requirements initiated by you, I think you might find yourself at the very least an accessory to such charges as rape, assault, what have you."

"Nonsense," Castleton said.

Steve shrugged. "Probably. But, as you say, that's neither here nor there. We're discussing the civil suit here, not the criminal charge. We're certainly not negotiating that. That would be compounding a felony and conspiring to conceal a crime. Something you and I would never dream of doing.

"Of course, that's assuming criminal charges are brought at all.

And from a legal standpoint, having reached a settlement with you in the civil suit and having given you a full release from any or all damages arising from the employment, Kelly-Blaine would be hard-pressed to come up with any grounds for pressing criminal charges in this matter."

Steve waved his hands. "But that's not what we're discussing. By all means, let's talk settlement."

"You have my offer. Twenty-five thousand."

"And you have mine."

"Yes. A hundred thousand. If you're not going to budge from it, there's nothing to talk about and we'll see you in court."

Steve smiled. "Did I say that, Mr. Castleton? We're all businessmen here. You've come up. I'll come down. Seventy-five thousand and call it a day."

Castleton shook his head. "Out of the question."

"Okay," Steve said. "I think the situation's clear. We have figures on the table neither one of us can live with. We need to come up with a compromise figure, or go to court."

"Such as?"

Steve shook his head. "Your move. I just came down to seventy-five, remember?"

"That's not even close."

Steve sighed. "We have a problem here. The way I see it, the only issue here is how many more bids it's gonna take us to get to fifty grand. You don't wanna say fifty because you're afraid if you do I'll say seventy and then we'll be arguing between those two figures trying to split at sixty. And I don't want to say fifty because then you'll say thirty and we'll be arguing between those two figures trying to split at forty." Steve threw up his hands. "It's a no-win situation. The way I see it, we could be here all day. So I'm not naming a figure. I'm suggesting if *you* named the figure fifty thousand, it might end negotiations."

"Are you stating such is the case?"

"Not at all. I'm talking tentatively and hypothetically."

"All right. Talking tentatively and hypothetically then, if I named the figure fifty thousand, would you accept it?"

"If you named it, yes."

"All right. Fifty thousand dollars, take it or leave it. Do we have a deal?"

"In principle."

Castleton frowned. "What do you mean, in principle?"

"The cash compromise is satisfactory. But the deal is predicated on my receiving Kelly Blaine's clothes and purse."

"And upon you furnishing me with a blanket release."

"Certainly," Steve said. He reached into his jacket pocket, pulled out the papers, handed them over.

Castleton glanced at the papers just long enough to verify what they were, then nodded to Danby. "Get it."

Danby turned and walked out the door with the air of a trained dog doing a trick. Castleton buried his head in the papers. He was still reading when Danby came back, carrying a purse and a shopping bag. He started to give them to Steve Winslow, but Castleton held up his hand. "One moment. I'm not done."

Castleton finished the last page, set the papers down. "All right, give him the stuff."

Steve took the shopping bag and the purse, walked over to a small table and set them down to examine them. In the shopping bag he found a skirt, sweater, bra, panties, stockings and shoes. The purse was of fabric rather than leather, a soft, flexible bag pulled closed with a drawstring that doubled as a shoulder strap. Steve spread the top open, reached in and examined the contents. He found the usual junk—tissues, lipstick, pens, paper, what have you. He also found a set of keys, a change purse with thirty-eight dollars and change in it, and a white envelope with Kelly Blaine's name on it and eight one-hundred-dollar bills inside.

Steve looked up from the purse. "Where's the wallet?"

"What?" Castleton said.

"There's no wallet. There's a change purse with money, but no wallet."

Castleton looked at Danby. "Phil?"

Danby shrugged. "Then she didn't have one. I assure you, her purse has not been touched."

"There's your answer," Castleton said.

"I have to check with my client," Steve said.

He walked over to the desk, picked up the phone, called the office and had Tracy put Kelly Blaine on the wire.

"Did you get it?" she asked breathlessly.

"Mr. Castleton and I have reached an agreement. I have your clothes and purse."

"Oh, thank God."

"There's one problem. I checked the purse. Your keys are in it, and your change purse and your day's pay. But your wallet isn't."

"That's all right, I left it at home."

"Fine," Steve said. "See you soon."

Steve hung up before she could ask any questions. He turned back to Milton Castleton. "All right, Mr. Castleton. We have a deal."

4

KELLY BLAINE CERTAINLY LOOKED DIFFERENT when she emerged
from the inner office where Steve Winslow and Tracy Garvin had
left her to dress. Of course, Steve had only seen her in a grungy
overcoat before, but still the change was amazing. She had taken
the time to fix her makeup and comb her hair. As a result, the
face that looked as if it could be attractive *was* attractive.

So was the figure. Her clothes, though discrete and conservative, covered a full-breasted, slim-waisted body that dressed differently could only be described as voluptuous.

Steve Winslow smiled. "Well, Miss Blaine, you do look better."

She smiled back. "I can't thank you enough. The whole thing
was such a nightmare. I can't believe it's over."

"Well, it is. Signed, sealed and delivered. I've had Miss Garvin
draw you up a check."

"Check?"

"Yes. Mr. Castleton naturally made the settlement out to me
as your attorney. As I told you, I'm retaining a third as my fee.
I've had Miss Garvin make you out a check for the balance."

Steve nodded to Tracy, who picked up the check from the desk
and handed it to Kelly. She took it, folded it, started to stick it in
her purse.

"You'd better look at it," Steve said.

"Why?" she said. She stopped, unfolded the check. Her eyes
widened. "Oh, my god!" She stared at the check a moment, then

looked up at Steve. "This check is for thirty-three thousand dollars."

"Thirty-three thousand and change. That's your share of the settlement. My share's sixteen thousand and change. The settlement was fifty thousand."

She stared at him. "I told you to settle for eight."

"I know. I'm a bad boy."

She shook her head. "You shouldn't have done that."

"Well, it's done."

"Yeah, but you could have blown the settlement."

"If I had, you could sue me for malpractice. As it is, you take the money and run."

Kelly Blaine looked at the check again. "Thirty-three thousand dollars."

"Yeah," Steve said. "I know I shouldn't have done it, but I couldn't help myself. It wasn't just that I wanted a bigger fee or that I wanted the money for you. I was just pissed off at the smug son of a bitch for what he did to you, and I wanted to bash him one."

"I see,'" Kelly said.

"What's the matter?" Steve said. "You don't look happy."

Kelly Blaine blinked. "I don't know. It's just . . . I guess I'm just a little stunned."

She took one more look at the check, then folded it, jammed it into her purse and pulled the drawstring shut.

"I'm sorry," she said. "I don't mean to seem ungrateful. It was terrific work. Unbelievable. I don't know how you did it. But if you'll excuse me, I gotta get home, relax, get this out of my mind."

She smiled at Steve, nodded to Tracy, then turned hurriedly and let herself out the door.

Steve Winslow and Tracy Garvin watched her go, then turned and looked at each other in puzzlement.

Considering she had gotten everything she came here for and more, Kelly Blaine did not look one bit happy.

5

MARK TAYLOR COULDN'T stop laughing. "I love it. What a concept. 'Miss Coosbaine, take a letter.' I mean, Jesus Christ."

"It's not funny, Mark."

Mark Taylor shifted his bulk in Steve Winslow's clients' chair and took a sip from the paper cup of coffee he was holding. "Sure, sure. It's not funny at all. Perfectly routine. I get a naked client once or twice a week. Tell me, what did she look like?"

"She looked good."

"I'll bet. Taylor chuckled. "I wonder if that would work in *my* office. Except that girl I got on the switchboard"—Taylor shook his head—"I'd pay to keep her clothes *on*." Taylor grinned. "I don't suppose *you* thought of tryin' it."

"You'd better watch out, Mark. You let Tracy hear you talk like that, you'll be in deep trouble."

Taylor shrugged. "I'm always in trouble with Tracy one way or another. First place, she won't date me. Second place, she fancies herself a private detective—she's always trying to one-up me. I don't see her as a private detective somehow. I see her more as a typist."

"Jesus, Mark."

"Okay, okay," Taylor said. "But you gotta admit it's funny. Anyway, if you got a settlement, I got a bill."

"What do you mean, if I got a settlement? I ever ask you to work on a contingency basis?"

"No, but we're friends, and I'm not gonna stick you. This

30

Castleton phone number thing—getting his unlisted number—well, that's a service and I can charge you for it. But as it happens, I've had occasion to look it up before and we had it in the rolodex. If you got a settlement and can afford to pay me for passing on the information, fine. If you didn't, I'd feel bad charging you for telling you something I already knew."

"The point is moot, since I made the settlement. What do you usually charge for an unlisted number trace?"

"Two hundred bucks."

"Fine. I'll have Tracy make you out a check."

Taylor's eyes gleamed. "She gonna type it?"

"Fuck you, Mark."

"Hey, lighten up. You gotta admit the whole thing's funny."

"It is and it isn't. You never met my client. This is a nice young woman. Someone this shouldn't have happened to. It's funny in the abstract, but when you start thinking of her as a person, it's not funny at all."

"Right. And it's not funny when someone dies, but somehow, eventually it always is."

"I know. On the other hand, you never met Castleton. Or did you?"

Taylor shook his head. "No. The case I got his number for, some attorney just wanted it for a negligence claim. I never even knew what the case was."

"But you know who Castleton is? I mean, you knew before I told you?"

"Yeah. Big-shot businessman, old and retired."

"Right. And he happens to like to look at naked women."

"I can't blame him."

"Yeah, well I can. See, Mark, that's the whole bit. You can say he's a rich eccentric, he likes to look at naked women, who doesn't, what's the big deal?"

"But there's more to it than that. If this guy just wanted to look at strippers, nude models, girls who do that kind of thing, yeah, what's the big deal? But he doesn't. That's not his bag. He doesn't want some girl who makes a living showing off her body. He wants some nice, decent, respectable secretary who wouldn't do that sort of thing in a million years. He wants to take her and offer her enough money to get her to do it. It's not just sex that gets the guy off. It's power, domination, humiliation. He wants to take a respectable girl and make her do what he wants. It's like the old joke about the guy in the casino goes up to the girl and says, 'I just hit it big at roulette and I wanna celebrate, would you come up to my room with me for a thousand bucks?' She says, 'Sure.' He says, 'Would you do it for five?' She says, 'What kind of a girl do you think I am?' He says, 'We've already established that. Now we're just haggling over price.' "

"Yeah, I heard it."

"Fine, well, that's Castleton. Money buys everything, money is power. He may be an old man, he may be sexually impotent, but he still has power. That's why he's a slime and a scum, and that's why I stuck him for every cent I could."

"Then I don't feel bad sticking him for two hundred bucks," Taylor said. He heaved himself out of the chair. "Well, I gotta get back to work. I'll send you a bill, you can send me a check."

"I can have Tracy make it out now," Steve said.

Taylor shook his head. "Cash flow's not that tight. I'll just send it along."

"Okay. Ask Tracy to step in on your way out, willya?"

"Sure," Taylor said. He jerked open the door to the outer office. "Hey, Tracy. Steve wants you."

Mark Taylor stood there as Tracy Garvin came in. As she went by he said mischievously, "I think he wants you to do some typing."

As Tracy turned to give him a look, Taylor grinned and ducked out the door.

Tracy turned back to Steve. She took off her glasses, folded them up. "You told him, didn't you?" she said accusingly.

"I had to tell him about the case. He worked on it."

"That's not the point. You told him about her working naked. You two have been sitting in here having a good laugh at your client's expense."

Steve sighed. He wasn't about to point out that Mark Taylor had been the one doing all the laughing. "Tracy," Steve said, "I don't want to go off on a big feminist thing here. The fact is, the girl was working nude."

"Woman."

"What?"

"She's not a girl. She's twenty-something years old. She's a woman."

"And if she was working with her clothes on, it wouldn't occur to you to get upset if I called her a girl. Because she was naked, the whole thing's about sex and you're ready to spring to her defense at the slightest provocation."

"Don't change the subject."

"What subject?"

"The fact is, she's a client, and you and Mark Taylor were making fun at her expense."

"What do you mean, at her expense? Mark Taylor never met her. He doesn't even know who she is."

"*You* know her."

"Yeah. So?"

"You didn't have to tell Mark Taylor. You tell him about the case, fine, but did you have to tell him she was naked?"

"Tracy," Steve said. "Mark Taylor's more than a business associate. He's my best friend. We were roommates at college, for Christ's sake."

"Exactly," Tracy said. "And that's how you treated it. Two college kids talking dirty about the coeds."

Steve threw up his hands. "Fine. Guilty as charged. Tracy, look. Yes, I told him she was typing naked. Maybe that was wrong, but I couldn't help myself. I'm a human being. It's not every day a lawyer gets a naked client. You expect me not to talk about it? To my best friend?

"And, as far as this Castleton business goes, it's the whole story. Aside from her being naked, this was probably the dullest, most boring, most straightforward, conservative case I've ever handled. A simple civil suit, to be settled out of court. A boring business negotiation. You know and I know if she hadn't been naked, I wouldn't have handled it."

"I know that, but—"

"But that's neither here nor there. The point is, I'm wrong, and I apologize. Okay?"

Tracy frowned. Steve could tell she wasn't really content to let it go at that but couldn't think of anything else to say.

"All right," Tracy said, reluctantly. She unfolded her glasses, started to put them on again.

"Now, about this letter Mark wanted you to type," Steve said.

Tracy snatched her glasses off again, glared at him. Steve's eyes twinkled. The corner of Tracy's mouth twitched. She suppressed a giggle. "All right, all right," she said. "It's funny, but it *shouldn't* be. That's the point."

"Absolutely," Steve said. "I think we're in complete agreement."

There came the sound of a door closing.

"Someone's in the outer office," Tracy said. "I hope they didn't hear that last exchange."

She went out, closing the door behind her. She returned a few minutes later.

"A young man to see you," she said.

"A young man?" Steve said.

"Yes. Young. If he were a woman, you'd call him a girl. Mid-twenties."

"Oh? And what is he wearing?"

"He's dressed."

"That's a relief. What does he want?"

"He wouldn't say. But I have an idea."

"Oh? And why is that?"

"Because his name is David Castleton."

6

DAVID CASTLETON SHOOK HANDS with Steve Winslow and sat in the clients' chair.

"So," Steve said. You wished to see me?"

"Yes."

"What about?"

David Castleton tugged at his shirt collar as if the tie he was wearing was slightly too tight. "Well," he said, "I'm David Castleton. Milton Castleton is my grandfather."

Steve nodded. That was no surprise, even though it was hard to relate the handsome, sandy-haired, open-faced youth to the bald, emaciated old man. "Yes?"

"I understand you just had some dealings with my grandfather."

Steve frowned. "You can understand anything you like. This is a law office. If you came here for information, you're in the wrong place."

David Castleton held up his hands. "No, no. I quite understand. That was just a preliminary remark. You don't have to tell me, I'll tell you. You recently handled a case against my grandfather. For a Miss Kelly Blaine. Settled out of court. That case is resolved. Over. Finished."

"So what's the point?"

David Castleton took a breath. "I'm interested in Kelly Blaine."

"I beg your pardon?"

"That's it. I'm not interested in the suit or anything. Just her."

"What about her?"

"I was hoping you could tell me something about her."

Steve looked at him narrowly. Could the man really be as young as all that? "I can't discuss a client with you. You should know that."

"I do, I do. It's just—I'm sorry, I'm saying this badly. I don't want you to discuss her. It's just—Well, I'd like you to speak to her for me."

"Speak to her?"

"Yes."

"Why?"

"Because I'd like to apologize for what happened and see if I can make it up to her in any way."

"Make it up to her?"

"Yes."

"How?"

David Castleton shifted uncomfortably in his chair. "I don't know. I just thought if I could talk to her. Take her out to dinner. I have contacts. Perhaps I could get her situated in another job."

Steve nodded. "That seems a very noble sentiment. Why don't you do that?"

David Castleton shifted position again. "Well, that's why I came to you."

"Oh?"

"Yes. I was hoping you could help me get in touch with her."

"Get in touch with her?"

"Yes."

"You don't have her address?"

"No."

"I don't understand."

David Castleton tugged at his shirt collar again. Steve wasn't sure if it was really bothering him, or if it was just a nervous habit. "Well, you see," he said, "I work for my grandfather. That is, I work for Castleton Industries. So I really work for my father, since grandfather's retired. That's another thing. Grandfather may be retired, but Dad never does anything without consulting him. He always has his thumb in—you know what I mean?"

Steve took a breath. "I know what you mean. I just don't know what you're getting at."

"What I'm getting at is, I don't work at grandfather's apartment, I work at the company. Kelly Blaine was grandfather's secretary. She wasn't part of Castleton Industries. This was something separate altogether. Castleton Industries has no record of her employment. The only one who would have that would be Grandpa and, of course, Phil Danby."

Steve held up his hand. "Wait a minute. Let me be sure I understand this. You're saying you want to contact Kelly Blaine, but you don't want your grandfather to know about it?"

David Castleton tugged at his shirt collar again. "Well, that's not the way I would have put it."

"Yes, but that's essentially it, isn't it? You just got through saying her address wasn't in the company records, that only your grandfather would have it. If you could ask him for it you wouldn't be here."

David Castleton grinned sheepishly. "Yeah, I guess that's right."

"So, the situation is, you wanna contact Kelly Blaine, and you came here to get her address and phone number."

"Well, her phone's not listed."

"No, I don't suppose it is. Tell me, did you really expect me to give you this information?"

"Actually, no. I quite understand if you wouldn't. But she's your client. You must know how to contact her. I thought if you could call her, give her *my* phone number. Explain who I am and tell her I want to contact her."

Steve frowned. "Explain who you are?"

"Yes. I mean the fact that I'm Milton Castleton's grandson."

"Wait a minute," Steve said. "Are you saying Kelly Blaine doesn't know you?"

"Well . . ."

"Well what? Have you ever met the woman?"

"Not exactly."

"Not exactly?"

"Well, as I said, I work for Castleton Industries. She didn't. She worked for grandfather. So, ordinarily I wouldn't have seen her. But, uh, my father occasionally sends me on errands over there."

"Oh? So you met her then?"

"No. I never met her, but—"

Steve's eyes hardened. "Are you trying to tell me you watched her through the window in your grandfather's office?"

David Castleton reacted as if his tie had just attempted to strangle him. He hooked his fingers inside the collar, tugged it down. "I resent that," he said. "I resent the implication. I saw Miss Blaine, I thought she was a nice young woman. I'd like to talk to her. That's all. She doesn't have to talk to me, but she might. I know you won't give me her phone number. That's fine. I'll give you mine."

He took a card out of his jacket pocket and set it on Steve's desk. "That's why I say if you could speak to her for me. Tell her who I am, that I have the best intentions, and that I'd just like to talk to her. And give her my phone number. If she wants to call me, she can."

David Castleton got up. "That's all. That's all I wanted to say, really. You can't make her call me. But you could put my case in the best light possible. Point out that calling me wouldn't obligate her to anything. If she'd at least listen to me and hear what I have to say—well, I'd appreciate it."

David Castleton nodded to Steve Winslow, nodded somewhat perfunctorily to Tracy Garvin and walked out the door.

7

TRACY GARVIN TURNED to look at Steve Winslow.

"Well, what about that?" Steve said.

Tracy frowned. "Just a minute. Let me make sure he's gone."

"I heard the door open and close."

"Even so."

Tracy got up, opened the door, looked out. She closed the door and shook her head. "Okay. I just wanted to be sure. He could have opened the outer door, closed it and come back."

"Why would he do that?"

Tracy shrugged. "Why was he here at all?"

"He told us."

"Yes. What do you make of all that?"

"The young man appears rather smitten with our client."

"Whom he has never met."

"But has seen."

"Yeah," Tracy said. "Isn't that interesting?"

"No, it isn't," Steve said. "Good lord, are we never going to be done with the Kelly Blaine case?"

"What's your obligation at this point?"

"Absolutely none. The man's given me a message to pass on to my client. I'm under no obligation to do it."

"So? You gonna?"

"Yeah, I am."

"Why?"

"It's not my decision to make. The guy wants to see her.

39

Whether she sees him or not is up to her. Let's just pass on the information and be done with it."

"I'm not sure you should do that."

"Why not?"

Tracy frowned. "I don't know. I just don't like this David Castleton."

"Why not?"

She shrugged. "Just a hunch."

"Based on what?"

"I don't know."

Steve smiled. "I do. It's 'cause you figure he's interested in her typing. Well, you could be right. But it's a decision our client will have to make for herself."

"Okay. You want me to call her?"

"I think I'd better be the one to talk to her. See if you can get her on the phone."

Tracy went over to the cabinet, pulled Kelly Blaine's file, looked up the number and called.

She let it ring ten times and hung up. "No answer."

"That figures," Steve said. "She either got another job, or she's out looking for one."

"More likely out shopping," Tracy said. "She just got a thirty-three-thousand-dollar settlement. Landing a new job real quick wouldn't be a high priority."

"Sure," Steve said. "And some jobs might require a more extensive wardrobe than her last one." Tracy shot him a look. "Sorry, couldn't help myself," he said. "Okay. Too bad she doesn't have an answering machine. We'll have to try her again later. In the meantime, you got her address there?"

"Sure."

"Let's drop her a note asking her to call the office."

"Fine," Tracy said, heading for the door.

"Where you going?"

"To get my steno pad."

"Hey, I don't have to dictate this. It's just, Kelly Blaine, please call my office."

"Okay," Tracy said.

She went out to her desk and typed the letter and the envelope, stamped and sealed it. She came back to find Steve sitting at his desk, reading the paper.

"I'm going to run this down to the post office," she said.

"It's not that urgent. You could drop it in the mail slot in the hall."

"Yeah, but then it won't get picked up till tomorrow."

"It's not that important," Steve said. Then, at the look in Tracy's eyes, "Oh, go ahead if you want to. Christ, you're determined to make a mystery out of this, aren't you?"

"Well, it is bizarre."

"It *was* bizarre. It's a closed case. Except for David Castleton. Which is really none of our business. I know you'd like to make something out of his interest for her. But I think basically what we have here is a horny young man who's got the hots for our client."

Tracy started to say something, but Steve held up his hands. "But, hey, don't let me rain on your parade. By all means, go and mail it."

Tracy Garvin was in a foul mood as she walked to the post office. Men. Why did Steve Winslow have to dismiss David Castleton as just a horny young man? Maybe he was, but even so. Wasn't the fact that the grandson of the man Steve had successfully sued was interested in the client who had sued him interesting? Shouldn't it be a top priority? As if there were any *other* priorities. Not that there was anything else going on in the office at the moment.

Besides, as far as Tracy was concerned, there was something about David Castleton that just didn't quite ring true. All right, maybe it was just sex. Maybe the guy *did* have the hots for her. Maybe he was looking for a one-night stand and was trying to give the impression he had more honorable intentions, and that's why he seemed slightly off.

Still maybe not.

Yeah, Tracy had to admit, maybe she did have a lot of romantic notions. Maybe she was influenced a lot by the murder mysteries she read. But hell, what was wrong with that? As far as she was concerned, the Kelly Blaine case was interesting, and she couldn't wait to see what happened next.

When Tracy got back to the office, Steve was in his inner office with the door closed. Fine. No need to report in. There was, as usual, no work to be done. She'd try Kelly Blaine again, then go back to her book. Tracy picked up the phone, punched in the number.

Once again, there was no answer.

Five rings. Six rings. Give it ten again, and then hang up.

On the seventh ring the phone was picked up.

It was a woman.

Speaking Spanish.

8

Steve Winslow looked up from his desk when Tracy Garvin came in the door.

"Yeah, Tracy?" he said.

"I got an answer at Kelly Blaine's."

"Oh?"

"Yeah. An Hispanic woman. She spoke no English, and I speak no Spanish, but we still managed to communicate. One thing for sure—the name Kelly Blaine means nothing to her."

"Oh yeah?"

"Yeah. Isn't that interesting?"

"Maybe you got the number wrong."

Tracy gave him a look.

Steve shrugged. "I'm sorry, but it happens."

"I didn't get the number wrong."

"Well, maybe she gave it to you wrong."

"Exactly," Tracy said. "And if she did, that's interesting."

Steve smiled. "Tracy, everything doesn't have to be a mystery. You gotta remember, the girl was really hassled. She'd just had a traumatic experience. It wouldn't be that unusual if she just happened to juggle a couple of numbers."

"Come on. You don't know your own phone number?"

"Maybe it's the area code."

"What?"

"Maybe she's got a seven-one-eight number but she didn't give you the area code. So you're dialing a two-one-two number and of course it's wrong."

Tracy shook her head. "No. Her address is Manhattan."

"Where is it?"

"East Seventy-seventh Street. If that's where she lives," she added.

"What do you mean by that?"

"Well, the phone number's wrong, what if the address is too?"

Steve smiled. "I think you're really stretching."

"I don't."

"Well, we'll know soon enough. You mail the letter?"

"Yeah. But I don't think we should wait for it."

"Whaddya mean?"

"Well, it's just across town. Why don't I run out there?"

"Now?"

"Hey, like we got anything else going on here?"

Steve sighed. "No, we certainly don't. All right, look, I'll take a run over there."

"I don't mind doing it."

"I know. But if she's there, I should be the one to talk to her."

Tracy bit her lip. "Oh."

Steve grinned. "All right, you win. As you say, there's nothing going on anyway. Put the answering machine on and close up the office. We'll run over on the way home."

They went out and hailed a cab on Broadway. Tracy started to give the cabbie the address, but Steve interrupted, saying, "Seventy-seventh and Third." When he did, she grinned and he felt sheepish. And annoyed. From past experience, when on a case Steve was loathe to give a cabbie the exact address he was going to, in case someone wanted to trace his movements later. He'd done that now out of force of habit, though there was no need to, just calling on Kelly Blaine. Tracy Garvin's grin told the story. As far as she was concerned, his fudging the address certified that however much he might protest to the contrary, he was treating the affair as a mystery and using all due caution.

Which pissed him off. As far as he was concerned, the Kelly Blaine affair was *not* a mystery. Just a mundane management/labor dispute, which never would have interested him at all if the woman hadn't been naked. So here he was, seduced by sex, doing a lot of things he normally wouldn't be doing.

Though really, of course, Steve's feelings were just like Tracy's. He wanted this to be a mystery. Anything to get out of the boring, deadly office routine. The problem was, unlike Tracy, he was realistic enough to know that it wasn't. In all likelihood, Kelly Blaine would be home, receive the news that Milton Castleton's grandson wanted to date her with predictably mixed emotions and be left trying to decide whether or not she wanted to do it. Which was entirely up to her, was none of Steve's damn business and would put an end to this affair for once and for all.

They pulled up at Third Avenue and 77th. Steve paid the driver, and he and Tracy got out.

"What's the number again?" Steve asked.

"Two-twenty-one."

"Okay. That's the uptown side of the street. Let's go."

"But you dinner she's not there."

Steve shook his head. "Bad bet. This time of the day, she's probably out."

"Okay. Bet you dinner she doesn't *live* there."

"On your salary?"

"I've been meaning to speak to you about that."

"You picked a bad time. Aside from Kelly Blaine, business isn't brisk."

"No shit. I take it you're ducking the bet?"

"I didn't say that. You wanna bet, you're on."

"Deal."

They walked up the block.

"Okay," Steve said. "There's two-eleven. Two-fifteen. Two-seventeen. It's gotta be that building over there."

It wasn't. That building over there was 219.

Two-twenty-one was a parking lot.

9

Mark Taylor ran his hand through his curly red hair. "I don't understand."

"It's perfectly simple," Steve said. "The girl gave us a phony address and phone number."

"That I understand. What I don't understand is, what's it got to do with you?"

"What do you mean?"

"The case is closed. You got a settlement. If she gave you the wrong address, what's the big deal?"

"I don't like to be played for a sucker."

Taylor shrugged. "Well, there's suckers and there's suckers. You made sixteen grand on the deal. That's not my definition of a sucker. A sucker is a guy who winds up *out* sixteen grand on the deal."

"That's not the point."

"Maybe not for you. You've got Sheila Benton's annual retainer to fall back on. You don't have to sweat a rent increase—you just pass it along. Me, I've got to hustle for clients and foot my own bills. Lot of clients are deadbeats who disappear without paying—that's a problem. A client who drops a hunk of change on me and then disappears is not a problem."

"How about a client who pays you to do something illegal?"

"Hey, I don't take that kind of work."

"Neither do I. And that's the problem." Steve leaned back in

46

his desk chair and ran his hand over his head. "This whole thing stinks from the word go. I mean, Jesus Christ, the girl comes in here and tells me a story about this old lecher who hired her to type naked. In the first place, she's not the type of girl to do that."

He shot a look at Tracy, who was sitting in, taking notes. She looked about to jump in. Steve held up his hand. "And let's not go off on a tangent about who *is* the type of girl to do that. The point is, she wasn't. But apparently she did. She's up here in my office in an old overcoat with nothing underneath it telling a fantastic story that's so bizarre it really shouldn't be true.

"But it is. I go and check it out and everything's exactly as she said. Plus, while Castleton and Danby deny the specific allegations, no one denies the fact that she was tying naked. But, rather than contesting her charges in any serious way, Castleton gives me fifty thousand dollars to sweep it under the rug. Case closed.

"Fine so far. Then the grandson shows up trying to reach the girl, it turns out the girl's a phony, and what the hell's been going on?"

"You got your money, what difference does it make?"

"Like I said before, I don't want to be played for a sucker, and I don't want to do anything illegal."

"What's illegal about it?"

"Come on, Mark. It's a perfect scam. The whole thing reeks of it. I mean, you strip away all of the trappings and what you have here is your plain and simple badger game. An attractive young woman places a wealthy man in a compromising position and then demands money. It's blackmail, plain and simple."

Taylor frowned. "Well, when you put it that way."

"How else can I put it? If the girl was legit, it's one thing. The minute she's bogus, what else *can* you think."

"The way I understand it, Castleton set up the situation. He advertised for secretaries. He paid them to take their clothes off."

"Right. And this woman heard about it and said, 'Wow, here's a way to make a hunk of change.'"

"But you acted in good faith."

"Tell it to the Bar Association."

"Well, if Castleton paid fifty grand to keep this quiet, he's not going to make a stink now."

"Great, Mark," Steve said irritably. "Now you're suggesting *I* blackmail him to keep quiet."

Taylor rubbed his head. "Jesus Christ."

"Don't mind him, Mark," Tracy said. "He's just in a bad mood today."

"Right," Taylor said. "So that's what you think now? That it was just a badger game?"

Steve sighed. "I would, except for one thing."

"What's that?"

"This is where the whole thing doesn't make sense, and this is why I'm going crazy, and this is why I'm really in a bad mood today."

"What's that," Taylor repeated.

"She didn't get the money."

"What?"

"The cash. The loot. The thirty-three grand. She didn't get it. Castleton made the settlement out to me. I gave her a check for her share. Tracy called the bank this morning. That check hasn't gone through."

"So? That's not unusual," Taylor said. "If she deposited it at her bank, it could take five business days to clear."

"But it won't."

"Why do you say that?"

"Because the address is phony, the phone number's phony, you can bet the name Kelly Blaine's phony, too. That's almost a sure thing, because when I picked up her purse there was no wallet in it, just a change purse. You can see why. She didn't want anyone to know who she was, and she didn't have any driver's license, credit card, what-have-you, in the name Kelly Blaine. And if Kelly Blaine's an alias and she's got no I.D. for it, there's no way in hell she can cash that check."

Taylor frowned. "That's right."

Steve shrugged. "So there you are. That's what's driving me crazy. Here's a perfectly straightforward, simple scam that went off without a hitch except for one thing. The person who pulled it off didn't get any money. I, on the other hand, am sitting on the whole fucking fifty grand."

Taylor chuckled. "An embarrassment of riches. Well, that's a new one. Okay, I get the picture. The only thing I don't understand is, what do you want me to do about it?"

"I want you to have Kelly Blaine in my office by four o'clock this afternoon."

Mark Taylor stared at him. "What?"

Steve grinned. "Just kidding. You can't do that. That's the problem. There's absolutely nothing to go on. So forget finding the girl. I've had Tracy type up her description just in case your men should happen to bump into her. But that's a slim chance at best. Yeah, run down the name Kelly Blaine, but I know you're gonna come up empty. No, the only lead right now is Castleton. I wanna know how he got in this mess, and why he paid off so easily. Start to work on him. Also David Castleton—that's the grandson. And Stanley Castleton—that's the son, now running the business. Though, from what the grandson told me, he's a figurehead and granddad is still the one pulling the strings.

"Also Phil Danby—that's Castleton's right-hand man. Milton Castleton, I mean. Go to work on him too."

"You want these guys followed?"

"That isn't necessary. Basically, I just want information. How you get it is up to you. Consider you got a free hand."

"That's pretty broad. What, specifically, do you want?"

"I want the dope on these guys. I want the dope on Castleton Industries. Look for anything that might give me a lead to my client. It's like looking for a needle in a haystack. Worse than that, cause the needle I'm looking for may not exist. Right now, I just want data. Somewhere in it maybe I'll find a clue as to why this girl did what she did.

"One other thing. Maybe I'll get a lead as to someone who might have been running her."

"Running her?"

"Yeah. Suppose it's a badger game like I said, but the girl isn't the principal, she's only a pawn in the game. Someone programmed her to set Castleton up."

Taylor frowned. "Set him up for what? A settlement check he can't cash?"

"That may not have been the idea, Mark. The idea may have been to put Castleton in an embarrassing position in order to gain some leverage. I may actually have scotched that plan by rushing in and getting an immediate settlement."

"That doesn't make any sense, either. The girl came to you. She sent you to Castleton. She agreed to the settlement. In fact, from what you said, she would have settled for less. If settling would have scotched the deal, why would she agree to it?"

"I don't know, Mark. That's the problem. The whole thing makes no sense at all. That's why I need the information. First off, I'd like to find my client—which is probably next to impossible. Barring that, I want all the information I can get."

"This is getting to be a bad habit with you," Taylor said.

"What's that?"

"Not knowing who your client is. Remember the Bradshaw case?"

"That was different."

"How so?"

"In that case I never met my client. All I had was an anonymous letter. Here, I've sat with my client, talked with her face to face, and I *still* don't know who she is."

"Well, I'll see what I can do. You got that description?"

Tracy passed over a sheet of paper. "Right here."

Taylor took it, read the description, whistled. "Some plum assignment. My men will be falling all over themselves to be the first one to find her." He cocked his head, grinned. "This is not a bad description, Tracy, but don't you think 'generously endowed' is a trifle euphemistic?"

Tracy gave him a look. "You expect me to put 'big tits' in a memo?"

Taylor raised his eyebrows and fluttered his fingers in front of his mouth as if he had a cigar. "You can put 'em anywhere you like."

Steve groaned. "Jesus Christ."

"My Groucho that bad?" Taylor said.

"Frankly, yes. But not as bad as this damn case." Steve shook his head. "And I've got a feeling it's only gonna get worse."

10

MARK TAYLOR WAS ON THE PHONE when Steve Winslow and Tracy Garvin walked into his office late that afternoon. He grunted acknowledgment, motioned them to sit down and kept on talking. The conversation was unilluminating as far as they were concerned. It consisted of Taylor grunting, "Uh huh," and scribbling notes on a pad. Finally he hung up.

"Okay. Thanks for coming up," Taylor said. "I can't leave here 'cause I got stuff coming in all the time."

"On my case?" Steve asked.

"Sure. I got eight operatives out now."

"Eight?"

"Sure. You said I got a free hand, so I'm using it. I got people going over newspaper files, I got people digging into Castleton Industries, I even got an operative primed for personal contact."

"With whom?"

"I got a girl's gonna make a play for David Castleton."

"Oh yeah? They make contact yet?"

Taylor shook his head. "Too early. What time is it, five o'clock? No, she's in place to pick him up when he leaves work. Which should be any time now."

The phone rang. Taylor scooped it up, grunted a few times, scribbled a few notes and hung up.

"See," Taylor said. "It's been like this all afternoon. Little dribs and drabs. But it adds up to a lot of dope. Not that it's gonna do you any good. As far as finding your client, I mean. But aside from that you should love it."

"Why is that?"

"Well, this Castleton's a character. Milton Castleton, I mean. The girl's typin' his memoirs, it's gotta be one hell of a book." Taylor flipped the pages of his notebook. "Milton Castleton, self-made man. Naturally. Born in Brooklyn in 1912 of poor but honest immigrants. Father ran a fruit stand. Mother took in wash. Fourth of five children. Never finished high school. Dropped out and joined the army. Got out just in time to get hit by the Depression."

Taylor shrugged and smiled. "Which is when he came into his own. Wouldn't you know it. Whole country's going bust except for Milton Castleton. Sets himself up in business as guess what?"

"What?"

"Shoe-shine boy. Don't you love it? Whole world's gone bust, no one can afford a quart of milk, people really gonna waste their money on a shoe shine. But Milton Castleton takes the money he saved up serving his stint in the army and opens a hole-in-the-wall-shoe-shine parlor on Flatbush Avenue. By rights he should go bust, right?"

"Right."

"Wrong. He prospers. The whole world goes in the toilet and Milton Castleton cleans up."

"Shining shoes?"

"No. I would imagine that wasn't so prosperous. But Milton Castleton had a sideline."

"What's that?"

"Bathtub gin."

Steve stared at him. "You're saying he was in the mob?"

Taylor shook his head. "No. That's the remarkable thing. He *wasn't*. He was totally independent."

"No shit. How the hell'd he do that? You move into that territory, you're just asking for it."

Taylor shrugged. "Apparently Milton Castleton could walk on water. He was smart, he didn't make waves, he didn't step on anybody's toes. Plus he was protected. If there were problems, they were on a lower level. It never got up to him."

"Jesus Christ. How long did he get away with it?"

"Till repeal. Which, of course, was the end. That's when the mob had to diversify, get into other things. Gambling had always been big, and drugs were the coming thing. A lot of bootleggers started leaning that way.

"But not Castleton. 'Cause all through the Depression he'd been using the money he'd been making to snap up real estate at bargain-basement prices. Now, with the economy slowly beginning to recover, he was able to rent out space to businesses— Castleton Realty. Also to start a few small businesses on his own—Castleton Manufacturing.

"At the same time he'd been dabbling in the stock market. He had a genius for it. He was making money hand over fist. So much so, people were noticing. People started coming to him for advice, which he was only too happy to give. As long as they wanted to join the fold—Castleton Investments and Securities.

"By the time World War Two came, Castleton had a lot of real estate, a lot of manufacturing companies, and a lot of friends in high places, and guess who wound up with a whole bunch of lucrative defense contracts?"

Taylor shrugged. "It goes on and on. Castleton Industries just kept growing, gobbling up property and business. Mergers, buy-outs, hostile takeovers, what have you."

Taylor turned the page. "Now, here's where we gotta talk. You told me I got a free hand. That's fine, but let's get serious here. A preliminary look into Castleton Industries tells me I could investigate it till doomsday. He's been pulling shit for nearly sixty years. That fifty-thousand dollar settlement's nothing. I could use up your share and your client's share, and never even scratch the surface. I figure what you want is whatever's most recent, so that's what I'm looking into. I'll give you what I got.

"Four years ago you got a hostile takeover of Fielding Tool and Die. Castleton bought up a controlling interest in the stock, then liquidated the company, took a tax loss and is using the shell of it for one of his other ventures. Fine on paper. In practice, it put ten thousand employees out of work. That's just one instance, one of the more recent. If you're looking for people with a grudge against Milton Castleton, you'd have to rent a football stadium to seat 'em.

"Three years back there was a scandal at Castleton Investments and Securities. Insider trading. Two vice presidents actually indicted. Nothing was proved, and the charges were eventually dropped. Both guys were promptly fired. Frank Heckstein and Alan Carr. Young men in their thirties, aggressive go-getters with a little too much initiative. Still, with the charges dropped, their dismissal has to be a kick in the teeth. I mean, what ever happened to innocent until proven guilty?"

"That doesn't work with employers. What else?"

"Two years back you got another scandal. Castleton Investments and Securities. A mere matter of a hundred-and-some-odd-grand embezzlement. That time the charges weren't dropped. The bookkeeper, one Herbert Clay, took the fall and is currently doing five to ten."

"Anything to that?"

Taylor shook his head. "The guy may be sore, but he's got no beef coming. He liked to play the ponies, apparently wasn't too good at it. Typical embezzlement situation. Misappropriation of funds. Hands-on bookkeeper diverts money into his own pocket for gambling—no problem if he wins and can pay it back. Faced with an audit, he plunges, loses, and that's all she wrote. Anyway the people who would have a beef would be the people who got ripped off, but Castleton made good on it, so that's that."

Taylor looked up from his notes. "Now, that's just scratching the surface. There's a lot more to get and I'm trying to get it, but I'm telling you, it's gonna be overwhelming. Castleton was a ruthless businessman. There's gonna be people he screwed on business deals, people he drove out of business, companies he bought and liquidated like this tool-and-die place, employees he fired and screwed over. A real mess. Anyway, I'm looking into it.

"Castleton retired two years ago, shortly after the embezzlement fiasco. That's why it's the last thing I dug up. Anything more recent would be while his son, Stanley Castleton, was in charge. Not that it necessarily makes a difference, but there you are. Anyway, in the last two years there's been nothing significant enough to hit the papers. But, as I say, we're still digging."

Taylor ran his hand over his head. "And that's just the business side." He flipped through the notebook. "On the personal side, the guy's been married four times. Two of the marriages ended in divorce. Two of his wives died."

"Anything there?"

"Suspicious, you mean?" Taylor shook his head. "One was cancer. The other was a car accident."

"The car accident sounds promising."

"Yeah, but it wasn't. This was over thirty years ago. His third wife. A four-car pileup on the Major Deegan. Three people killed, she was one of them. Now, with a one car-accident you can say, sure, maybe someone tampered with the brakes or something. But a four-car pileup, you gotta figure it's legit."

"Yeah, I guess so. What else?"

"The four marriages produced one child. Stanley Castleton, currently running the company. That was with his second wife, Ellen. She's still alive, by the way, living quite happily on her alimony, thank you very much. She's ten years younger than Castleton, which makes her sixty-eight.

"The other wife still alive is wife number four." Taylor grinned. "Betsy Ross, if you can believe that. She's a lot younger than Castleton. Like forty years. She married him when he was sixty-four, stayed with him for two years and hit him up for a pocketful of change. All of which was spelled out in the prenuptial agreement, by the way. No illusions there. In her case, he didn't buy, he leased. Anyway, she's currently residing in California, where she calls herself an actress. She's not getting any work, but with the terms of her settlement she doesn't ever have to.

"Aside from the marriages, there were numerous affairs and assignations. All of which, I gather, were to be detailed in the memoirs your client was typing. Whether there's anything in that, I don't know."

"I don't, either, but it's an interesting thought. Is that it?"

"That's it so far. As I said, I'm still digging."

"All right. What about my client?"

"A big zero. As expected, Kelly Blaine's not her right name. Not unless she skipped some of the usual things people do, like getting a driver's license, applying for a social security number or getting born."

"Shit."

"Yeah, but it's what we expected. Only hope I see is through the personal contact."

"Which is happening now?"

Taylor looked at his watch. Shrugged. "Any time now."

11

MARCIE KELLER DIDN'T WANT to push it. The guy was interested, yeah, but it was a casual interest. Not like he was seriously thinking of picking her up.

Which was strange. Because David Castleton seemed like the playboy type. And if he was, Marcie should have been right up his alley. Blonde, slim, with a fashion model's face. But in no way cold and distant. Laughing eyes, slightly bored expression—the completely indifferent ploy that usually drove men nuts. Hell, he should have been all over her.

Especially in a place like this. It was a singles bar on Third Avenue. High-class, but definitely a pickup bar. It was early evening and the place was jammed. It would thin out later when people made contacts and wandered off together. But most of them would have a few good drinks first.

David Castleton was on his second. So was Marcie, though she was trying to take it easy. After all, this was business. Marcie had bought the first drink herself. David Castleton had paid for the second.

She'd tailed him here from work, picked him up when he came out of the building on Third Avenue where Castleton Industries held their offices, recognized him from the picture one of Mark Taylor's men had managed to dig up from the newspaper morgue. Newspaper pictures can be deceiving, but it was a good likeness, and she'd been ninety percent sure it was him. Still, ninety percent wasn't good enough, and it had been a relief when she'd tailed him to an address on Fifth Avenue, an address that turned out to be that of Milton Castleton's apartment. Which made it a hundred percent sure thing.

David Castleton had been in there for something over an hour, then come out and walked over to Third Avenue, then down to the bar, which was actually only a few blocks from the office.

They'd been there fifteen to twenty minutes. She'd played it cool, taken it slow. The place had been pretty crowded when they got there, so there was no danger of him spotting her right away, no chance of him seeing she had come in at the same time. David Castleton had pushed his way into the center of the bar and ordered a drink. She'd hung out at the far end and ordered one, too.

She'd waited until he was nearly finished with his drink before making her way down the bar and squeezing in beside him to hold up her empty glass for the bartender. It was the simplest of pickup routines. "Excuse me," as she jostled his arm, was all she'd had to say.

She'd fed him some bullshit line about being an actress and a model. He'd shown only polite interest. And hadn't opened up at all about himself. Hadn't tried to impress her with the Castleton millions. Which would only have been natural for a young stud like him.

Which was annoying. This should have been an easy assignment. Instead it was like pulling teeth.

"So, what do you do?" Marcie ventured. It was the second time she'd asked.

He tugged at his tie. "I told you. I'm in business."

"You didn't say what business."

He shrugged. "Hey, the way I see it, business is business."

"A junkyard's a business. You don't look like you do that."

"Naw. White-collar, I mean."

David Castleton ran his finger under his white collar, unbuttoned it, loosened his tie. Marcie couldn't tell if he'd done it to make a joke, or if he'd been totally oblivious of the connection. Not wanting to rock the boat, she let it go.

"Let me guess," she said. "Advertising?"

"No."

"Maybe I just want it to be advertising so you can get me a commercial."

"Uh huh."

He wasn't really listening. He glanced at his watch, then at the door.

Marcie frowned. Shit. He was meeting someone. That's why he wasn't interested. Of all the rotten breaks. If she was gonna get anything out of him, she was gonna have to move fast.

Which wasn't gonna work. She was gonna have to wash the evening out, come back and try again tomorrow. Providing he came to this bar. Then she could talk to him again. But if he went anywhere else, there was no way she was gonna get away with the coincidence of bumping into him there.

No, the way Marcie saw it, there was only one way to go. Take the bull by the horns and try the 'you're waiting for someone, aren't you?' routine.

She was just about to do that when he said, "Excuse me," and moved away from the bar.

And that was that. Win some, lose some. Wash out this assignment. Even though it wasn't her fault, Marcie felt bad. She was good at what she did, and she liked to deliver the goods. Well, not this time.

Marcie watched as David Castleton pushed his way through the crowd, making his way to the door. Shit. He couldn't be leaving, could he? If he did she'd have to follow, and that'd be a bitch, following him without being spotted after trying to pick him up. Relax, she told herself. He couldn't be leaving, he's waiting for someone. That's it. They just came in. They just came in and he's meeting them now.

As she watched, David Castleton raised his hand, called and waved to someone standing near the door. He squeezed his way past a young couple and reached the doorway. There. The young woman. Of course. No wonder she couldn't make any time.

A girl standing in her line of vision stepped to the side and she could see the woman clearly. So, that's what she was competing with. Slim figure, large breasts, and—

Oh shit!

Marcie took a breath. Jesus Christ, it was her, wasn't it? It was the woman she'd been told to look out for. Christ, what did she do now? If they stayed here, she'd already made contact, so maybe she could get close and listen in.

But what if they left? She couldn't really follow. She would if she had to, but it wouldn't be wise. She should call for backup.

Which wouldn't be easy. The phone was in the back of the bar near the rest rooms. She'd already scouted it out. It would be a bitch to get to in this crowd. But she had no choice. If they stayed, she'd have to phone. If they left, she'd have to follow. Either way, she had to be ready.

She swallowed the rest of her drink, put the glass down and moved away from the bar. It was tough to see them through the crowd. It would be tougher still to get to the door, if that's where they were heading.

But they weren't. He was leading her through the crowd back to the bar.

Okay. They're staying. Go for the phone.

Marcie threaded her way through the crowd. She reached the pay phone in the back of the bar, dropped in a quarter, punched in the number. It rang twice and the switchboard picked up.

"Taylor Detective Agency."

"It's Marcie. It's urgent. Get me Mark."

Marcie craned her neck, looked down the bar just in time to see David Castleton toss down his drink, throw a couple of bucks on the bar and pick up the check.

Shit. They *were* leaving. He'd gone back to get his bar bill.

Mark Taylor's voice was just saying, "Hello?" when Marcie dropped the receiver and began fighting her way through the crowd.

Knowing it was futile. Knowing she could never get there in time.

She was right.

By the time she got to the front door, they were gone.

12

"I FUCKED UP."

Steve Winslow frowned. Well, at least she wasn't mincing any words.

Steve had just finished dinner and gotten back to his Greenwich Village apartment when Mark Taylor had called to tell him what happened. He'd taken a cab back uptown and gotten to the Taylor Detective Agency just in time for Marcie Keller's debriefing.

Which wasn't pleasant. Mark Taylor wasn't in the best of moods. He obviously agreed with Marcie's succinct assessment of the situation, and Steve figured it was only his presence that was keeping Taylor from taking her head off. So Steve found himself in the uncomfortable position of being a buffer between them. Which wasn't easy, since he was pretty pissed off too.

"Tell me about it," Steve said.

Marcie grimaced. "It was a bonehead play. I blew it."

"We know that," Taylor snapped. "Just give us the details."

"Tell it from the beginning," Steve said. "How did you pick him up and what happened?"

Marcie took a breath. "Okay. I staked out Castleton Industries on Third Avenue as instructed. I spotted him leaving work at approximately five-fifteen. I tailed him from there to an address on Fifth Avenue that turned out to be the apartment of Milton Castleton. He went in, came out an hour and five minutes later, and walked to a singles bar on Third Avenue about two blocks up from Castleton Industries.

"I followed him in, approached him at the bar, tried to lure him into conversation. He wasn't having any. Which was strange, 'cause I was making myself look like an easy score. He wasn't interested, so I figured he was either gay or he was meeting someone.

"Turned out he was meeting someone. Girl comes in. Short brown hair. Attractive face. Subtle makeup. Slim body, big breasts. I figure it's her, the one I was told to look out for.

"So I got a big decision to make. If they leave there I gotta tail them, but it's gonna be hard not to be spotted after trying to pick up the guy. What I should do is call for backup, but if they're leaving right away there's no time. The only phone's in the back of the bar, the bar's crowded and it's not an easy call. I gotta watch and see what they're gonna do. If they leave, I'm gone. If they stay, I call.

"Now he's gone to meet her by the door, and they're standing there and talking so I'm ready to go. But then he's bringing her back to the bar where he'd been drinking. I figure they're staying, I figure I'm shot as a tail, I gotta call for backup, then go back to my place at the bar, listen in on the conversation if I can, maybe even get an introduction. So I go to a phone to make the call.

"I figure wrong. The guy just went back for his bar bill. He grabs it, heads for the door. I drop the phone, try to follow, but it's crowded, he's got a head start, and by the time I get out the door they're gone."

She shrugged. "And that's it. That's the story. I fucked up, plain and simple."

"That's for sure," Taylor said. "How many drinks you have?"

Marcie stiffened somewhat. Her chin came up. "Two."

"Two what?"

"Martinis."

Taylor snorted. "Shit."

"I'm not drunk," Marcie said. "I can hold it. I was trying for a pickup. I wasn't gonna impress the guy as an easy lay sitting there drinking Diet Coke."

Taylor opened his mouth to say something, but Steve held up his hand.

"Now hang on, Mark," Steve said. "It's a fuckup, but the way she tells it, I don't see what else she could have done. Let's stop worrying about what we didn't get, and see what we got."

Steve turned to Marcie. "Now, the girl who came in—can you describe her any better?"

Marcie frowned. "Brown hair. Blue eyes. Clear complexion. Not pale, but not heavily tanned either. Her face was attractive, but not glamorous. Plain, simple, but nice. She was wearing a light blue business suit. Stylish but conservative. Big breasts, like I said, but deemphasized by the clothing. The impression I got was a practical, no-nonsense woman."

Steve nodded. "That's her, all right. Damn."

"I know," Taylor said. "It's frustrating as hell."

"I take it I'm off the case?" Marcie said. 'Off the case' was wishful thinking. She was hoping she wasn't fired.

Taylor might have been about to say exactly that, but Steve jumped in. "No, Mark, keep her on."

Taylor frowned. "Why?"

"Cause she made contact. And the bar's only two blocks from Castleton Industries. Which means maybe it's a place David Castleton regularly hangs out. Pops in for a drink after work. If so, it's too good to pass up." He jerked his thumb at Marcie Keller. "Now, there's no way she could meet him anywhere else. That would be too big a coincidence and make him suspicious. But in the same bar it would be perfectly natural. So, Marcie, I want you to go hang out in the same bar tomorrow night. If Castleton comes in, make a play for him again."

"He wasn't interested," Taylor said.

"Sure, because he was waiting for Kelly Blaine. If he weren't, he might be *very* interested. If so, try to open him up, kid him along. Pull a 'who was that chick you stood me up for last night?' routine on him. Think you could handle that?"

"Piece of cake."

"Fine, Mark. That's what I want her to do."

Taylor shrugged. "Okay. It's your money." He turned to Marcie. "But if the girl shows up, you stick with her—I don't care what it takes. Don't rush to the phone and let her go."

"We can solve that now," Steve said. "Have a guy in the bar with her. Not with her, of course, but ready to move if the girl shows up."

"Okay, if that's what you want."

"That's what I want."

Taylor gave Marcie her instructions and she left, obviously relieved to get out of there. He watched her go and shook his head. "I think you're being too easy on her, Steve. For my money, she fucked up."

"Yes and no."

"What do you mean by that?"

"As it turns out, she should have followed them instead of calling for backup. On the other hand, you could have had a man already staked out in the bar, like we're doing tomorrow night, and she wouldn't have had to make that decision."

Taylor's eyes narrowed. "You're telling me *I* fucked up?"

"No, I'm just telling you what you didn't do. Before you get hot under the collar about it, I could have told you to have backup in the bar, but I didn't do it either. And I wouldn't have done it, even if I'd known about it. Because there was no reason to suspect the guy would be meeting Kelly Blaine. So we didn't prepare for it, and it's really nobody's fault."

"Maybe not, but I can tell you're still pretty pissed."

"Yeah, I am."

"Why?"

"Because I wanna find Kelly Blaine. You got eight trained operatives out scouring the city for her. They can't find her, but David Castleton does just like that."

Taylor shook his head. "He couldn't have found her. She must have called him."

"She didn't *know* him. They'd never met. According to David Castleton, she didn't even know he existed."

"That's just his story."

"Yeah, but why would he lie about it? I mean, if he knew her, the whole thing makes even less sense."

"Which is saying something."

"Right. I mean, the guy came here looking for her. If he knew how to find her, he wouldn't have done that. So he obviously doesn't know how to find her. But twenty-four hours later he's meeting her in a bar."

"Maybe he found her through his grandfather."

"He claimed he didn't want his grandfather to know about it.

Acted embarrassed about the whole thing. That's just what he claimed, but still. Say he went to his grandfather's, wanted to look up Kelly Blaine's address in the records. That wouldn't do him any good either."

"Why not?"

"Cause she gave me a phony name and address, it's a cinch she gave Castleton one too. So the grandfather wouldn't know how to find her any more than the grandson would."

"So maybe she called *him*."

"Grandpa?"

"Sure."

"Yeah, that's the only explanation. But if she did that, the question is why? She'd been fired from her job, she'd gotten a settlement. If she couldn't cash the check, that was too bad, but it wasn't Castleton's fault and there was nothing he could do about it."

"Maybe that's it, though," Taylor said. "Maybe she wanted him to make good with cash."

"Whaddya mean?"

"Tell him the check was worthless to her, she wanted her settlement, she wanted him to make good with thirty-three grand in cash."

"Why the hell would he do that?"

"Well, she had him in a pretty embarrassing position."

" 'Had' is the operative word. We'd made a settlement. He had a signed release letting him off the hook."

"Signed with a phony name," Taylor pointed out.

"True, but still binding," Steve said. "Castleton entered into the settlement in good faith. He can't be held accountable if my client's actions are fraudulent."

"Maybe he didn't know that."

Steve waved it away. "Even so. I mean, give me a break. The girl rings him up and says, 'I'm not really Kelly Blaine and I tricked you on the settlement and I want more money,' and Castleton says, 'Fine, why don't you go for drinks with my grandson.' "

Taylor frowned. "I see your point."

Steve threw up his hands. "It's a fucking nightmare. Nothing makes sense. I got a respectable young woman prancing around naked in front of a one-way glass for the benefit of a lecherous octogenarian who can't get it up anymore but who still likes to look. I got a horny grandson running around looking for her who hasn't got a prayer of finding her but who does just like that. And I got a fifty-thousand-dollar cash settlement that nobody seems to want."

"Right. So what does it all mean?"

Steve took a breath, blew it out again. He shook his head. "I haven't the faintest idea. And *that*, Mark, is what is *really* pissing me off."

13

TRACY GARVIN WAS in a bad mood when Steve Winslow walked into the office the next morning. "You're late," she said accusingly.

Steve frowned. He was not in the best of moods himself. "Yeah, so?" he said.

"Mark Taylor's called three times already. Wants to see you right away."

"Oh yeah? What about?"

Tracy's eyes blazed. "He wouldn't say."

Steve couldn't help grinning. No wonder she was pissed. Mark Taylor had some information she wasn't going to hear till he got there, and he was late.

"Oh," Steve said. "Is he coming down?"

"No, he's hanging on the phones again. He wants you to stop up."

"Anything happening here? Any calls?"

"No. Just Mark. Absolutely *nothing* is happening here."

Steve grinned. "Okay, you win. Put the answering machine on and let's go."

Mark Taylor was grinning from ear to ear when they walked in. "Hi, Steve. Hi, Tracy. Sorry to hold out on you, but I had to be the one to tell him."

"Tell me what?"

"We found her?"

"You're kidding."

"Nope. I got you one naked typist, as ordered. Signed, sealed, delivered."

"Where is she?"

"Apartment on East Eighty-eighth Street."

"She there now?"

"Yeah."

"Son of a bitch. How the hell'd you do that?"

Taylor shrugged. "Easy as pie. And lucky as hell, to tell the truth. When Marcie lost them last night, I sent a man to stake out David Castleton's building. It was a long shot—the way things stood, I didn't think there was a chance in hell the guy'd get her up to his apartment. But it was too obvious a play to pass up. So I staked a man out in front of the building, and sure enough, ten-thirty they come walking up together large as life and go in."

"No shit."

"None. An hour later the girl comes out alone and my man tails her home."

"And it's her? I mean, there's no chance it's the wrong girl?"

"Well, there's a chance it's not your client. We didn't have a picture to go on, just a description. But it's the same girl he picked up in the bar, all right."

"How do you know that?"

Taylor grinned. "Marcie Keller. The girl takes her job seriously. She knew she'd fucked up, and she felt bad. So when I sent her home last night she went out to David Castleton's apartment. She didn't know I'd assigned a man to it, though she could have figured it out if she'd thought about it. Anyway, she went out there on her own 'cause she knew she'd fucked up and she wanted to get out of the doghouse. So she went out there and ran into my man."

"What happened?"

"He told her to relax, he had it covered, go home and forget about it. She wouldn't hear of it. Said she was the only one who'd seen the girl, and if she showed up, she should be there to make the I.D. Anyway, they wound up staking out the place together, and she was there when Castleton showed up with the girl at ten-thirty."

"Jesus Christ. She follow her home, too?"

"Sure. She stayed there until the girl came out, and the two of them followed her to her apartment." He shook his head. "That's when they had a falling out. Marcie and my guy, I mean. This guy, Dan Fuller, figures he found the girl and got her address, that's the assignment, they should phone it in and go home. Marcie won't hear of it. What if she doesn't live there, she's calling on a girlfriend and ten minutes after they leave she comes out again? Dan argues with her but it's no go—Marcie's blown it once, she's not gonna blow it again, and the long and short of it is Dan hangs it up and Marcie sits there all night watching the apartment."

"You're kidding."

"Not at all."

"Why didn't she phone in and ask for instructions?"

"Switchboard's closed that time of night. Service picks up, and they'll ring me if it's an emergency. Marcie doesn't figure it's an emergency, just routine. Actually, she couldn't bear to ring me at midnight to tell me she'd done something she felt she should have done in the first place. Instead she sits there all night long, and I don't hear of it until I get in this morning."

"She still there?"

"Naw, she's home now. She wouldn't leave till I sent a man to relieve her. Even then, she put up a fight, saying the guy wouldn't know the girl and she ought to be there to finger her for him."

"How'd you settle that?"

"I sent Dan. He'd seen the girl, too, and she couldn't argue with that."

"You sure she's still there?"

"Absolutely. Otherwise Dan would have called."

"You know what apartment she's in?"

"Yeah. Two-A."

"How do you know?"

"It's a brownstone. When the girl went in, a light came on on the second floor front. That's Two-A."

"That should knock out the theory of her calling on a friend."

"Yeah, that's what Dan said. But Marcie wasn't taking any chances. Anyway, the name on the bell is K. Wilder. So at least the name Kelly might be right."

"You check it out?"

"Just with information. Which doesn't help much. They have a listing at that address, but it's K. Wilder, too."

Steve frowned. "Okay. Hold down the fort, Mark. Tracy and I will take a run out there."

"Sure you don't need another witness?" Taylor said. "I wouldn't mind coming along."

Steve grinned. "I'm sure you wouldn't. And I'm sure your interest is strictly professional. But she doesn't know you, and I don't want to spook her."

"Killjoy."

"Come on, Tracy. Let's go."

They went out and hailed a cab. Once again, Steve had the cabbie let them off a block from the apartment. But this time it was for real. Steve didn't like the situation at all, and he wasn't taking any chances.

They'd been silent in the cab. As soon as it drove off, Tracy said, "How you gonna play it?"

"I don't know. It depends on what she does. She's gotta be surprised to see us."

"That's for sure."

"So we take it slow and easy, see how she reacts. If possible, let her start explaining before we even ask her anything."

"Think she will?"

"She should. She gave us a phony name and address. She's gotta try to explain that away."

"Oh yeah? Bet you another dinner the first thing she says is 'How did you find me?' "

"No takers. Anyway, we sidestep that question and counter by asking her why she didn't cash the check."

"Gotcha."

They turned the corner onto 88th Street.

Steve grabbed Tracy's arm. "Son of a bitch!"

Halfway down the block there were two police cars with their lights flashing parked in front of a brownstone. While Steve and Tracy watched, a plainclothes cop came out followed by two uniformed cops leading a handcuffed Kelly Blaine.

14

"Shit's hit the fan, Mark."

"I know. Dan called in right after you left. Says the place is lousy with cops."

"Yeah, and they got our girl. They just led her out in handcuffs."

"Shit. So that's why Dan called back."

"Oh?"

"He's on hold. I took your call first. Where you calling from?"

"Pay phone on the corner."

"So is he. Must be the other end of the block. You wanna hook up with him?"

"Fuck, no. Get him out of there, call him in. Then get a line into headquarters and find out what the hell's going on. It shouldn't be hard. Whatever it is, it's something big."

"Gotcha."

"Get a move on. We'll be right there."

Steve slammed the phone down, hopped out in the street and hailed a cab. He and Tracy got in and headed back to the office.

Tracy tried to talk on the way, but Steve cut her off with a meaningful look at the cabbie. They rode in silence, Tracy smoldering.

The switchboard operator at the Taylor Detective Agency looked particularly harried. There were calls flashing on hold, and she was talking on another. As they walked in, yet another line rang. She said, "Hold, please," pushed the button, said, "Taylor Detective Agency, please hold," pushed another button, jerked her thumb in the vague direction of Mark Taylor's office, said, "Go on in," pushed another button and said, "Yes, who is it?"

Steve and Tracy walked into the office to find Mark Taylor holding two phones. "Okay, get back to me," he barked into one and slammed it down. Without missing a beat he shifted the other phone, said, "That's a theory, I need a confirmation. Get it," and slammed that one down too. He grabbed a paper cup of coffee from the desk, took a sip, swallowed, exhaled. "We are in deep shit."

"What's up, Mark?"

"David Castleton's dead."

"What?!"

Taylor grimaced, ran his hand over his head. "Cleaning lady showed up at David Castleton's apartment nine o'clock this morning, let herself in with a key. Found him lying on the floor in a pool of blood. Shot once through the heart with a thirty-two-caliber automatic. Gun found lying next to the body."

"Self-inflicted?"

Taylor shook his head. "Not a prayer. There was a pillow used to muffle the shot. Sofa cushion, actually. Suicides don't do that. Suicides don't give a shit who hears the shot. Besides, you usually shoot yourself in the head, not the heart."

"Speak for yourself. When did it happen?"

"I don't know. I'm trying to find out. What's it been, fifteen minutes since you called me? They arrested the girl, I got a line into headquarters, this is the result."

The intercom buzzed. Taylor snatched up the phone, punched a button. "Yeah?" He listened a moment, then covered the mouthpiece and said, "Dan Fuller's here. Wanna see him?"

"Yeah, but not yet. Have him wait."

Taylor nodded, said into the phone, "Tell him to hang out till I want him. And no gossip."

"No gossip?" Steve said.

"Which means don't talk about the fucking case. Which is a big problem, which is what you and I gotta talk about right now."

"Yeah, I know," Steve said. "But let's get the facts first. What about Marcie Keller?"

"What about her?"

"Where is she?"

"Most likely home asleep."

"You didn't call her?"

"In my spare time?" Taylor said sarcastically.

"Call her now. Get her in here."

Taylor snatched up the phone, pressed the button, said, "Call Marcie, get her in here double quick." He listened a moment, said, "Yeah, I'll take it," pushed another line on the phone, said, "Taylor, speak to me . . . Okay, keep digging," and slammed down the phone.

"What was that?" Steve said.

"Fatal bullet's still in the body. That means they can match the gun."

"Big deal with the gun right there. Unless there's prints on it."

"Yeah. Or unless they can trace ownership."

"Most likely not."

"Why do you say that?"

"You kidding? If it's your gun, you don't leave it behind."

"True. Shit, I hope that isn't it."

"What?"

"How the cops got a lead to Kelly Blaine."

"How *did* they get the lead."

"How the fuck should I know? That's what I'm working on now. So far, I can't even get a confirmation the Castleton murder is why they picked her up."

"If not, it's one hell of a coincidence."

"I'll say. Steve, what the hell you gonna do?"

"What do you mean?"

"You know what I mean. About Marcie Keller and Dan Fuller."

"That depends on what they have to say."

"You *know* what they have to say. They saw the girl go into his apartment with him."

"The building. Not his apartment."

"Right," Taylor said irritably. "She went up there and stood in the hall for an hour."

"We're talking legal obligation here, Mark. They don't *know* she went to his apartment. They just know she went in the front door."

Taylor stared at him. "That better not mean what I think it does."

Steve held up his hand. "Mark. Let's not jump the gun. It's early here. We don't know what's going on yet. For all we know, this has nothing to do with the murder."

"Give me a break. We have evidence Kelly Blaine was the last person to see Castleton alive."

"Hardly evidence, Mark. Your detectives left the building at eleven-thirty. Anyone could have come in and out after that."

"Bullshit. We're not talking speculation here. We have hard evidence that Kelly Blaine was seen with David Castleton around the time of the murder."

"There again you're speculating, Mark. We don't know the time of the murder yet."

"No, we don't. But you wanna bet it turns out to be right around eleven o'clock?"

"No, I don't, and neither do you. There's no reason to assume it was. You start thinking that way, and then you *will* be in hot water."

"I'm in it already."

"Not at all. We have no information, and there's no reason to believe the murder took place then. We're investigating, we're looking into it. Let's take it slow and not go off the deep end."

Taylor looked very unhappy. He took a sip of coffee, grimaced, shook his head. "Steve—"

"Mark," Tracy said. "Come on. Steve wouldn't steer you wrong."

"You kidding?" Taylor snorted. "He'd slit his own grandmother's throat for a client." He looked at Steve. "And what about it, huh? You did some work for this girl, but it's finished. So who the hell's your client?"

Steve took a breath. "That's why I say, Mark, there's no reason to be hasty about this thing. Let's take time here and find out where we stand." He turned to Tracy. "But that's a good point.

No client. I'm sorry to spoil your fun, but I think you better get downstairs and check the answering machine in case the cops give Kelly Blaine her one phone call."

"Shit," Tracy said.

"Sorry," Steve told her.

She smiled, shook her head. "The problem is, you're right."

Tracy went out. The intercom buzzed. Taylor picked up the phone, said, "Yeah?" listened a moment, said, "Okay, stick her in storage," and hung up. "Marcie Keller's here."

"Okay, Mark. We're gonna talk to her. Now you just listen careful, hear what I have to say, don't go flying off the handle, everything's gonna be all right."

"You gonna send 'em to the cops?"

"I'm gonna see that everyone's protected, make sure we're doing the right thing."

"That's no answer."

"Sure it is."

"I asked a yes-or-no question."

"There aren't always yes-or-no answers."

The intercom buzzed again. Taylor snatched it up. "Yeah?" He listened, said, "Okay, I'll take it," and started to punch the button.

"Hold on," Steve said.

Taylor looked at him. "What's the matter? It's important. Preliminary medical report."

"Buzz the switchboard, tell 'em to call back in half an hour."

Taylor stared at him. "What?"

"We got more important business to take care of." Steve jerked his thumb. "Those detectives you're so worried about. Let's take care of them first."

Taylor couldn't believe it. "This is the guy with the line to the medical examiner. He may have the time of death."

Steve shrugged. "Yeah, and then again he may not. He may have just called to tell you they started the autopsy. There's no reason to speculate. Let's take care of business."

"But—"

"Mark," Steve interrupted. "It's important here to get everything in the proper order. *We don't know the time of death.* We're hoping to learn it, but right now *we don't know.* So let's go talk to your detectives *before we do anything else.*"

Mark Taylor looked at Steve Winslow. He sighed and shook his head. "Damn it," he said. "That's what I thought you were saying."

15

STEVE WINSLOW SIZED UP Dan Fuller as he and Marcie Keller filed into Mark Taylor's office and sat down. Fuller was a stocky, muscular young man, with a broad, open face and curly brown hair. He had a sort of insolent macho air about him. The initial impression Steve got was handsome but not that swift. Steve smiled, thinking how this guy must have reacted to Marcie's suggestion during last night's surveillance.

When the detectives were seated, Mark Taylor looked at Steve Winslow, sighed heavily, and ran his hand over his head.

"Okay," Taylor said. "You're here because of the job you did last night and the job you did this morning. I want you to listen very carefully to what I have to say.

"Marcie, you met Steve Winslow, but Dan, you haven't. For your information, Mr. Winslow is the client in the case in question. He is an attorney, he knows the law, and he has a few things he'd like to say to you.

"Before he does, I have a few things to say to you.

"First off, we have just learned that David Castleton, the man you were following last night, was found murdered in his apartment early this morning."

Dan Fuller's jaw dropped open. "What?"

Taylor nodded. "I'm afraid that's right. Cleaning lady went in nine o'clock this morning, found him lying in a pool of blood, shot once in the heart."

Fuller exhaled noisily, shook his head. "We've got to go to the cops."

"Shut up, Dan," Marcie said.

Fuller turned on her. "Hey!"

"You talk too much," Marcie said. "Mark asked you to listen. Now shut up and listen."

Mark Taylor held up his hands. "All right, you two. Let's not bicker. You'll get a chance to talk. Right now I'd like you to listen carefully and hear what I have to say."

"I second that," Steve put in. "It's important that you hear exactly what Mark Taylor has to say. Later on, if someone should ask you, you may need to remember what he said. You may also need to remember what he *didn't* say. So listen up."

"All right," Taylor said. "Here's the situation. You were assigned to conduct a surveillance on the decedent, David Castleton. It is possible that your surveillance might turn out to have some bearing on the murder investigation. In the event that it did, it would be your duty to turn over what information you have to the police."

Fuller frowned. "Are you saying that's the case?"

"I thought I made myself clear," Steve said. "I told you to listen carefully to what Mark Taylor said so you'd know what he *didn't* say. I think Mark has given you a very fair and accurate assessment of the situation.

"But let me add to it. I am the client in this case, and I am an attorney at law. Anything I know I have the right to withhold from the police because of my attorney/client privilege. You're detectives. You don't have that privilege. Therefore, you must be very careful at all times to make sure you are not obstructing justice and withholding evidence from the police. If you willfully withhold information from the police, knowing it to be evidence, you could be in serious trouble. As an attorney, I am advising you *not* to do that. I am also advising you to be very clear in your own minds about what is and what isn't evidence so you are able to make the right decision.

"In making that determination, there are certain facts I want you to remember. First of all, will you please make note of the fact that as soon as he learned of the murder, the first thing Mark Taylor did was to call you in here and inform you of it. The second thing he did was tell you that should the information you had turn out to be evidence, it was your duty to report it to the police. Also make note of the fact that Mark Taylor immediately informed you of all the facts of the case in order to help you in making that decision.

"Now, the next thing Mark Taylor was about to do was to ask you if you had any questions. In order to make sure you understood the situation thoroughly and in order to further assist you in making your decisions. Am I right, Mark?"

"Absolutely," Taylor said. "If you have any questions, the time for them is now. So, do you have any questions?"

"Yeah," Fuller said. "Should we go to the cops?"

Mark Taylor frowned.

"That is a question better addressed to me," Steve Winslow said. "As an attorney, I have to look out for my client's interest. I also have to look out for your interests, and Mark Taylor's as well. We have a situation here that might require your communicating with the police. In the event that it does, Mark Taylor and I both advise you to do so. At the present time, we are collecting information and examining facts in order to make that determination."

Mark Taylor rubbed his head. He looked very unhappy. "Any more questions?"

"Yeah," Marcie Keller said. "You say you've given us all the facts at your disposal?"

"That's right."

"What about the time of death?"

"We don't know the time of death. We're looking into it, but as yet we have no information on the subject."

"All right," Marcie said. "Then at the present time, I don't think the information we have is sufficient to warrant us going to the police. We had David Castleton under surveillance yesterday. For all we know, he was killed early this morning. Is that right?"

Taylor shrugged. "It's entirely possible. We don't know."

"Let me point out the time element is of major importance," Steve Winslow said. "For instance, if it should turn out David Castleton was killed early this morning, or even any time after midnight, the surveillance you conducted on him would be wholly irrelevant.

"Unless, of course, Kelly Blaine were to be charged with the crime. Then your testimony would be of prime importance. Because you had Kelly Blaine under surveillance from the time she left David Castleton's apartment building last night until after his body was discovered this morning. In that case, she could not have done it, and your testimony could clear her. Because between the two of you, you can account for her whereabouts every minute from the time she left Castleton's building until the time of her arrest."

Marcie Keller's eyes widened. "Arrest?"

"Yeah," Fuller said. "See, you *don't* know everything. See why I said we gotta tell the cops?"

"Is that true?" Marcie asked. "Is she under arrest?"

"I'm sorry," Taylor said. "I forgot. Dan knew that, you didn't. I didn't mean to keep it from you, I'm just somewhat rattled and I didn't realize you didn't know. Yeah, the cops picked Kelly Blaine up about a half hour ago."

Marcie Keller frowned. "On what charge?"

Taylor shrugged and held up his hands. "That's just it. We don't know. It just happened, and we have no information as of yet."

"Which is why," Steve put in, "we are not in a position to advise you at this point. Other than what we already have. We are making the facts available to you as we have them, so you are able to act in your best interests. So that you may obey the letter of the law."

Marcie Keller looked at Steve Winslow. "This Kelly Blaine—is she your client?"

Steve Winslow took a breath. "I have represented Kelly Blaine in the past. It is conceivable I might represent her in the future. In the meantime, I am doing everything legally possible to protect her interests in the event that situation should arise. At the present time, it is my every intention to protect her as my client."

Marcie nodded. "And you've told us everything you know?"

"We've given you all the information we have at the present time."

"I see," Marcie said. She turned to Mark Taylor. "Mr. Taylor, when I began work for you, I told you that I was an actress, that

I took this job part-time to supplement my earnings, but my primary concern was my acting career. I feel my acting has suffered as of late. Because of my work for you, I've had to miss auditions and haven't had the time to make the rounds. I need to get back on track. For that reason, I regret to inform you that until further notice I will be unable to work for your agency. It's not that I didn't like working here, and I certainly hope there will be a job opening for me after I get things straightened out. But right now, I really have to concentrate on my career."

She turned to Dan Fuller, who was staring at her open-mouthed. "Come on, Dan. Let's get out of here. These guys got work to do."

Dan blinked. "What the hell are you doing?"

"Come on, Dan. There's no use sitting here. These guys have told us everything they know. Let's go get some breakfast."

"Breakfast?"

"Yeah. I don't know about you, but I just got yanked out of bed and dragged down here on ten minutes' notice. I haven't eaten anything and I'm starved."

"Yeah, but—"

"Come on, Dan," Marcie said. She grabbed his arm and literally yanked him out of his chair. "Let's get something to eat and talk this over. If you're not hungry, you can have some coffee and keep me company."

Marcie practically dragged him out the door.

"That," Steve said, "is one hell of a girl."

"I'll say," Taylor said. "Christ, Steve, on top of everything else you just cost me an operative. If not two."

"More than likely," Steve said.

"Think she'll whip Fuller into line?"

"Hell, yes." Steve grinned. "The way she's going I wouldn't be surprised if by the time breakfast's over she talks him into getting married so they wouldn't have to testify against each other."

Taylor shook his head. "Steve, I don't like this."

"Relax, Mark. You're in the clear. You just told them everything you knew and advised them to contact the police if the information should warrant it. If they fail to do it, you've still discharged your duty."

"I could still go to the police myself."

"With what? Hearsay? You don't know anything, Mark. You only know what other people have told you."

Steve clamped his hands together. "Okay, Mark. That's out of the way. Let's see if we can get that medical report."

16

Tracy Garvin was at her desk when Steve Winslow pushed open the door.

"She call yet?" Steve said.

"No. What's up?"

"What about Mark? Did he call?"

"I thought you were just with him."

"I was. I mean while I came down in the elevator."

Tracy looked at him. "No, he didn't call. What's going on?"

Steve ran his hand over his head, exhaled. "I'm sorry. I'm a little worked up. We're waiting on the medical report."

"Oh?"

"Yeah. Mark's man called in the with the medical report, but we were tied up and couldn't take it. The guy hasn't called back yet, and Mark can't reach him."

"Then what are you doing down here?"

"I wanted to see if the girl called."

"You could have called me."

Steve waved his hand. "I know, I know. I just had to get out of there. Mark was driving me nuts."

"Oh yeah? What about?"

"I more or less sent his detectives underground."

"What?"

"Marcie Keller and Dan Fuller. Mark and I had a talk with

them. Afterward they took off. If Marcie Keller has her way, I doubt if we'll be seeing them again for a while."

Tracy took off her glasses, folded them up. "Wait a minute. Are you telling me you told them not to talk?"

"No. We told them exactly what had happened, told them everything we knew and advised them if it became relevant it was their duty to go to the cops."

"Then why is Mark upset?"

"Because Marcie Keller's interpretation of what's relevant is apt to be rather narrow."

"So, you basically threw on a coat of legal whitewash and told the detectives to disappear."

"I'm sure that's how the police would interpret it."

"No wonder Mark's upset."

The phone rang. Tracy scooped it up, said, "Steve Winslow's office." She looked up at Steve. "It's Mark."

Steve was too worked up to bother going into his office to take the call. He walked over to the desk and took the phone from Tracy. "Yeah, Mark."

"The guy called back with the medical report."

"And?"

"It's the worst. They put the time of death last night between eleven and twelve."

"Shit."

"Yeah. We're in it now, so what the hell do we do?"

"Notify your detectives immediately."

"I don't know where they are."

"That, of course, makes it harder."

"Damn it, Steve, it's not funny. What do I do?"

"I told you. Notify your detectives. Make every effort to reach 'em. That's all you can do right now."

"Steve, I don't like it."

"I hate it like hell, but there you are. They charge the girl yet?"

"Not that I know of."

"Okay, keep digging."

Steve hung up the phone.

"So?" Tracy said.

"They put the time of death between eleven and twelve last night."

"Shit."

"Yeah."

"So what're you gonna do?"

"You heard what I told Mark."

"Yeah. So what about you? What's your responsibility in this?"

"Absolutely none. I have professional privilege. I'm protecting the confidence of a client."

"Is she a client?"

Steve sighed and shook his head. "Damn it. You know, you always ask the key questions. She *was* a client. And I have every expectation she's gonna be calling me any minute. But the fact of the matter is, no, my job for her was finished and all this other shit I did on my own. Damn, why hasn't she called yet?"

"Why wait?"

"What?"

"Why wait for the phone call? Why don't you just go down there and see her?"

"As her attorney?"

"Yes."

Steve sighed again. "That's the whole thing, Tracy. I don't know what her story is. It sure wasn't what she told us—at least, not entirely. So what have we got? We've got some woman prancing around in the nude, extorting money from businessmen, having rendezvous with young playboys who wind up dead. I don't know what's going on, but until I hear her story I don't wanna commit myself to being her lawyer. If it turns out she killed David Castleton, I don't wanna have anything to do with her."

"There may have been extenuating circumstances."

"Maybe so. But you know, I don't give a shit. Self-defense, maybe, but I still don't like it. The guy's unarmed and she plugs him with a thirty-two? She'd have to have a damn good story to get me to argue self-defense on that."

Steve shrugged. "If she calls me up, it's a different story. I'll go down, listen to what she has to say. If I don't like it, I'll tell her to look elsewhere."

"What if she doesn't call?"

"I don't know. We're getting more information all the time.

Sooner or later I'll figure out what the hell I'm going to do. But right now I don't know."

The phone rang. Tracy picked it up, said, "Steve Winslow's office," listened a moment, said, "Hold on."

She covered the mouthpiece and looked up at Steve. "It's her."

17

"I DIDN'T do it."

Steven Winslow frowned. He looked at Kelly Blaine through the wire mesh screen in the visiting room of the lockup. "They charge you yet?"

"Yes."

"What's the charge?"

"Murdering David Castleton."

"That's what you didn't do?"

Kelly frowned. "Why are you talking like that? Like you didn't believe me? You're my lawyer."

"Hang on," Steve said. "Let's get something clear. I'm not your lawyer. I did a job for you. That job is finished. Now you're consulting me again. I may take the case and I may not. That's still up in the air. I'm not your lawyer till I tell you I am."

"But—"

"Hold on. Let me finish. You're now consulting me as an attorney. Whether I take the case or not, anything you tell me is confidential. It can't implicate you, and I can't divulge it. So there's no reason to hold anything back. You can talk as freely as if I were your attorney."

"I don't understand. Why wouldn't you take the case?"

"We have a slight credibility problem here. You come into my office, tell me a story. I act on it, get you a settlement. As it turns out, I have no idea how much of your story is true. All I know is, you gave me a phony name and address and then you didn't cash your settlement check. Next thing I know you're palling around with David Castleton and he's dead.

"That's in the debit column. You expect me to have any dealings with you, you better start filling in the credit side of the ledger."

Steve took a breath. "Okay. Let's start with your name. You told me Kelly Blaine. The cops have you down as Kelly Wilder. Which is it?"

"It's Wilder."

"And what's Blaine?"

"Nothing. I made it up."

"Why?"

"It's a long story."

Steve gestured at the surroundings. "Yeah, well it looks like you're gonna have plenty of time. So start explaining."

Kelly took a breath. "Well, I guess you could start with my name."

Steve's eyes narrowed. "It isn't Wilder either?"

"No, it is. But it's my married name." She wrinkled her nose. "I was married two years. To an actor. A total creep. I don't know why it took me that long to figure it out. It was just one of those things. Anyhow, I'm divorced. Almost a year now. I just haven't gotten around to changing my name."

"Yeah? So what?"

"My maiden name is Clay."

Steve frowned. "Clay? Why is that name familiar?"

"My brother's name is Herbert Clay."

"Herbert Clay." Steve's eyes widened. "The bookkeeper for Castleton industries, went to jail for embezzlement?"

"That's right."

"Good lord. Do the cops know that?"

"I don't know."

"They're sure as hell gonna find out." Steve shook his head. "Jesus Christ."

"What's the matter?"

"What's the matter? That's the motive. Indignant sister of jailed brother wages one-woman war against industry that put him away."

"That's not true."

"I didn't say it was true. I just told you how it's gonna sound. But we're not talkin' true here. Which from you would be a real innovation. So far, all I've had from you is a bunch of bullshit. Start at the beginning and tell me what the hell happened."

"You know about my brother?"

"I know he worked for Castleton Industries, went to jail for embezzlement. That was about two years ago, right?"

"Right. I was in California. Married to a schmuck." Kelly shook her head. "Alan Wilder. The great Alan Wilder. Teen heartthrob, rising screen star. What a fool. There I was, working, supporting both of us. And there he was, making the rounds, going to Hollywood parties alone to further his career. Snorting cocaine and screwing starlets. And I shouldn't stand in his way, his chance to make the big time. I don't know why it took me so long to wise up."

Steve shifted restlessly.

Kelly held up her hands. "All right, all right. Anyway, the point is, I was in California when it happened. The thing with my brother, I mean. I knew about it, I knew he was in trouble and all that. But I was a million miles away, and I had my own problems.

"But I knew Herb. I knew he wouldn't do anything like that. I figured it was all a big mistake, and everything would get straightened out. Next thing I know he's in jail.

"Well, I wanted to do something to help, but like I say, I had my own problems.

"And that's what did it. What woke me up, I mean. Because I wanted to come here, see Herb, see if there was anything I could do to help, and Alan wouldn't hear of it. What was I thinking of, going to New York? We didn't have the money. He didn't have the time. He couldn't come with me, he didn't want me going alone. And he didn't want me calling attention to myself. He had his career to think of, for god's sake. He didn't want people associating him as the guy married to the sister of an embezzler.

"Anyway, that was the beginning of the end. We separated, we eventually divorced, and I started saving money to come out here. Which wasn't easy. New York is not cheap. I got a one-room apartment—lucky to get it—that costs me close to a thousand a month.

"I hit town about four months ago, went to see Herb."

Her eyes misted over and her lips trembled. "Jesus. I couldn't believe it. What jail had done to him. Oh, nothing physical. He wasn't beat up. He wasn't even thin. But his eyes. They were dead. Defeated. Yeah, he was glad to see me and he was animated, but it lasted about a minute. After that there was nothing but dull resignation. Hopelessness."

"So what?"

Kelly's eyes widened. "So what? What do you mean, so what? This is my brother we're talking about. He's in jail and he didn't do it." Kelly's jaw tightened. "Yeah, go on, look at me like that. I'm telling you he didn't do it. I don't care what you think, I know."

"How do you know?"

"I just know." Kelly held up her hand. She took a breath. "I know, that's no answer. But it is for me. I know my brother. If he'd done it, he'd have told me. Look, you want the truth? My brother's no saint. He's been in scrapes before. But he wouldn't try to lie out of it. Not to me. He wouldn't say, 'I didn't do it, you gotta help me.' He'd say, 'Kelly, I did this, I'm in a mess, now what can I do?' You understand? If he'd done this, he'd tell me everything he'd done to see if there was anything we could do about it. If he tells me he didn't do it, I gotta believe him."

"He was found guilty in a court of law."

"Yeah, sure," Kelly said contemptuously. "Probably the first time the courts ever made a mistake."

"What was the evidence against him?"

Kelly's eyes shifted.

"Well?" Steve prompted.

"Well, he was in charge of the books. And . . ."

"And?"

Kelly took a breath. "Well, my brother is weak. He likes to gamble."

"Oh?"

Her eyes blazed. "See? You made up your mind already. Just like the jury did. Which wasn't fair. All right, I'll tell you. Herb liked to play the ponies. It was a weakness with him. He tried to control it, but it was always there.

"Anyway, he was in charge of the books, so if he was a little short until payday, he'd sometimes dip into the petty cash to cover his losses. It wasn't that much, and he always made good by Friday when he got paid."

"That came out in court?"

"Yeah. He got arrested on Thursday. He was short, as usual. A couple of hundred bucks. Anyway, there'd have been no trouble the next day, but as it was he was screwed."

"He didn't go to jail for two hundred bucks."

"No. That was the tip of the iceberg. It was over a hundred thousand."

"How was that possible?"

"Stocks had been manipulated, transactions misreported, entries carried on the books that weren't accurate. Over a hundred grand of investors' money had been siphoned out of the company."

"And the bookkeeper in charge had a history of playing the ponies and dipping into petty cash to cover his losses?"

She took a breath. "Yes. I know it sounds bad. Hell, the jury didn't have to hear any more than that. They brought in a verdict without even thinking. But the fact is, he didn't do it."

Steve held up his hand. "Fine. Let's not argue the merits of the case any more. What has this got to do with you working for Castleton?"

She looked at him. "Isn't it obvious? To get my brother out of jail. To find something to prove he didn't do it."

Steve looked at her skeptically. "Wasn't that a hell of a long shot."

"Not at all. I knew exactly what I was looking for."

"What was that?"

"Well, you gotta understand. The way Herb tells it, he knew something was fishy with the books long before this happened. It was all somewhat complicated, he couldn't be sure what was going on, but the way the entries were coming in, he had a suspicion everything wasn't entirely kosher."

"So?"

"So, about two weeks before his arrest he wrote a memo to Milton Castleton, telling him this."

"Was that brought out in the trial?"

"Yes and no. Herb claimed he wrote the memo. His lawyer subpoenaed Castleton's files. Of course, it wasn't there."

"I see."

"No, you don't. They were making a case against him. If the memo had been in the files, they'd have destroyed it."

"Did his lawyer point that out?"

Kelly sighed. "In a halfhearted way. He was just going through the motions. Look, I have to be honest with you. The way Herb tells it, his lawyer thought he was guilty too."

"Yeah, fine," Steve said. "But what's the point? Of you working there, I mean? If the memo was destroyed, what good was it gonna do?"

"That's the thing," Kelly said. "Herb remembered something. He hadn't during the trial. Probably because his lawyer was a piece of shit and didn't believe in him to begin with. But I talked to Herb. Drew him out. I know how to do it. And I got something."

"What's that?"

"He faxed it."

"What?"

"The memo. He faxed the memo."

"To whom."

"Milton Castleton. Look, you gotta understand the setup. This was two years ago. Milton Castleton was still head of the company then. He hadn't stepped down yet. He was still running things.

"But he was sick. His health was bad. I don't know what he's got, no one seems to know, he's real quiet about it. But the last year before he stepped down, when his health got bad, he stopped going into the office. He ran things from his apartment on Fifth Avenue. Had his office set up there.

"Well, fax machines were the new craze, and of course Castleton had one, to get reports directly from the company. Herb remembers he faxed the memo to him."

"What difference does that make?"

"It's recorded. There's a record. See, Castleton Industries is all computerized. The latest state-of-the-art equipment. Very sophisticated. We're not talking a desktop computer here. Castleton's got a setup in his office like they got in the Pentagon. You could run an army with it.

"And it's tied into everything. Including the fax system. When a fax comes through, it's automatically copied."

"How do you know all this?"

"I'm not just a typist. Back in California—when I was supporting the schmuck—I was working as a computer programmer."

Steve's eyes widened. "So that's why you took the job."

"Of course. See, after I pumped Herb for everything he could give me, I knew what I had to do. I went out and investigated Castleton Industries. I was looking for some way to get a job, to get in.

"I managed to make friends with one of the secretaries there. What she told me wasn't that promising. The only thing I'd be able to get would be in the typing pool, the girls in the pool wouldn't have access to anything. It'd be a hell of a long shot. Still, it was better than nothing."

Kelly lowered her eyes. "Then she told me something else. She'd heard rumors about Milton Castleton. His memoirs, the whole bit. She said he advertised in the *New York Times*, just like it was a regular job. But when girls answered the ad, well, you know."

Kelly shook her head. "Well, it was so bizarre I couldn't believe it. Or I didn't want to believe it. But I kept watching the *Times*. Five days later, there it was. Secretary wanted to type memoirs. Castleton's name wasn't mentioned, but it gave the address and it was his building.

"Well, I had to think about it, but not too long. It certainly wouldn't hurt to go to the interview.

"I called the number. Phil Danby answered. I gave him the name Kelly Blaine. I rattled off a list of qualifications. Some I made up, some were actually mine.

"He asked my age. When I told him, he said fine and set up an interview.

"It was at Castleton's apartment. The morning I went, there were four other women there. Two of them were rather plain. Danby took them first. He was the one conducting the interviews. Castleton was not in evidence. Anyway, we were all sitting in a drawing room. Danby came in, smiled at one of the women, led her off. Was back two minutes later to get the other.

I doubt if he even took them into the office. Just told them in the hallway they weren't suitable and sent them home. Anyway, they never came back.

"The next person he took was me. He led me to the office—the one where I worked—and explained the situation. It was just like the secretary said. There was a window in the wall with a one-way glass to Castleton's office, he was eccentric and liked his secretaries to work nude, for which he paid a hundred bucks an hour, and if I had any problem with this there were no hard feelings and he was sorry he'd wasted my time, but did I want to hear more?

"Well, I was willing to listen. And he explained the setup. I would work there in the office at a word processor. I'd be typing up dictation from a microcassette. I would be in a locked room and no one would disturb me. I'd make eight hundred bucks a day."

Kelly looked up at Steve with pleading eyes. "Well, it's not the sort of thing I would have done. I mean, what the hell did I want to be in a locked office for. If I could have worked in *his* office, if there had been an opportunity to be alone, to have access to the files. But to run around naked in front of that dirty old man . . . well, there was no way I was going to do it."

She paused. Took a breath. "Except for one thing. The word processor. The first thing I noticed was it didn't have a printer. I asked him about it, aren't I supposed to print out what I type? He said, no, that wasn't necessary. The word processor was hooked up to the main computer in Castleton's office. Everything I typed would be monitored and printed out there.

"Well, that was the key. The deciding factor. I wasn't just working a word processor. I was working a computer terminal. I know computers. I would have access.

"I took the job."

"And the rest of it?"

"What?"

"When you got fired. Thrown out. Was it true?"

"Not entirely."

"How not entirely?"

"Well, a lot not entirely. He did lock me out in the hall—Phil

Danby. I did play tag in the stairwells and find a coat in the basement. All of that was true."

"But the attempted rape? The sexual advance?"

"Never happened. You met Danby. Can you imagine him trying that? No, what happened was I found it."

"Found what?"

"The memo. The one Herb wrote. I found it in the computer."

"You're kidding."

"Not at all. I knew it was there, I looked for it and I found it."

"How."

"Well, the way the whole thing was set up, I couldn't access their computer. But they could access mine. To monitor my work. And I had a way to 'tell when they were monitoring. Of course, that meant leaving the document I was working on and playing around with DOS."

"DOS?"

"Yeah. Direct Operating System. I could get into DOS, tell if I was working solo or if they'd accessed my terminal. If they had, it established a link. The line was open. When they accessed my terminal, I could access theirs."

"You're kidding."

"Not at all. But it was risky. Because everything I was doing would be flashing on my screen."

"And flashing on theirs?"

"No. If they accessed my document, that's what they'd be seeing. If I exited the document and went into DOS, that wouldn't show up on their terminal. Unless they knew how to look for it, they wouldn't find it, and they wouldn't know how to look.

"But it was on *my* screen, and even from a distance you could tell the difference. Of course, I couldn't see through the window, couldn't tell if anyone was looking through the other side. And I couldn't turn my monitor away from the window, that would be a dead giveaway. I tried to keep my head in front of the screen, block it the best I could, but even so it was a risk. Besides, if they were looking at the last page of my document, if they stopped to think about it, they could see that nothing new was being typed."

"Yeah, so?"

"So I had to work fast. Before they caught on, and before they broke the link. Which wasn't easy. They didn't keep it open long. It took me half a dozen times before I got in."

"Into what?"

"Into Fax-log."

"And?"

"And it wasn't there."

"Oh?"

"Yeah. I found copies of every fax that was sent during the dates in question. Herb's memo wasn't there."

"Maybe he didn't send it after all."

"Yes, he did. They erased it. They deleted it from the file. Isn't that great? That's ten times more damning than if it had been there. They knew it was important, so they erased it."

Steve Winslow frowned. "That's really inverted logic. What you're looking for isn't there, so you claim it was destroyed. I thought you said you found it."

"But I *did*." Kelly's eyes were gleaming. "Don't you understand? I found the damn thing!"

"What are you talking about? You just said it was erased."

"Yeah, it was. From the file. But you gotta understand. These computers are very sophisticated. They all have backup systems. Suppose you accidentally delete a file, wipe it out. Well, it's gone from the main system, and if you didn't know any better, you'd think that was it. But it's still saved in the automatic backup, and if you know computers and know how to get into it, you can bring it back."

"And you did?"

"Yeah."

"When?"

"The day I got fired."

Steve took a breath. "Okay. Tell me about that. What really happened?"

She held up her hands. "All right. Look. You remember, Castleton was gone for the day. Or so I was told—how the hell should I know? But as far as I knew, Castleton wasn't there. So I didn't expect to get anything because I didn't expect to be monitored. But I kept checking off and on all day, and finally I hit it—someone was on the line. I didn't know if Castleton had come back or if it was Danby or what the hell, but I didn't care. I was in and I had to work fast.

"By then I really knew what I was doing. I'd been close before. I riffled through the files and I found it.

"I was really scared. I didn't know if I was being watched. If Castleton wasn't there, I shouldn't have been. Those were the ground rules. If Danby was in his office, the curtain on the window should have been closed. I couldn't count on that, but I had to take a chance.

"So I put a floppy disk in the computer and downloaded the memo."

Steve's eyes widened. "You what?"

"That's right. I had a floppy disk in my purse. I mean, why not? They never searched me or anything. It's just when I was working it was like being in a fishbowl. Anyway, as soon as I hit it I got up, grabbed my purse and went into the bathroom. I took the floppy disk out of my purse, went back to the computer and downloaded the memo. As soon as I had it, I ripped the disk out of the machine, went back in the bathroom and put it in my purse. I put the purse back in the closet and was just sitting down at the machine when the door opened and Danby came in."

Steve was listening, too fascinated now to even think of a question. "Go on," he said.

"I was scared to death. I didn't know what had happened. Was the curtain open? Had he seen me? Had he been monitoring my terminal or what?

"I screamed, covered myself and backed away from the machine.

"That's when I saw. Shit. I was still in DOS. I was so eager to get the disk out of the computer I hadn't exited the program.

"I lunged for the machine, pushed the button, and the letter I'd been typing came back on.

"Danby tried to stop me. He grabbed my wrist, said, 'Don't touch that.' But it was too late. I'd switched the screen. Anyway, he grabbed me and I slapped him. When I did he let go. But then I didn't know what to do. I was panicked. My purse and clothes were in the closet, but I couldn't get by him to get to them. And he was coming at me. And I don't want to answer questions, and

I'm naked for Christ's sake, and I'm scared out of my mind and I don't know what to do.

"So I ran. I ran out of there. Just like I told you before. I found a coat, came to your office and you know the rest."

"No, I don't know the rest. You told me a bullshit story and I acted on it. I see now why you did it, but tell me anyway."

"I wanted the purse, of course. That's why I didn't give a damn about the settlement. All I wanted was the disk in my purse."

"Yeah, but you didn't get it."

"Yes, I did."

Steve frowned. "I searched your purse. It wasn't there."

"Yes it was. It was in the lining. It's the only smart thing I did. It was a big, floppy purse. I cut a slit in the lining. I had the disk hidden there. You didn't find it and they didn't find it. That's why I was so damn pleased when you got me my clothes back. I looked in my purse and it was there."

Steve thought that over. "Okay. That explains what happened then." He spread his hands to indicate the surroundings. "How did we get to this?"

Kelly bit her lip. Shook her head. "I was stupid. I should have gotten help. I should have told you what was going on. Either that, or I should have gone to Herb's lawyer. But he was such a numbnuts—I mean, the guy thought Herb was guilty. Anyway, I tried to do it on my own."

"Do what?"

"Bluff them."

"Bluff them?"

"Yeah. See, I was stupid again. I had the memo, but what did it prove? It was just that, a memo. Nothing to prove where it came from. I could have typed it myself on some other machine. If I'd been smart and I'd had time, what I should have done was downloaded the whole file. Then I'd have had copies of all these other fax that would have matched the ones in Castleton's files. Even that wouldn't be real proof—I could have just added this memo to it. But even so. I'd have had more credibility.

"Anyway, I had the memo. I didn't know if they knew I had it. I mean, Danby knew I'd been screwing around with the computer, but he didn't know what I was after. He wouldn't know about the backup file.

"And Castleton. Well, Castleton hadn't embezzled a hundred grand. Not him. Not from his own company. If someone had, and I could prove it to him and prove it wasn't Herb, well, he'd have no reason not to listen."

"Yeah? So?"

"So I called."

"And?"

"I got Phil Danby. Of course. But he wasn't rude and abusive and he didn't cut me off. That was a good sign. Instead, he seemed interested to find out what was going on.

"Which was perfect for me. It meant they were still in the dark. They had a feeling they'd been had somehow, but they still didn't know why or what it was all about. And they were interested enough to want to find out.

"Anyway, I wasn't about to deal with Danby. I told him I wanted to talk to Milton Castleton directly. He said no way, any dealings with Castleton went through him."

"What did you do?"

"I said, 'Too bad,' and hung up. I gave him a few hours to think it over and called back. That time Danby's attitude was quite different. He said he'd talked to Castleton and Castleton was willing to talk to me, but not on the phone. But if I'd come to the apartment, Castleton would see me personally."

"What did you tell him?"

"Told him to forget it. There was no way I was going back in that apartment. I told him I wanted to meet Castleton in a public place where I'd feel safe, and I wanted to meet him alone.

"Danby said that was impossible. Castleton was in poor health, he couldn't go traipsing around the city and certainly not alone.

"I said, 'Too bad,' and hung up. I let 'em stew about it and called back the next day.

"I got Danby again. He said he'd relayed my message to Castleton and what I wanted was out of the question.

"But Castleton had a compromise. If I wanted to meet in a public place, he couldn't meet me but he'd send his grandson in his place."

Steve's eyes narrowed. "Oh yeah?"

"Yeah."

"The meeting was for last night?"

"That's right."

Steve thought that over. "Why his grandson? Why not his son?"

"I don't know. Only, the way I hear it, the son is not too swift. Just a yes man for dad. But David Castleton is pretty sharp." She bit her lip. "Was."

"Yeah. So you agreed to this?"

"Yes."

"Why?"

"Because I figured it was true what Danby said, that I'd never get to Castleton himself. And there was another thing."

"What was that?"

"David was the one I wanted."

"What do you mean?"

"David Castleton was Herb's boss. David Castleton had a reputation of being a playboy. Of being a little wild. There were rumors grandpa had him on a short leash."

"You mean . . . ?"

"Absolutely. He was the one Herb suspected of the embezzlement. The way Herb saw it, he certainly was the most likely. Particularly in light of what happened. Because if Castleton's own grandson was involved, what would happen then? You'd get a whitewash, a cover-up and a convenient scapegoat. Which is exactly what happened."

"Your brother have any proof?"

"Of course not. No more than they had proof against him. My brother liked to gamble, live above his means and had access to the books. So did David Castleton. My brother wasn't anybody's grandson, he was just a little guy without connections, and he took the rap."

"All right," Steve said. "So you figured you'd confront him with this?"

She shook her head. "I didn't know what I would do. But this was a guy I wanted access to, and here he was. I didn't know how much I would tell him, I didn't know how much I would let on. I figured I'd play it by ear. The key thing I had going for me was David Castleton didn't know who I was. Didn't know I was Herb's sister, I mean. So I figured I'd talk to him, sound him out, try to see what made him tick. I'd never met the guy, you know. Anyway, I figured it was a step in the right direction."

"So what happened?"

"So I met him last night. Seven o'clock. Singles bar on Third Avenue. His suggestion. Well, it was noisy, crowded. I couldn't talk there. I told him so. He said, no problem, we'd go somewhere quiet, have dinner, talk it over. We went out, hopped in a cab, went uptown to a small Italian place. Not fancy, but nice. Quiet, unpretentious. We sat there and had dinner."

"And?"

"I took it real slow. During dinner I didn't bring up why I was there. And neither did he. We just made small talk. Which was kind of one-sided, 'cause I wouldn't tell him anything about myself. So we talked about him. His grandfather. The company. Which was great, 'cause that was what I wanted to know."

She stopped. Took a breath.

"And?" Steve prompted.

She frowned. Shook her head. "And he was nice. Not at all what I expected. It could have been an act, considering the circumstances. But I was looking for that. I was expecting that. But I didn't think so. The guy was basically nice."

"So?"

"So, it was a slow, leisurely dinner. Then we had coffee. We still hadn't brought anything up. Finally, he smiles and says, 'Why are you here?' "

"And?"

"And I got into it. Not directly. I still didn't tell him who I was, what I was after. But he'd been talking about the company, so I picked up on that, and then I brought up the embezzlement."

"What happened then?"

She shook her head again. "It didn't seem to bother him. I was watching closely, trying to judge his reaction. And there wasn't any. He knew all about the embezzlement, of course. But my bringing it up didn't seem to faze him. He was very matter-of-fact about it. Yeah, there'd been an embezzlement, and it was sort of an embarrassment to him because it had been in his branch of the company, but they got the guy who did it and he was in jail and it really hadn't hurt him much."

"Did you believe him?"

"That's the problem. I did. I didn't want to, but I did. I kept telling myself, the guy's shrewd, he's acting, he's conning you. But I couldn't make myself believe it. The guy just came across as sincere."

"So what'd you do?"

"I still didn't let on who I was. But I admitted what I was after. I had reason to believe that he had been conned and Herbert Clay had been framed and the embezzlement had actually been the work of someone else."

"How did he take that?"

"He was very skeptical. And his attitude changed. He was still nice, but very condescending, you know what I mean? It was obvious I was sincere, but I was misguided and misinformed. He felt sorry for me, and he just wished there was something he could do to convince me I was wrong and I was wasting my time."

"What happened then?"

"We went to his apartment."

"Why?"

"Because he had a computer."

"What?"

"I had the floppy disk in my purse. The way things were going, I decided to show it to him."

"You tell him what you had?"

"No, I just asked him if he had a computer. When he said yes, I said, fine, I want to show you something. We took a cab to his apartment."

"What time did you get there?"

"Ten-thirty."

"Go on. What happened?"

"We went up there and he turned on the machine. I stuck the floppy disk in and called up the memo."

"And?"

"It floored him. At least that's how he acted. He'd never seen the memo before, he had no idea it existed, he couldn't believe I'd pulled it out of the files."

"You believed him?"

"Yeah, I did. Because he was angry, you know? He was outraged this could have happened. He promised me he'd get to the bottom of it."

"Is that when you told him who you were?"

"No. I never did."

"Really?"

"Yeah, really. I mean, I trusted him but only so far."

"Then how'd the police get to you so fast?"

"I don't know."

"They didn't tell you?"

"No."

"They talk to you?"

"Yeah."

"Ask you questions?"

"They tried."

"You tell 'em anything?"

"Absolutely not. I said, I'm not talking and I want to call my lawyer."

"Good for you. Just keep telling 'em that."

"You gonna represent me?"

"Let's hear the rest of your story first."

"That's it."

"No, that isn't it. You're in jail under suspicion of murder. Let's find out how you got here. The last you told me, you were up in David Castleton's apartment and he seems real sincere and he wants to help you."

Kelly drew back from the screen. "What's the matter? You sound sarcastic."

"Do I? Well, that's the problem with your story. When you hear it repeated back, it doesn't sound that good."

"You don't believe me?"

"I didn't say that. But I'd like a few more details. Right now I got you and David Castleton up in his apartment looking at a computer disk. Suddenly, he's real compassionate and wants to help you?"

"So?"

"You go to bed with him?"

Kelly set her jaw. "What the hell kind of question is that?"

"It's a question you're gonna be asked. It would help to have the answer."

"The answer is no, goddamn it. And I resent that. You're only asking me that because I typed nude. You're saying a girl who would do that's a loose woman, you could expect her to hop into bed with every man she meets. Well, I'm not like that. I told you why I took that job, and that's not fair."

Steve shrugged. "Yes, but it's a two-edged sword."

"What do you mean?"

"You'd be asked that question anyway. The only reason you're so pissed off and defensive is *because* you typed nude. Otherwise, the question wouldn't bother you."

"Yeah, but—"

"Look," Steve said. "There's some hard realities here. Hard reality number one is you're charged with murder. Hard reality number two is whatever reason you may have had, you *did* type nude. When that gets out, you are gonna be on the front page of every tabloid in the city."

Kelly's eyes widened. "Oh, shit."

"Yeah," Steve said. "So you better get used to it, and you better figure out how you're gonna handle it. Let me tell you something—righteous indignation is not an act that's gonna play."

Steve paused and took a breath. "Okay. Now hold all that for a moment. How did you leave things with David Castleton?"

"That's just it. I left him the disk."

"The floppy disk?"

"Yeah."

"You trusted him with that?"

"It was a copy. I had the original. I wasn't bringing that with me. I duped a copy to bring to show."

"And you left him that?"

"Yeah."

"Why?"

"To show his grandfather. That's what he said he'd do. First thing the next morning. He said there was no way his grandfather would have let this thing happen. Not if he'd seen that memo. He said his grandfather was hard, ruthless, cutthroat, but fair. He would not frame an innocent man and he would not let it happen. I tell you, he was very upset."

"Okay," Steve said. "Say all this is true. If he believed you, your brother didn't do it. If you believed him, he didn't do it. So who could have done it? Who had access? Who did he think it could be?"

Kelly shook her head. "He wouldn't say. But that's just it. That's why he was so upset. Not just that this had happened. Because of the implications."

"What implications?"

"Like you said. Who had access? See, David's immediate superior was his father, Stanley Castleton."

"What?!" Steve said incredulously.

"That's right. In charge of the division, being groomed to take over the company."

"Why in hell would a man in that position risk something like that?"

"I don't know, and I tell you, it's nothing that David said. It's just the impression I got. And would account for him being so upset. You asked me, so I told you."

Steve rubbed his head. "Jesus Christ."

"Yeah. It's a mess, isn't it?"

"I'll say. So you left him the disk?"

"Right."

"And you left his apartment?"

"Yes."

"What time?"

"Eleven-fifteen, eleven-thirty. Somewhere in there."

"And you went straight home?" Steve said. He knew the answer, of course, but he didn't want her to know he knew.

"That's right. I went home, went to bed. Next thing I know, cops are knocking on the door."

"And you never told David Castleton who you were?"

"No."

"And you never told him your address?"

"No."

"Or phone number?"

"No."

"Or any way to get in touch with you?"

"No. I told him I'd get in touch with him."

Steve shook his head. "It doesn't make sense."

"What?"

"How the cops got onto you so fast. Tell me something, you ever own a gun?"

"A gun? Why?"

"Why do you think? David Castleton was shot. With a thirty-two-caliber automatic. So tell me. You ever own a gun?"

"Of course not."

"Ever borrow one?"

"No."

"There was a gun found next to the body. Are you telling me there's no way that gun could be traced to you?"

"Absolutely not. How could there be?"

"I don't know. But it would explain how the cops got onto you."

"I see that. But the answer is no. I've never had any connection with any gun. It had to be something else."

"Yeah. Great. You sure you didn't talk to the cops. Tell 'em anything?"

"Nothing. So what about it. Will you be my lawyer?"

Steve ran his hand over his head, sighed. "Yeah, I'm your lawyer. Tell me, where's the other floppy disk? The original."

"In my apartment."

"How will I find it? Is it marked?"

"Yeah. It's in a box of disks in my top dresser drawer. It's marked with an X."

"An X?"

"Yeah. In gold pen. There's a special gold marker you can use to write on floppy disks. It shows up against the black. You can write right on the disk itself. I didn't label the thing, I just marked it with an X. Right on the tab. You'll see it riffling through the disks."

"What about the other one? The one you left with David? Was that marked?"

"Yeah."

"How?"

"X dash one."

"In gold pen?"

"Right."

"Then the cops should have found it. I'll check on that."

Steve took out a pen and pencil and slipped it through the wire mesh screen. "Here. Write out a note to your super, stating I'm your attorney and you're authorizing me to get stuff out of your apartment."

Kelly scribbled the note, pushed the pen and paper back through the screen.

"You'll get the disk?" Kelly said.

"Yeah. I'll get the disk."

She looked at him with pleading eyes. "And then you'll get me out of here?"

Steve sighed. "That may be a little harder."

18

Steve dropped a quarter in the pay phone, called the office.

"Tracy, it's Steve. Did Mark call?"

"I'll say. Every two minutes. Did you take the case?"

"Yeah. She's our client. What's Mark want?"

"You, basically. He's having a shit-fit. What should I tell him?"

"Tell him to hang in there, keep getting the dope, do nothing till he hears from me."

"Should I tell him you took the case?"

"Sure."

"You coming back to the office?"

"In a bit. I got something to do first."

"Where you going?"

"Tell you later."

Steve hung up the phone, stepped out in the street and hailed a cab. He paid it off a block from Kelly's apartment, walked over and rang the super's bell. He was in luck—the super was in. He was a skinny Hispanic with a moustache. He read Kelly's note, then looked up at Steve Winslow with suspicious eyes.

"How I know she wrote this?"

"You don't know her handwriting?"

"How should I?"

"Didn't she ever leave you a note?"

"Sure, but I should remember?" He shook his head. "Nice girl. What the cops want with her?"

"Murder."

His eyes widened. "No?"

"Yeah. And I'm her lawyer and I need to get in."

"You don't look like no lawyer."

"I know," Steve said. He whipped out his wallet. "Here's my I.D. Steve Winslow." He jerked his thumb at the phone. "Call the cops. Ask 'em who Kelly's lawyer is."

The super thought that over. He nodded. "Okay. You say that, it must be true."

Which was a relief. Steve was bluffing. He didn't really want the super asking the cops if he could get into Kelly's apartment. Not that they had any right to deny him permission. He just didn't want to start them speculating on what he was after.

It was also a relief when the super unlocked Kelly's door and went back downstairs, leaving him to search alone.

Which wasn't hard. It was, as Kelly had said, the most modest of one-room apartments. The furniture consisted of a single bed, a dresser and an end table.

The box of computer disks was in the top dresser drawer, just where Kelly had said it would be. Steve opened the box, riffled through the disks.

The disk with the gold X wasn't there.

19

STEVE PUSHED OPEN the office door. "Mark call again?"

Tracy looked up at him. "Are you kidding? I can hardly get off the line with him before he calls again."

The phone rang.

"See?" Tracy said. "There he is now." She snatched it up. "Steve Winslow's office . . . Yes, Mark, he's here."

"Tell him to come down," Steve said.

"He just got in, he says come on down." Tracy listened a moment, covered the phone, said with some exasperation, "Mark says he's got too much stuff coming in right now, you should go up."

"Tell him to put a man on the phone and come down. Tell him you're pissed off at being left in the lurch and I'm afraid you might quit on me."

The phone squawked.

Tracy hung up. "He heard that, and he's coming down."

"Great."

Steve walked into his inner office, slumped into his desk chair, leaned back, closed his eyes and rubbed his head.

Tracy followed him in and stood there looking at him. "What's the matter?" she said.

Steve opened his eyes, sighed, shook his head. "This fucking case. It's really getting to me."

"What about it?"

"I listen to this girl, and she's either totally innocent or she's the most accomplished liar I ever heard."

"Oh?"

"The first story she told us was hogwash, or at least most of it."

"She didn't type nude?"

"Yeah, she did." Steve held up his hands in exasperation. "That's just it. The parts of her story that sound like outlandish, preposterous lies turn out to be true. It's the reasonable stuff that turn out to be lies."

"So what's going on? You gonna tell me?"

"Of course. That's why I had Mark come down. Turns out I got a lot to tell."

"Like what?"

"Like—"

Then came the sound of the outer door banging open.

"There's Mark now."

Seconds later Mark Taylor came barreling into the room.

"All right, Steve. What the fuck is going on?"

"Take it easy, Mark. What's the matter?"

"What's the matter? The girl's charged with murder, I'm sitting on a bunch of key evidence, and you ask me what's the matter?"

"We've been through all that."

"Yeah. Before she was charged. Now she is, and there's gonna be hell to pay."

"You call your detectives?"

"Yeah. I can't reach 'em."

"Then you've done your job. You got information for me?"

"I'll say. And more coming in every minute. Tracy tells me you took the case. Is that right?"

"Yeah, I took it."

"Great. So you want me to sit on the evidence?"

"I'm not asking you to sit on anything. I told you to tell the detectives."

"Right. Which I can't do, 'cause you told 'em to skip out."

"I never told 'em that."

"They knew what you wanted."

"I'm not legally responsible for what someone infers. I'm only responsible for what I said."

"Steve, I got a license."

"I know that. Look, let's stop talking in the dark. We got information, let's pool it. Then we can work out what we gotta do. You say you got information for me?"

"Lots of it."

"How about the fact Kelly Wilder happens to be the sister of Herbert Clay?"

"Who?"

"You're the one who told me, Mark. The Castleton bookkeeper, went to jail for embezzlement."

Mark Taylor's eyes widened. "Are you shitting me?"

Steve shook his head. "Not at all."

"Jesus Christ, it's even worse. That's the motive."

"That's how it looks to you?"

"Of course it does."

"Then that's how it's gonna look to the cops. But as far as you know, they haven't got it yet?"

"If they do, I haven't heard."

"Your pipeline good?"

"The best."

"Then they probably don't. Okay. You know how the cops got a line on the girl?"

"No, I don't."

"Damn. The whole thing doesn't make sense."

"What whole thing? What the hell's going on?"

Steve held up his hands. "Okay. You win. Me first. Here's what happened."

Steve gave them a rundown on Kelly Wilder's story. He told them everything, up to and including the floppy disk that wasn't there.

Taylor shook his head and said, "Shit."

"What's the matter?"

"The more I hear, the worse I feel."

"Why is that?"

"This girl does not exactly inspire confidence. She tells you one story, it turns out to be bullshit. Then she tells another story. How do you know it's not bullshit, too?"

"I don't."

"Exactly. And then this fairy tale about a floppy disk that don't exist."

"Maybe it did. Maybe she had it and someone stole it."

"Sure," Taylor said. "The conspiracy theory. Someone framed her brother. Someone framed her. Maybe you can sell that to a jury, but you'll have a tough time selling me."

Steve took a breath. "Mark, I have a tough time selling myself. I'm just telling you what I've got. Now what have you got?"

Taylor pulled out his notebook, flipped it open to a page that was filled with seemingly indecipherable scrawl and proceeded to decipher them. "Okay. Time of death you know about. That's the worst, and that's what fries our ass. And hers.

"Cause of death—gunshot wound to the heart. Thirty-two-caliber automatic found next to the body. One shot discharged—you knew that. News is, it's the murder gun. Ballistics matched up the bullet.

"No prints on gun—thank god for that, one for the good guys. Girl's prints in the apartment, score one for the bad team. Paraffin test on hands shows corpse did not recently fire gun."

"Unless wearing gloves," Steve said.

"Great," Taylor said sarcastically. "Good theory. Decedent wearing gloves shot self through heart, then removed and hid gloves before expiring on the floor."

"I'm not saying he fired that shot from that gun, but he could have fired *a* gun."

"Sure. At an assailant, making it self-defense. Assailant then removed gloves and gun, leaving murder weapon behind."

"Admittedly not the best defense. I'm just talking. Go on, Mark."

"Bartender at singles bar recalls David Castleton drinking there early in the evening, but did not see who he left with."

"You're kidding."

"No."

"How the hell'd they get a line on him?"

Taylor shrugged. "That I haven't got. Best guess is Castleton talked."

Steve nodded. "Yeah, that makes sense. But you can't confirm it?"

Taylor shook his head. "That's the one thing I can't get a line on. Anything about Milton Castleton's being handled with kid gloves. Anything he told 'em is very hush-hush. The reporters don't have it and I don't have it."

"Yeah, but that's got to be it. David Castleton left work, went right to his grandfather's apartment, then went to meet the girl. The way I see it, it means Castleton was running him all along."

"What do you mean?"

"When he first came to my office. David Castleton, I mean. Trying to get a line on the girl. That bit about admiring her from afar was bullshit. Grandpa was running him."

"Why?"

"Basically to find out what the hell was going on." Steve took a breath. "The problem is, we're sifting through these stories, and everyone is lying and misrepresenting and holding out. So we have a Watergate situation here—who knew what when?

"Let's start from the beginning. With Kelly Blaine Clay Wilder whatever getting fired. Her original story and Danby's version of what happened were presumably both lies. If her second story's true, that she was tapping into the computer system and Danby caught her at it, well what happened then? I would assume Danby told Castleton exactly what happened. So Castleton's clued into that, but still doesn't know what's going on. Then I show up and try to bulldoze a settlement. Which confused Castleton. First he thinks the girl's an industrial spy, now he thinks it's a badger game. Whatever, he's playing 'em close to the vest. He won't let Danby admit the girl was fired for going through the files and has him tell his improbable story of her making sexual advances to him. He then settles the civil suit as cheaply and as quickly as he can, figuring if that's all there is to it, they're actually lucky and they got off easy.

"But as soon as it's settled, he starts checking to make sure that's what actually happened. So he starts checking on the girl. Which is well before *I* start checking on the girl. And it doesn't take long to check out. She gave a phony name, address and telephone number. The girl is completely bogus.

"Now Castleton *really* wants her checked out, but he's got no way to do it. The girl is my client, so presumably I should be able to reach her. But he knows I won't tell him. So he gets his grandson, who's young and handsome, to come in and make a pitch about wanting to date the girl. The guy is awkward and embarrassed about it, but under the circumstances that goes pretty well with the role he's playing. Anyway, as it turns out, I can't reach Kelly any more than he can. In the meantime, she contacts him.

"Which is just what Castleton feared. This thing is more than just a simple badger game. The girl wants to meet him. The girl won't come to his apartment. Wants to meet in a public place. He won't go. And there's no way she'll deal with Danby. So Castleton rings in his grandson again.

"When David Castleton gets off work, he goes to his grandpa's, where he and Danby program him for the evening and send him out to meet the girl."

"Fine, I see all that," Taylor said. "What's the point?"

"The point is, if what I just said is the situation, that accounts for the cops getting a line on the bartender. Castleton told his story, which included his grandson going to the singles bar to meet the girl."

"Right."

"But it doesn't explain how the cops got a line on her. Castleton knew her only as Kelly Blaine, didn't have her name, didn't have her address."

"As far as you know."

"Yeah, but it stands to reason. If Castleton knew how to contact the girl, he wouldn't have to go through the charade with the grandson."

"Yeah, but you're talking about when he talked to the cops."

"So?"

"So, maybe he knew then."

"How?"

"From his grandson. His grandson meets the girl last night, learns her name and address. Assuming she didn't kill him—and that's a big if—after she leaves he calls grandpa and gives him the dope."

"But she didn't tell him."

"So she says. She's said a lot of things. Some of them are not noted for being true."

"I like that theory."

"Why?"

"It leaves David Castleton alive after she left."

"Yeah, well don't go on *my* say-so. The way I see it, it works as well if she excused herself to use the bathroom and David picks up the phone and says, 'Got it, Grandpa, her name's Kelly Wilder and here's the address.' "

"Then she comes out of the bathroom and plugs him with a thirty-two?"

"Why not?"

Steve thought a moment. "One thing against it."

"What is that?"

"As far as you know, the cops haven't put together the fact her brother is Herbert Clay, right?"

"If they have, I haven't got it."

"Then they probably haven't. Because that's the type of fact they wouldn't sit on. It don't hurt Castleton none, and it's front-page news. Now David didn't know Herbert Clay was her brother, but he knew that was what she was after.

"But apparently Castleton didn't. Or the name Herbert Clay would have come up. And once it did, it wouldn't take the police long to make the connection. If they haven't, it means it didn't."

Taylor shook his head. "Again, you're going by what the girl told you. I don't think you can take any of it at face value."

"Maybe not, but the point is, we still got a big, unanswered question—how did the cops get a line on the girl?"

"I don't know."

"Great. So what else have you got?"

"That's it. But I got stuff coming in all the time. Can I get back to my office now?"

"Won't they ring you here?"

"Not if it's routine. They're just collecting data. They won't call down unless it's something hot."

The phone rang.

Steve looked at Taylor. Grinned. "A movie moment. Wanna bet that's for you?" He turned to Tracy, who had scooped the phone. "Is it for him?"

"You called it," Tracy said. She passed over the receiver.

Taylor took it, listened for some time, said, "Okay, thanks," and hung up the phone.

"Well," Steve said.

"A major kick in the chops, Steve. Your client's the biggest liar in seventeen counties. No real surprise there. But I got the answer to your question—how did the cops get a line on the girl? She told you didn't give him her address, right? Well, she did. He had it written down on a piece of paper in his pants pocket."

"You're kidding."

Taylor shook his head. "Not at all. And that's the least of it. I'm begging you. Steve. Bail out of this, let me go to the cops and give 'em everything I know."

"I can't do it, Mark. I took the case. Sink or swim, I'm in it now."

"That's what I thought you'd say. Well, tell me how you're gonna deal with this. The cops traced the gun."

"And?"

"Speculation was with the gun left there, it'd be a cold piece—either stolen, unlicensed, unregistered, impossible to trace, or it would turn out to belong to David Castleton himself."

"And it didn't?"

"Hell, no. I don't know if the cops have put it together yet, but they're bound to, and when they do, you're sunk. For your information, the murder weapon was duly licensed and registered to one Herbert Clay."

20

"IT ISN'T true."

Steve Winslow frowned at Kelly Wilder through the wire mesh screen. "What isn't true?"

"Any of it. It's not true."

"So you say."

"You don't believe me?"

"We have a small problem here. The cops have evidence. You don't have anything."

"I'm telling you the truth."

"That would be a refreshing change."

"Damn it, I—"

"Hold on," Steve said. "The facts are the facts. The cops found your address in David Castleton's pocket."

"I didn't give it to him."

"Then where did he get it?"

"How the hell should I know?"

Steve took a breath. "Look. We got a problem here. Every time you tell me something it turns out not to be true. Your first story, you admit, was a lie. Now you're in a jam, you tell another story. When I start checking it out, all I get are contradictions."

"That's not my fault."

"It's not mine either. But guess what? I'm not in jail charged with murder. You are. If you wanna get out, you gotta help me."

"I'm trying to help you."

"Fine. Then how did David Castleton get your address? And

don't say how the hell should I know. We're trying to think this out together. 'Cause if we can't, you're sunk. So give me some help here. How could he have got your address?"

Kelly looked at him. Blinked. She took a breath. Blinked again. Her face contorted and her eyes filled with tears. "Damn it," she said. "You think I don't *want* to help you? I don't know. The simple fact is, I don't know. This is like a nightmare. Things keep happening to me and they don't make any sense. You want me to make sense out of them, well how the hell can I?"

She took a breath, rubbed her eyes and looked straight at Steve. "I didn't give David Castleton my address. That's the bottom line. You wanna figure out how he got it, well, you help me figure it out, because my brain is Jell-O."

"Okay," Steve said. "When you were up in his apartment. Did you have a purse?"

"Yes, I did."

"Did you have your wallet in it? With your real identification? Your name and address and all that?"

"Yes, I did."

"Fine. Now is there any time he could have looked in your purse? Like maybe you went to the bathroom, left your purse on the desk next to the computer."

Kelly thought, shook her head. "No. I remember. I went in the bathroom once, but I took my purse with me."

"That's the only time? Maybe you went in the kitchen for a moment?"

"No, I didn't."

"How about in the restaurant?"

"What?"

"During dinner. Did you maybe go to the ladies' room, or the telephone or something, leave your purse at the table?"

"No, I didn't."

"You sure?"

"Yeah, I'm sure."

"That's no help."

"I can't help that. It's the truth. You want me to say I did if I didn't?"

"No."

She looked at him closely. "Some attorneys do that, don't they?

They look at the facts of the case and then tell their clients what they have to say to account for them. Is that what you want me to do?"

"No, it isn't. And we're not talking about what story you're gonna tell. We're talking about what actually happened.

"And get this. I'm not going to put you on the stand and have you tell a lie. If that's the kind of defense you want, get another lawyer."

Kelly frowned. "Are you telling me you wouldn't argue to the jury that David Castleton must have learned my address some other way?"

"Of course not," Steve said. "I don't care what you're telling me now. I'll go in front of a jury and argue that David Castleton must have looked in your purse during dinner while you were in the bathroom. I'll do everything I can to raise the inference that that must have happened. I got no problem there."

He pointed his finger at her. "What I *won't* do is put you on the stand and have you swear to it."

"What's the difference?"

"Big difference. One way I'm making a perfectly legitimate legal argument. The other way I'm suborning perjury on the one hand and laying my client wide open to be ripped apart and caught in a lie on cross-examination on the other."

Kelly frowned. "I see."

"But that's not your concern," Steve said. "Never mind the legal ramifications. That's my job. We're not in court now, it's just between you and me and we wanna know what the hell happened. Now, you say the idea he got a peek in your purse is out. Fine. But I still want you to think about it, see if there's any way that could have happened. But for the time being, say it didn't. All right then, what about the phone calls?"

"Phone calls?"

"Yeah. When you called him, set this meeting up—any chance those calls could have been traced?"

She shook her head. "No."

"You sure?"

"Absolutely. I called from pay phones."

"Oh?"

"I was *afraid* the calls would be traced. I wasn't taking any chances. I called from pay phones on the street, and never the same ones."

"And how long were you on the line?"

"What's the difference? Even if they traced the call, they couldn't get to where I was."

"Maybe not, but even so. How long were you on the line?"

"Five minutes tops."

"Long enough to trace the call."

"But not to get there. If I'd used the same phone, sure. They trace the call and stake someone out there for when I call again. But I didn't do that. The phones weren't even near each other. There's no way that could have happened."

Steve sighed. "Great. Nice work. You understand it would be better for us if it could?"

"Yeah, but it's you and me talkin' here. And you don't want some nice theory, you want the facts. Well, those are the facts."

"Great," Steve said. "And then we have the little matter of the gun."

"I can't understand that."

"You and me both. How did David Castleton come to get shot with your brother's gun?"

"I have no idea."

"What a surprise."

Kelly opened her mouth to say something. Steve held up his hand. "Look, let's not go through the same bullshit over this. The fact is, he *was*. The cops are gonna say you pulled the trigger. Now, how would you have had access to Herbert's gun?"

"I didn't."

"Fine. I know that. But the cops are gonna *claim* you did. Now, how are they gonna base that claim?"

"They can't."

"Did you ever see the gun?"

"Of course not. I didn't even know he had one."

"He didn't tell you?"

"No."

"You never saw it?"

"No. I told you that."

"Okay. After you came to New York and you went to see Herbert . . ."

"Yes?"

"Did you go to his apartment?"

Her eyes faltered. "Oh."

"Shit."

"Well, how was I to know?" she said indignantly.

"You weren't. But here we are. I take it you went there?"

"Yes."

"Why?"

"It's a two-bedroom apartment. Herb was sharing it with this other guy. When Herb went to jail, of course he stopped paying rent. His roommate was pissed off, didn't want to go it alone, wanted to rent the room. Anyway, the guy was putting all of Herbert's stuff in storage."

"So?"

"So I packed for him."

"Oh, hell."

"It was the least I could do. Sort through things, make sure nothing got left behind."

"The roommate knows this?"

"Of course. He was there when I did it."

"He didn't watch you all the time, did he?"

"No. Why should he?"

"But he can swear you went through every inch of your brother's stuff. Which is all the cops will need to convince the jury you would have found the gun."

"But I didn't. It wasn't there. If it was, it was in some box I didn't open."

"But it wasn't."

"Why do you say that?"

"Because if the gun was packed away in storage, it wouldn't have killed David Castleton. No, there's only two theories. Either the gun was there and you found it, or it was already gone."

"It was already gone."

"So you say. Who would have taken it?"

"I don't know."

"What about Herb's roommate?"

"What about him?"

"He could have taken the gun."

"Why would he?"

"I don't know. But he had access to the gun. That makes him as good a suspect as any."

"But killing David Castleton—why the hell would he do that?"

"I don't know. Who is he, anyway?"

"Some guy. I don't even know his name."

"He work for Castleton Industries?"

"I don't think so. In fact, no. He's an actor."

"You sure?"

"Yeah. I remember now. I didn't like him. I didn't like him because Herb told me he was an actor. My husband was an actor and he was a schmuck, and when I heard he was an actor I immediately didn't like him."

"Was he a schmuck?"

"Who?"

"The roommate."

Kelly shrugged. "He was a nice enough guy. But he was an actor and he was throwing Herb out, so why should I like him?"

"I see," Steve said. He sighed and got up.

"You going?"

"Yeah. It's real nice talking to you and all that, but the problem is you don't know anything." Steve shrugged. "Looks like I'm gonna have to have a talk with your brother."

21

"She didn't do it."

Steve Winslow frowned. He looked through the plexiglass at Herbert Clay, who was sitting opposite him, holding the other telephone. He remembered what Kelly said—dead, defeated. Yeah, that was Herbert Clay all right. But in Steve's mind it wasn't just prison. There was something about Herbert Clay that wasn't quite right. Steve couldn't put his finger on it. He wasn't handsome, but he wasn't ugly. He didn't look bright, but he didn't look dull either. He just looked a little off. An inept con man. A sharpie not quite sharp enough to make it.

A loser.

That's what it was.

Your basic loser.

"Oh yeah?" Steve said. He chuckled and shook his head. "I don't know what it is with your family, but that's what they all say."

"Huh?"

"She says you're innocent. You say she's innocent. Big deal."

"But she is. Kelly wouldn't hurt anyone."

"Well that's reassuring. Great. You've made my day."

Clay frowned. "Hey. What's with the sarcasm?"

"This may surprise you, but I don't exactly need you as a character witness."

"Character witness?"

"Yeah." Steve gestured around an imaginary courtroom. "And

now, Your Honor, I'd like to call Herbert Clay, a convicted embezzler, to testify that in his opinion the defendant, his sister, did not commit the crime." Steve widened his eyes in mock surprise. "You have *that*, Mr. Winslow? Why didn't you say so? Case dismissed." Steve looked back at Herbert Clay. "See what I mean?"

Clay scowled. "Hey, what the fuck you doin', man. Whose side you on?"

"I'm on your sister's side. I'm trying to help her. If you want to help her, you'll come down to earth and answer my questions. I've been talking to you five minutes now, all I hear is what a great girl she is and how she wouldn't do it. Big deal. Tell me something I want to know."

Clay's eyes hardened. "Son of a bitch." He held up his finger. "Look. I want to help Kelly, but I don't have to take this shit. A convicted embezzler. Just for your information, I didn't do it. Maybe that's what they all say, but in my case it happens to be true. I didn't do it."

"Maybe not, but if you weren't dipping into the till and playing the ponies you wouldn't have taken the fall. Now I'm not your lawyer. I'm Kelly's. You want to help her or not?"

Clay glared at him a few moments, then dropped his eyes. "Yeah. Go on."

"Tell me about the gun."

Clay shook his head. "I can't understand that."

"That makes two of us. Tell me, how did David Castleton get killed with your gun?"

"I have no idea."

"Well the cops have. Your sister took it and killed him with it. How's that sound to you?"

"That's ridiculous. Kelly—"

"—wouldn't do such a thing," Steve finished for him. "Right. So who would?"

"I don't know."

"Well, let's figure it out. Tell me about the gun."

"What about it?"

"What do you think? Why did you have a gun, what were you doing with it, where did you keep it, who had access to it, who could have taken it?"

Clay took a breath. "I had it for my job."

"Why?"

"Occasionally I had to make deposits, withdrawals, carry large sums of money. Mostly during the day, but sometimes at night after work I'd make deposits. I didn't feel safe walking around with the money on me, so I got a gun."

"Who knew you had it?"

"I don't know. David Castleton, of course. He was my boss. Aside from him I wouldn't know. It wasn't any secret or anything."

"How about his father?"

"Whose father?"

"David's father. Wasn't he in charge of that division?"

"Yeah. But he wasn't really hands-on, you know what I mean? He was a cream puff. Only had his job because he was the old man's son."

"Yeah, but did he know about the gun?"

Clay frowned. "You think he killed his son?"

"We're running possibilities here. You tell me Kelly didn't do it. You want to tell me Stanley Castleton didn't either?"

"This doesn't make any sense."

"Maybe not. Tell me something. Are you innocent?"

Clay stared at him. "I told you that."

"You didn't steal over a hundred grand from Castleton Industries?"

"Hell no."

"Well, someone did. If it wasn't you, who was it?"

"I thought it was David."

"Well, he's dead. Who's next on your list?"

"I don't know."

"How about Stanley Castleton?"

"I can't see that. I mean, the guy's such a wimp."

"How well did you know him?"

"Hardly at all. But—"

"Then let's not cross him off the list. Did he have access to the gun?"

"I suppose so. But I still can't see it. I mean, Stanley Castleton, for Christ's sake."

Steve sighed. "Let's forget the parties involved and talk about the gun. Where did you keep the gun?"

"On my belt. I had a clip-on holster. My jacket covered it."

"You walked around all day long with a gun clipped to your belt?"

"No. Just when I had to carry cash."

"Fine. That's what I mean. When you weren't wearing the gun, where did you keep it?"

"In my desk."

"You kept the gun in your desk?"

"Yeah."

"Anyone know you kept the gun in your desk?"

"I don't know."

"Anyone ever *see* you put the gun in your desk?"

"I don't remember."

"Or take it out and clip it on?"

"Maybe. I don't remember."

"Ever show off with the gun? You're talking to someone you wanted to impress, you say, 'I gotta make a deposit,' you'd open the drawer and take out the gun and clip it on your belt?"

"I don't think so."

"Any secretary there you were sweet on, you might want to impress?"

Clay flushed. "No."

Steve held up his hand. "Hey. I'm not attacking your personal life here. I'm trying to get a handle on what's happening. I need to establish that someone else had access to the gun. And more than just access, I'd like to establish that they would have known about it."

"You want me to say I showed someone the gun?"

Steve took a breath, rubbed his head. "I don't want you to *say* anything. I'm not asking for perjured testimony here. Frankly, it wouldn't be worth a shit anyway. What I want are the facts. So stop trying to figure out what you want to say and what I want to hear, and just concentrate on the basic problem. Someone knew you had that gun and took it. Now, who could have done that?"

"Well, David."

"Right," Steve said. "But the suicide theory is out. So unless David took it and someone found it in his apartment and killed him with it, that doesn't help us. In fact, it hurts us, 'cause the most likely person would still be Kelly. Now who else?"

Clay's brow furrowed. He shook his head. "I don't know. Anyone could have known, could have done it, but I simply don't know."

"Great," Steve said. "Now when was the last time you saw the gun?"

"I don't know."

"You don't know?"

"I don't remember. It's been a long time. I hadn't thought about it."

"Well, think about it now."

"I don't know. I used it for cash transactions. They all sort of blend into each other. I can't remember the last time. I had my own problems. I was distracted."

"Right. With the embezzlement. Go on, think about the embezzlement."

"What about it?"

"You got wind something was up, and you sent a memo to Milton Castleton."

"Yeah."

"And you faxed it."

"Yes, I did."

"Fine. Now from that point on, did you have reason to use your gun?"

He frowned. "I don't think so."

"You don't think so?"

"As a matter of fact, no, I'm pretty sure not."

"Why is that?"

"Because that was one of the things. That was worrying me, I mean. One of the reasons I wrote the memo. There seemed to be something funny with the figures and no one had asked me to make a deposit for a while. Which had me paranoid. I was afraid they might peg me."

"You weren't paranoid. They did."

"Yeah."

"But from the time you sent the memo, you don't recall ever seeing the gun?"

"When you ask me like that, no, I guess I didn't."

"Okay. Good. Now let me ask you something else. When you weren't using the gun, did you always leave it in your desk—"

"Yes."

"Let me finish. Or did you ever leave it at home?"

"Oh."

"Well, did you?"

"I don't know."

"Well, think about it. After you made a deposit—at night, after work—did you go back to the office to put the gun away or would you go straight home?"

"I'd go home."

"So you'd take the gun home."

"Yeah."

"You bring it back the next morning?"

"Sure."

"When you took off the gun at home, where would you leave it?"

"On my dresser."

"On your dresser?"

"Or in the drawer."

"Which was it?"

"Either. Both. It was no big deal, you know. I never thought about it."

"You ever forget and leave the gun at home?"

"Not that I remember."

"But you could have?"

"I could have, sure."

"That's too bad."

"Why?"

"Why do you think? Your sister cleaned out your room, packed your stuff for storage. If you left the gun home, that's when she would have got it."

"Then I'll say I didn't."

"What?"

"If they ask me, if they put me on the stand, I'll say I didn't. I'll say I never kept the gun at home."

Steve frowned. "I told you, I'm not asking for perjury."

"I know. You're not asking nothing. I'm just telling you what I'm gonna say."

Steve held up his hand. There was an edge in his voice. "Let me tell you again. I'm not interested in what you're gonna say. I'm interested in the facts. Just between you and me, is it possible you left the gun at home?"

"Yeah, it's possible. But I'll never say that. I promise."

"Thanks for your support," Steve said dryly. "Okay. Now we got the gun. It could be at the office, it could be home, you're not sure which. Am I right?"

"Yeah."

"All right. Never mind now who you think you're helping. Where do you *think* the gun was?"

"At the office."

"That's your best guess?"

"Yeah. It's possible it was home, but I don't think so. If you ask me, I think I left it at the office. If *they* ask me, I'll *swear* I left it at the office."

"Okay. Fine. But say you left it at home. Your roommate—what's his name?"

"Jeff Bowers."

"Okay. This Jeff Bowers—what about him?"

"What about him?"

"Could he have taken the gun?"

"Sure, but why the hell would he?"

"You tell me. What's his connection with Castleton Industries?"

"None. He didn't have any. He's an actor."

"Yeah, but they do job-jobs. Drive taxis. Wait tables. In between work."

"Yeah. So?"

"Any of his job-jobs have anything to do with Castleton Industries?"

Clay's eyes widened. "You trying to prove Jeff did it?"

"I'm not trying to prove anything," Steve said. "I'm trying to raise an inference. If the prosecution raises the inference the gun was at home, I want to raise the inference that Jeff could have taken it. You know what that means, to raise an inference?"

Clay frowned. "Hey, I'm not stupid."

Steve let that pass. "Good," he said dryly. "Then you see what I'm trying to do. Did your roommate ever work any job remotely connected to Castleton Industries?"

"Not that I know of."

"Ever date one of the secretaries?"

"I don't think so."

"You ever introduce him to anyone you knew from work?"

"No. We had separate lives. We shared the apartment, and that was it."

Steve sighed. "Yeah, that's it. Okay. Thanks for your help."

"Listen," Clay said. "I'd do anything for Kelly. Anything. You put me on the stand, I promise I won't hurt you one bit. If you need me, just put me on the stand."

"Yeah, sure," Steve said. He hung up the phone, pushed back his chair and stood up.

Under his breath he said, "Like hell."

22

MARK TAYLOR LOOKED like he'd been run over by a truck. He took a sip of coffee from the paper cup and ran his hand over his face, which only served to spread out some of the grime.

"Well," he said, "I ain't got much."

"Oh?" Steve said.

"Well, I do, it's just you've heard it all. They've got an open and shut case against Kelly Wilder, the grand jury's ready to indict, what more is there to say?"

"Your detectives check in yet?"

"If they had, would I look like this?" Taylor exhaled noisily. "I been up all night. Not 'cause there's so much comin' in—there isn't. But 'cause I can't sleep. This thing has me tied up in knots, and I don't care what happens, I don't ever want to go through it again."

"That bad?"

"Worse. And the thing is, it's too late now."

"What do you mean?"

"I mean the clock is ticking, and it's just run out. I know it and you know it. I'm sittin' here last night waitin' to see if Marcie and Dan call in, and all the time I'm thinkin', shit, if they do, what the hell am I gonna tell 'em? And," Taylor said, "I'm gonna tell 'em hang up, get lost, you never heard from me, you never made this phone call." He exhaled again and shook his head. "It's too damn late. I can't go to the cops with this now, I have to withhold it. Why? Because it's too damn late, I'm *already* withholding it. I go to them now, they wanna know why I didn't go to them before. I got no answer and I'm in the soup."

"You made every effort to contact your detectives and—"

"Yeah, yeah, tell me about it," Taylor said irritably. "Try tellin' that to the cops. Anyway, as far as I'm concerned, we're past the point of no return. I'm just trying not to think about it. Which isn't easy."

Taylor took another sip of coffee, leaned back in his chair and said, "What did you get out of Clay?"

Steve sighed. "Nothing much. He's a punk and a loser. For my money, the guy may have done it."

Taylor stared at him. "Are you serious?"

"Absolutely. He's just the type."

"Jesus Christ. What about the immortal memo?"

"So far, we only have my client's word for that."

"You tellin' me you don't believe her?"

"I'm telling you I'm really depressed, Mark." Steve shook his head. "You wanna get really depressed sometime, just have a nice talk with Herbert Clay."

"I don't need that to get depressed. I'm doin' just fine on my own."

"You really got nothing new?"

"Nothing worth talking about. Which really isn't surprising. We already got the kick in the balls with it being her brother's gun. Aside from an eyewitness who saw her pull the trigger, there's not much more they can do to us."

"Shit."

"One thing though. The big news is, your client typed nude."

Steve stared at him. "What?"

"That's right. Naked as a jaybird. Boffo. In the buff."

"Mark. We know that."

"Yeah, well the cops didn't. They do now. So does the press. It may not be big news to you, but it sure is to them. The killing of a millionaire's grandson was gonna get big press anyway. Think what it's gonna get now. You won't have to open the *Post* tomorrow morning to read about the case, it will be right there on the front page."

Steve sighed. "Oh, shit."

"There is one silver lining."

"Yeah? What's that?"

"You won't have to face the D.A."

"Oh?"

"Yeah. Word is, Dirkson's gonna pass. If he does, you can thank her typin' nude for it. Otherwise, it's just the type of case for the District Attorney to handle himself. The victim's rich. It's an open and shut case—sorry, but the facts are the facts. And you're the defense attorney. Dirkson would love to beat you in court. Hell, he probably feels he *has* to beat you in court after the way you handled him last time. Here's a case he figures he can't lose, and ordinarily he'd snap it up like that." Taylor shrugged. "Except for her typin' nude. Suddenly it's not a case anymore, it's a media circus. However they play it, people are gonna be laughing at it and making fun of it. Dirkson's a politician, he can't afford to look ridiculous. So the word is, as much as he'd like to nail your hide to the wall, he'll pass it on to an A.D.A."

"That's good?" Steve said.

Taylor shrugged. "Dirkson's smart. You may have beat him before, but the guy is smart. The A.D.A. may be sharp, but he won't be used to the spotlight. It'll rattle him some. Plus, he won't be used to you. Your kind of tricks. So the way I see it, we caught a break."

Steve thought that over. "You could be right, Mark. If you are, it's the first one we got in this damn case."

23

District Attorney Harry Dirkson looked across his desk at A.D.A. Frank Crawford and thought once again, Christ, did I make the right choice?

He was sure he had. Crawford was one of his top A.D.A.s, with a conviction record second to none. He was bright, sharp, aggressive.

But young.

Shit, that was the problem. Young. Not much older than Steve Winslow. And the thing was, he looked it too. Thin and wiry, that was no problem, that was actually good—the lean and hungry look. But the face. The smooth boyish features. And the hair. That was the worst of it. The sleek, black hair. Not even a touch of gray at the temples.

For a second the thought flashed, could they spray some on? Dirkson frowned, angry at himself. Christ. Get serious. Get some control.

Dirkson took a breath, looked hard at the young man sitting opposite him. He held up his hand. "The bottom line," he said, "is somber."

"Sir?" Crawford said.

"Not somber, exactly, but serious. Deadly serious. The thing is, we got a big problem here. Not with the case. The way I see it, the case is open and shut. We got a problem with our image. I don't like to hear that, and I don't like to say it, but it's you and me talking here, so let's talk turkey.

"We don't want to come out of this looking like schmucks. The fact is, the girl typed nude. Which means we got a media circus here. There is a serious danger of this case becoming a big joke. We'll still win it, but it'll be a big joke. We can't let that happen."

Crawford nodded. "So we play down the fact she was typing nude?"

Dirkson took a breath. Shit, the guy didn't get it. "Not at all," Dirkson said. "We want to win the case. We probably would anyway, but why take a chance? You use everything you got. The fact the girl typed nude will go a long way toward prejudicing the jury against her. That's how juries think—a girl who would type nude would kill someone.

"So, no, you don't play it down. Hammer it in. But keep it solemn. That's the word I wanted. Not somber, solemn. 'Ladies and gentlemen, this woman typed nude.' You gotta work on it so you can do it without cracking a smile. That'll be hard. The defendant's got big tits, visions of Playboy centerfolds are gonna be dancing in everyone's heads. But you keep it solemn. It's a serious business. The woman killed someone, that's the bottom line. No matter how attractive she may be, no matter how hilarious the media wants to portray her prancing around in the nude, the fact is she took a gun, put it to David Castleton's head and pulled the trigger, bang."

Dirkson shot the A.D.A. Crawford with his finger. He sighted down the finger, stared hard into the young A.D.A.'s eyes. "You got that?"

"Yes, sir."

"You got any problem with what I told you so far?"

A.D.A. Crawford cleared his throat. "Ah, I think he was shot in the heart, not the head."

Dirkson sighed, shook his head. "Yeah. Right," he said dryly. The intercom buzzed.

Dirkson frowned, snatched up the phone. "Reese, I told you to hold all calls."

"It's Milton Castleton, sir."

"Shit. What line is he on?"

"He's here, sir."

"Here?"

"Yes, sir."

Dirkson would have liked a little more than that, but realized Reese couldn't say anything with Castleton right there. "All right," he said. "Show him in."

Dirkson had never seen Castleton before. He knew who he was, of course, but had never actually met him.

It was a bit of a shock. Dirkson's first thought was, Christ, he should be in a wheelchair. Castleton was walking, but obviously with great effort. Two men were supporting him, one on either side, which made it hard getting in the door. One man was plump and bald, the other tall and thin. They guided Castleton up to the desk and seated him in the chair A.D.A. Crawford had vacated when they entered the room.

Castleton gripped the arms of the chair and held on tight. The man was so frail, the impression Dirkson got was that he was holding on to keep from falling off.

The plump, bald man spoke. "Mr. Dirkson, this is Milton Castleton." Then, indicating the tall man, "His son, Stanley Castleton. I'm Mr. Castleton's business associate, Phil Danby."

Danby didn't feel the need to indicate which Mr. Castleton he meant. That was obvious. In fact, Dirkson was surprised to find the tall, ineffectual man with the weak chin was Castleton's son and Danby the associate, rather than the other way around.

"Yes, Mr. Castleton," Dirkson said. "This is a pleasure." Then, realizing it wasn't, added, "I'm sorry we have to meet at such trying times."

Castleton might not have heard him. He dug his fingers into the arm of the chair, pulled his slim, frail body erect. "She killed my grandson," he said.

"Yes, sir. I know."

"She has to pay."

"She will, sir. That I promise."

"Good," Castleton said. "We will help. Anything you need, you've got." Castleton's right hand pointed slightly to Phil Danby. "This is Mr. Danby. You want me, you call him. Anything you want, he will do."

"Yes, sir," Dirkson said. He waited for another directive regarding Stanley Castleton, the son. None came.

Dirkson took a breath, wondering what to say next. "Is there anything we can do, Mr. Castleton?"

"Convict her."

"Yes, sir."

"If you need me to testify, I will testify. I am old. I am sick. But I *can* do it. Don't keep me off the stand because you think I'm a sick old man."

"Yes, sir," Dirkson said. "Ah, what would you testify to?"

"How she tricked me into hiring her and then sued me. Part of a vindictive campaign because of her brother. That she made threats leading us to believe that she had been involved in industrial espionage. That she set up the meeting with my grandson and then killed him."

"I see," Dirkson said.

"Most of this, Phil Danby will testify to, as the go-between. But I confirm what he says. My name lends weight."

"Yes, sir," Dirkson said. He hesitated. "You understand, the testimony regarding her employment . . . ?"

"Yes?"

"It is going to come out that the employment was somewhat unusual."

"She worked nude," Castleton said. "My secretaries work nude. I'm an old man, but I still like to look at naked women. Does that bother you?"

Dirkson gulped. "No, sir."

"Good. Then it doesn't bother me. And I don't give a damn who knows it. So don't pull your punches any."

A.D.A. Crawford had been hovering in the corner. Castleton seemed to see him for the first time. He jerked his thumb in his direction. "Who's he?"

"Oh," Dirkson said. "This is A.D.A. Crawford. I was just briefing him on the case. He'll be handling the prosecution."

Castleton didn't even look at Crawford. He stared straight up at Dirkson. "You," he said.

"Sir?"

"You will be prosecuting."

Dirkson cleared his throat. "No, sir. I will be *supervising* the prosecution as district attorney, and Mr. Crawford will be reporting directly to me."

Castleton didn't bother shaking his head, but the eyes in the emaciated face burned into those of the district attorney. "*You* will be prosecuting*,*" he said evenly.

Dirkson took a breath. Castleton was not just a wealthy man, he was a *connected* wealthy man. Without actually checking, it would be impossible to tell just how many campaign contributions were directly influenced by him. Even with checking, it might be impossible to tell. But the man's influence was certainly extensive.

Dirkson nodded. "Yes, sir. Me."

24

Steve Winslow looked at the newspapers spread out on Mark Taylor's desk. "NAKED TYPIST SLAY SUSPECT" was the headline in the *Post*. The *Daily News* had "CASTLETON KILLER TYPED NUDE."

Steve shook his head. "Jesus Christ."

"Yeah," Taylor said. "And that's just the ones they're printing. You should hear some of the stuff the guys are making up."

"Oh yeah? Like what?"

"Oh," Taylor said. He ran his hand over an imaginary headline. "Like, 'COPS HAVE NOTHING ON HER AND NEITHER HAS SHE.' "

"Nice."

"Yeah. Or, 'AT LEAST SHE WASN'T CARRYING ANY CONCEALED WEAPONS.' "

"That's not a headline."

"Hey, let's not quibble. The point is, it's just as bad as you feared. Your client's a laughingstock, the story's page one, and this case is going to be decided in the press before it ever gets to trial."

"I know, Mark."

"The other bad news is, we're dead wrong as usual. Dirkson's gonna prosecute."

"You sure?"

"Yeah. It's not official yet, but I have it on good authority.

Word is he wasn't gonna, but Castleton paid him a little visit yesterday and turned him around."

"Oh, hell."

"Yeah, it's bad news in more ways than one. You're going up against the D.A. with Castleton's weight behind him. That's a formidable combination. The scary part is, Dirkson's sharp. If there's the slightest leak about my involvement in this case, Dirkson will pick up on it. A young A.D.A. might miss it, but Dirkson won't."

"Let's not go through that again."

"No, let's not. Believe me, I'm *never* going through this again."

"Yeah, fine," Steve said impatiently. "You got anything for me besides the voice of doom?"

"Yeah, but it ain't good." Taylor flipped open his notebook. "Stanley Castleton. Basic wimp. Weak, ineffectual, yes man to Milton Castleton. Position in company due solely to accident of birth. Puppet, at best. Wouldn't go to the bathroom without checking with dad. Fifty-two years old, married thirty years to same woman, Helen Castleton, née Greenfield, union produced one son, David."

Taylor flipped the page. "House in White Plains. Marriage still intact. Stanley Castleton not known to have any mistress, girlfriend, or otherwise fool around. No predilection for gambling, dope or booze. Staid family man. Hobbies are—get this—coin and stamp collecting."

Taylor looked up from his notes. "You wanna make a case a man like that killed his only son, good luck."

"Yeah," Steve said. "What about the stamp and coin collecting?"

"What about it?"

"How extensive is this collection? Castleton plunkin' down any large sums for any rare coins?"

"Nice try, but the answer's no. The guy's a tightwad and a penny-pincher. Best information we got, the most he ever spent on a coin was fifty bucks. And then it took him two weeks to decide if he was gonna spring for the damn thing."

"Shit."

"Yeah, I know, Steve. We've gone through his background

with a fine-tooth comb. I wish I could tell you the guy had some weakness, that he'd been claiming business trips and actually nippin' off to Atlantic City to the casinos, but it just isn't so. The guy is your basic stick-in-the-mud."

"But he's the nominal head of Castleton Industries."

"Very nominal. Milton Castleton still runs the show, and everyone knows it."

"Yeah. Until he dies."

"What?"

"Milton Castleton is a sick man. He's not gonna last forever. So what happens when he dies? What does Stanley Castleton do then?"

"That'll be up to him. Daddy may have left him some guidelines, but he doesn't have to follow them. It'll be his company then."

"Will it?"

"Whaddya mean?"

"Just a thought, Mark. Right now Stanley Castleton's in charge. Nominally, as you say. And one assumes he'd take over when the old man dies. But would he?"

Mark Taylor frowned. "Whaddya mean?"

"Well, he would now, that's for sure. But if David hadn't died."

"What are you getting at, Steve?"

"From everything you told me, there's no way Stanley Castleton could run the company."

"So?"

"So Milton Castleton must know that. He must have been taking that into account. He's old and sick, and he can't last much longer. But he's a fighter, and he's got an interest in this empire he built up."

"I'm trying to follow this, but—"

"I'm talking about the line of succession. You say Stanley Castleton would take over after his father's death, but what if he wouldn't? I mean, here's Castleton's son—weak, ineffectual, everything Castleton isn't. And here's the grandson—young, sharp, aggressive, just coming in to his own. A go-getter, playboy type, a chip off the old block."

"Are you saying—"

"Sure I am. What if Castleton's plan was to bypass old Stanley and put David in charge?"

"Could he do that?"

"How the hell should I know? It's just an idea. If he was planning that and Stanley found out, he just might not like it too much."

"So he kills his own son?"

"Hey, Mark, isn't it the quiet, repressed types that always take a chainsaw to their family and wind up on the front page of the *Daily News?*"

Taylor shook his head gloomily. "I suppose so. As a theory, I can't say I like it much."

"Me neither. But let's not pass it up. Get your men digging around, see what you can get."

Taylor scribbled a note. "Okay, will do."

"What about Danby?"

Taylor shook his head. "There again, it's a dead end. Company man, fifteen years with the firm. Business manager, trouble-shooter, whatever you want to call him—has no official title I can tell. Basically, Milton Castleton's right hand. No personal interest in the company. Just your basic hundred-grand-a-year wage slave.

"Vices, none. Doesn't drink, smoke, gamble or do drugs. Single, never been married, doesn't chase after women. Not gay, either, just not interested. Workaholic. Married to his job."

"Shit."

"Yeah, why couldn't one of these guys turn out to be a child molester or something you could use? Anyway, I got nothing."

"Where was he that night?"

"If you mean an alibi, I assume he hasn't got one. The guy lives alone. But these people are all hostile and won't talk to us. And the cops aren't askin' 'cause they don't give a shit—they got their murderer. So there you are."

"Yeah. What about the roommate? Jeff Bowers?"

"A little better there. He's a young guy, twenty-nine, an actor, hangs around with the theater crowd and might be into drugs. But what the hell does that get you? He's got no connection at all to Castleton Industries except for Herbert Clay."

"That could be enough."

"Anyway, he's got an alibi for the time of the murder. He was on stage in a show."

"That late at night?"

"So he says. I'm checkin' it out, but why would he claim something so easy to verify if it wasn't true?"

Steve rubbed his head. "Jesus. One dead end after another. You got anything else?"

Taylor frowned. "I got a suggestion. I'm not sure you'll like it."

"Whaddya mean?"

"Well, it's really none of my business. But we're friends, so I'm gonna say it."

"What's that, Mark?"

"I been thinking this ever since I heard Dirkson was prosecuting himself." He gestured to the newspapers on his desk—"And ever since I saw this.

"You got a problem with this case, Steve. In more ways than one. The girl typin' nude—well, that's a big bummer. You can fight to keep it out of court, but so what. It'll be like the Oliver North trial. You're not gonna find twelve people in all of Manhattan who haven't heard about it."

"I know that. So?"

"So the people on the jury are gonna know. And human nature bein' what it is, at least half of them are gonna think a girl who runs around nude is the type of girl who'd kill someone."

"I know that Mark. What's the point?"

"The point is, you got a big image problem. You want to build your client up, make her seem respectable, make her seem the type of girl who *wouldn't* kill someone. It's not gonna be easy, and, frankly, you being her lawyer isn't gonna help."

Steve looked at him. Taylor held up his hands. "Hey, no offense, but I gotta say it. Imagewise, you're the wrong lawyer for the case. You look like a refugee from the sixties. Ordinarily that's all right, but this time it isn't gonna play. The girl doesn't need a hippie standing next to her. She needs someone respectable and conservative. Some pillar of the community whose presence would build up her image."

"You telling me to get off the case, Mark?"

Taylor shook his head. "No. I'm only suggesting you might secure associate counsel."

"You mean Fitzpatrick?"

"I was thinking of Fitzpatrick. He's just the right image. The white hair, the three-piece suit. Plus he's overweight and got chubby cheeks, the well-fed, prosperous look. Fitzpatrick, Blackburn and Weed is a prestigious, conservative firm. His standing up for the girl would lend weight.

"Of course, I'm not sure if Fitzpatrick would want to work with you again."

"Thanks a lot, Mark."

"You know what I mean. Look, Steve, maybe I'm out of line, it just seems to me having Fitzpatrick on the team might help. I hope you're not offended."

Steve thought a moment. "No, I'm not offended, Mark. In fact, that's exactly what I'm gonna do."

25

HAROLD FITZPATRICK RAN a hand through his curly white hair, cocked his head at Steve Winslow and said, "I understand you have a case."

Steve Winslow looked at him for a moment, then burst out laughing.

"What's so funny?" Fitzpatrick said.

"You," Steve said. He jerked his thumb at the newspaper lying on Fitzpatrick's desk. "It's on the front page of the *Daily News*, but you *understand* I have a case."

Fitzpatrick smiled. "You don't like my choice of words? All right, I *know* you have a case. This girl—the naked one—tell me, how is she?"

"Not too well. She's in jail."

"I know that. I mean, what is she like?"

"She has large breasts."

Fitzpatrick shook his head. "Dear, dear."

"And she's spunky."

"Spunky?" Fitzpatrick grimaced. "Even worse. Juries don't like spunky."

"Yeah," Steve said. "I can strap her down and dress her like a Sunday-school teacher, but it's not gonna fool anyone."

Fitzpatrick jerked his thumb at the newspaper. "Not with this kind of publicity. So how you gonna play it?"

"I haven't decided yet."

"I see."

146

Steve Winslow glanced around Fitzpatrick's sumptuously furnished office. "So how's things with the firm?"

"Could be worse, " Fitzpatrick said. "Could be a lot worse. In point of fact, we're actually doing very well."

"I'm not surprised," Steve said. "A firm like this, I would imagine things were pretty steady."

"What do you mean?"

"Well, you have an established clientele. You don't take on new clients all the time."

Fitzpatrick nodded. "That's largely true. A good percentage of our clients have been with the firm twenty, thirty years. That's the way it is with firms of our type. Of course, we do pick up a new client now and then."

"Did appearing in court with me hurt you any?"

Fitzpatrick shook his head. "Not at all. It might have if we'd lost, but we won. We actually picked up clients from it."

"Oh?"

Fitzpatrick chuckled. "Yeah. I was a celebrity for a while. People would come up to me at cocktail parties, say, 'You defended in the Harding case, didn't you?' People actually came over to our firm, which is strange when you think of it. Because our type of client isn't looking for a criminal lawyer. Quite the contrary. I guess it was a status thing. Snob appeal. Like saying F. Lee Bailey's my lawyer, you know?" Fitzpatrick shook his head. "No, that case didn't hurt me at all."

Fitzpatrick grinned. His eyes were shining. "Why do you ask?"

"Oh, just making conversation."

Fitzpatrick nodded judiciously. "Right, right. You got a murder case you're defending, so you just pop over here to make a little conversation."

"Well, I was wondering about your courtroom experience."

"What about it?"

"When the case was over, you expressed the opinion that you doubted if we'd be working together again soon."

"As I recall, I did say something like that."

"I was wondering if you were still of that opinion."

Fitzpatrick pursed his lips. "Are you asking me to work on this case?"

"No."

Fitzpatrick frowned. "No?"

"No," Steve said. "It would be highly detrimental to my client to ask for help from such a prestigious firm and be turned down. And I do hate lying to the press."

"That's a failing in a lawyer," Fitzpatrick deadpanned.

"Anyway, I prefer to talk hypothetically. I'm wondering if that were the case, what your reaction would be."

Fitzpatrick leaned back in his chair, ran his hand through his curly white hair. "You know," he said, "I have to admit, I liked it. The Harding case, I mean. Being in court. The whole thing. Not the sort of thing I want to do every day, but it sure was a kick.

"Oh course, that was a lot different. I was the original lawyer on the case, and then you came in. This case, it's the other way around. Not that I mind playing second fiddle, but I'd still like to play *something*."

"What do you mean?"

Fitzpatrick smiled. "I know why you're here. I knew the minute you walked in the door. Hell, I knew before you came." He shook his head. "Look, if you really needed help, it would be one thing. But I know you. I've seen you in court. You need my help like you need a hole in the head.

"Look, I'm not the greatest trial lawyer in the world. Hell, I'm not even a trial lawyer. In point of fact, I haven't been back in court since our last case.

"And now you're in here, asking me without actually asking me if I'd like to work with you again.

"If I could do something, yeah. But to be a prop. An ornament. That's all I'd be, wouldn't I? I mean, that's the situation here. The girl's got a credibility problem. You need some conservative old fart like me to sit next to her and lend an air of respectability.

"I mean, that's all you really want me for, isn't it?"

Steve grinned at Fitzpatrick. "Not at all."

26

District Attorney Harry Dirkson was nervous.

It wasn't because the courtroom was jammed, with every available seat taken—Dirkson was a veteran campaigner, he'd played to packed houses before. And it wasn't because the case was a political bombshell, what with the girl typing nude—though surely that was part of it. No, what made Dirkson nervous was one frail old man, sitting dead center on the aisle in the second row. A pale, emaciated elderly man who somehow radiated more power that anyone else in the courtroom. Milton Castleton would be watching his every move. It was enough to make even an experienced prosecutor like Harry Dirkson self-conscious.

Dirkson didn't show it though. It was with every appearance of confidence and poise that he rose to make his opening argument. He strode into the middle of the courtroom, acknowledged the judge and the jurors, then stood there a moment, waiting until he was sure he had everyone's attention.

"What is the oldest motivation in the world?" Dirkson said. He glanced around the courtroom, as if looking for an answer. "Is it greed?" He shook his head. "No. It's not greed. It's not lust, either. It's not jealousy and it's not even hatred. So what is it?" Dirkson glanced around one more time, as if the question were not rhetorical. Then he held up one finger. "Revenge. That is the primal motive. Revenge. Take the lowliest creature—if you strike at it, it will strike back. 'The smallest worm will turn, being

trodden on.' Shakespeare was right. Revenge is the basic, in-
stinctual motivation. You hurt me, I hurt you. Revenge.

"Well, ladies and gentlemen of the jury, that is the motive we
expect to lay before you in this case."

Dirkson paused, looked around again. He seemed to switch
gears, dropping the ponderous, oratorical tone and swinging into
his no-nonsense, hard-line-prosecutor mode. "Ladies and gentlemen of the jury, we expect to prove that on the night of June
twenty-eighth, the defendant, Kelly Clay Wilder, murdered the
decedent, David Castleton, by shooting him in the heart with a
loaded gun.

"And why did she do this, ladies and gentlemen of the jury?
She did it for revenge. We expect to show that Kelly Clay
Wilder's brother, one Herbert Clay, was a bookkeeper with
Castleton Industries. His immediate superior in the company was
none other than David Castleton. We expect to show that Herbert Clay embezzled over one hundred thousand dollars from
Castleton Industries and was subsequently arrested and sent to
jail for that crime. We expect to show that because of this, and
out of devotion for her brother, the defendant, Kelly Clay Wilder,
developed a deep-seated resentment against Castleton Industries
in general and against David Castleton in particular.

"There was no basis for this resentment. It was not rational.
Castleton Industries was the victim, not her brother. He tried to
steal from them, got caught, and went to jail. Surely, that could
not be considered Castleton Industries' fault. It is not rational.
But we expect to show that the defendant, Kelly Clay Wilder, is
not an entirely rational woman. In her somewhat warped opinion,
her brother had been wronged, the one who wronged him was
Castleton Industries, so she proceeded to exact her revenge.

"Now, ladies and gentlemen, the manner in which she did so is
so bizarre that it defies comprehension. When you hear it, you
will say, 'No, it cannot be,' but I assure you, these things are facts
and can be proven.

"The first thing Kelly Clay Wilder did in her plot for revenge
was to attempt to insinuate her way into Castleton Industries.
Now, the founder and head of Castleton Industries, Milton
Castleton, is presently retired, but was still the active head of the
company two years ago when Herbert Clay was found guilty of

embezzlement. So he and David Castleton were the two men Kelly Clay Wilder would blame most for her brother's imprisonment.

"Her first target was Milton Castleton. The defendant, Kelly Clay Wilder, learned that Milton Castleton was writing his memoirs and employing secretaries to type them. So she applied for the job."

Dirkson paused and took a breath. "It turned out to be a peculiar job. Milton Castleton's secretaries typed nude." Dirkson paused and looked around. He did a good job of it. There was not a trace of amusement on his face. He looked as solemn as could be.

Dirkson nodded gravely. "That's right, ladies and gentlemen. You heard me correctly. Nude. Naked."

Dirkson turned and pointed at the defendant, just in case any of the jurors had missed the point. Not that any of them had. In point of fact, Dirkson noted with some satisfaction, they were all looking at her already.

"When Kelly Clay Wilder applied for the job, she learned that if she got it she would be required to sit naked at her word processor while she did her typing."

"Did that dissuade her from taking the job? No, it did not. She took it. She came in to work every day. And she took off her clothes. And she walked around her office naked. And she sat at her typewriter naked. And she typed naked. From nine o'clock in the morning till five o'clock at night when she went home."

Dirkson paused and looked over at Kelly Wilder. "Now, you might ask yourself, why would a young woman do such a thing? The answer is simple. Revenge. It was the first step in her campaign of revenge. And how did she enact that revenge? Simple. After a few weeks of parading around naked, she quit her job, hurled an accusation of sexual harassment against her employer, Milton Castleton, and finagled a settlement of fifty thousand dollars from him."

Dirkson shook his head. "Fifty thousand dollars. Surely a fair price for walking around naked, don't you think? Had any other woman done it, you would have to consider it extortion. But for the sister of Herbert Clay, it would be considered revenge.

"But the revenge wasn't sweet enough. We expect to show that shortly after receiving her settlement, Kelly Clay Wilder began placing phone calls to Milton Castleton, implying that through her employment she had learned industrial secrets about Castleton Industries, which she would reveal unless Milton Castleton acceded to her wishes.

"And what did she want? What was it that she demanded?" Dirkson held up his finger. "Nothing less than a private meeting with Milton Castleton. One to one. Somewhere away from his apartment."

Dirkson shook his head. "Well, ladies and gentlemen, there is little doubt what would have happened had he acceded to that request. But as it was, ill health prevented him from even considering such a proposal. Instead, and to his great regret, he sent his grandson in his place.

"What happened then, ladies and gentlemen? Well, the facts are all too clear, and we shall lay them out for you. We expect to show that at approximately seven o'clock on the evening of June twenty-eighth, the decedent, David Castleton, met the defendant, Kelly Clay Wilder, at a singles bar on Third Avenue, that they left the bar almost immediately and took a taxi uptown to a small Italian restaurant and had a long and leisurely dinner. This fact will be attested to by both the waiter and the maître d'. Both knew David Castleton by sight—this was a favorite restaurant of his, he dined there often. And both the waiter and the maître d' will positively identify the defendant, Kelly Clay Wilder, as the young woman who dined with David Castleton that night.

"You will hear the testimony of the cab driver who picked up David Castleton and Kelly Clay Wilder outside the restaurant at approximately ten-twenty that evening. We will introduce his trip sheet, on which is recorded in his own handwriting the destination, which recorded not only the street, but also the actual address of David Castleton's apartment. We shall show beyond a shadow of a doubt that the decedent, David Castleton, and the defendant, Kelly Clay Wilder, returned to David Castleton's apartment at approximately ten-thirty on the night of the murder."

Dirkson spread his arms. "What happened next is up to you to infer. This is a case of circumstantial evidence. Most murder cases are. What that means is that there is no eyewitness to the crime. No one saw Kelly Clay Wilder actually shoot David Castleton. This is not unusual. Murderers don't usually shoot their victims when someone is watching. Therefore, most murder cases must be proved by circumstantial evidence."

Dirkson smiled and shook his head. "Well, I doubt if the circumstances have ever been more overwhelming than they are in this case. As I already started, we will show that David Castleton and Kelly Clay Wilder returned to his apartment at ten-thirty on the evening of the murder. We will show by the testimony of the medical examiner that David Castleton met his death some time between the hours of eleven and twelve o'clock that night. We will show that he died of a single bullet fired into his heart. We will show that the murder gun, the gun that fired the fatal bullet, was left behind, next to the body."

Dirkson paused, raised his finger. "Again, not an unusual circumstance. Most murderers leave the gun. No one wants to be caught with the murder weapon in their possession."

Dirkson smiled. "However, in this instance, leaving the murder weapon there was a big mistake. See, Kelly Clay Wilder must have figured that it was what we refer to as a cold piece—that is, that it was an illegal, unregistered gun that could never be traced. Unfortunately for her, this is not the case. We will be able to show that the murder weapon was indeed duly licensed and registered. And who was the gun purchased by, licensed and registered to? None other than the defendant's brother, Herbert Clay."

Dirkson shrugged his shoulders, spread his hands wide. "Ladies and gentlemen of the jury, I don't want to insult your intelligence by pointing out what all these facts mean. It is very simple. We have a young woman hell-bent on revenge. So obsessed with the idea of revenge, that she was willing to run around naked in order to extort money from Milton Castleton, head of Castleton Industries, and subsequently set up an assignation and murder his grandson, David Castleton.

"We shall prove all these things beyond a reasonable doubt, and we shall expect a verdict of guilty at your hands."

Dirkson bowed to the jury and sat down. As he did, a low murmur broke out in the courtroom.

Judge Wallingsford silenced it with his gavel.

Dirkson grinned. He couldn't have drawn a better judge for this case. Wallingsford was an older judge, stern, severe, and quick with the gavel. He would brook no nonsense in his courtroom. Moreover, his judicial impartiality nothwithstanding, Wallingsford's cold, disapproving appearance implied a high moral tone, which would only serve to point up the defendant's improprieties. All in all, Dirkson could not have done better.

Judge Wallingsford glanced over at the defense table, where Kelly Clay Wilder sat flanked by Steve Winslow, dressed as usual in corduroy jacket and jeans, and Harold Fitzpatrick, as usual the model of propriety in his three-piece suit. "Does the defense wish to make an opening statement?"

Fitzpatrick stood up. "The defense does, Your Honor."

Dirkson smiled again. No surprise that Fitzpatrick would be handling the opening statement. That's what he'd been hired for. To match Dirkson's high moral tone and try to clothe the defendant in a cloak of respectability. In Dirkson's mind, it was a hollow tactic, and one that wasn't particularly going to work. So he was pleased to see the defense trying it.

Fitzpatrick walked out into the middle of the courtroom. Indeed, he looked just as solemn as Dirkson had, a frown of disapproval on his brow. Dirkson knew what would come next would be a weighty, ponderous argument.

Fitzpatrick did indeed begin slowly and ponderously. "Ladies and gentlemen of the jury," he said. "I just heard District Attorney Harry Dirkson's opening statement, and I have to tell you it is the most unusual opening argument I have ever heard." His disapproving frown gave way to one of puzzlement. "I don't know about you, but I don't think I've ever head the word *naked* used so often. I wasn't counting, so I can't tell you exactly how many times Harry Dirkson used the word naked, but I do know this— he used the word *naked* more times than he used the word *murder*." Fitzpatrick shook his head. "Well, that's mighty strange. From the opening argument, it would seem this defendant was charged not with the crime of murder, but with the crime of being naked."

Fitzpatrick held up his hands. "Well, I would just like to set the record straight on this point. We do not wish to contest the allegation that the defendant typed naked. She did. There is no question about it. She typed naked. Stark naked. Nude. Boffo. In the buff."

Fitzpatrick paused and glanced around the courtroom. Everyone, including Harry Dirkson, was staring at him incredulously. Dirkson's mouth was actually open.

Fitzpatrick held his hands wide and looked around. He was smiling, and he looked not so much an attorney than a vaudeville hoofer about to take off on a buck-and-wing. "You all got that?" he said. "I know Harry Dirkson did his best to hammer it in, but I want to make sure there's no mistake. The defendant typed naked. Absolutely naked." He held up one finger. "And what's more, when she was naked, she didn't have any clothes on."

Fitzpatrick smiled, glanced around again. "Everybody got that? I want to make sure everybody got that. I want to be very clear on this point." Fitzpatrick wheeled around, pointed his finger at Kelly Clay Wilder. "I'm going to ask the defendant to stand up and take her clothes off. Miss Wilder, would you please stand up—"

"Objection!" Dirkson thundered. He lunged to his feet. "Your Honor, I—"

Judge Wallingsford's gavel cut him off. Simultaneously, a roar erupted in the courtroom, as the spectators, who had been stunned by what Fitzpatrick had said, all began talking at once. Judge Wallingsford banged the gavel furiously, shouted for order, but it was several seconds before the courtroom quieted down.

"That will do," Judge Wallingsford said. His face was iron and his eyes were blazing. "Let the spectators be warned. Another such outburst, and I will clear this courtroom." He shifted his eyes to glare down at Fitzpatrick. "Attorneys, I will see you in my chambers. Now."

With that he got up and stalked from the courtroom.

27

Judge Wallingsford was controlling himself with a great effort. "Mr. Fitzpatrick," he said. "I must say I would not have expected this sort of behavior from so conservative and respected a member of the bar."

Fitzpatrick played it well—polite and deferential, but still cool and unperturbed. "I beg your pardon, Your Honor," he said, "but to what do you refer?"

Judge Wallingsford nearly gagged. "What?" he sputtered. "To what do I refer? You just stood up in my courtroom and asked the woman you are defending to take her clothes off."

"Oh, that," Fitzpatrick said.

Judge Wallingsford took a breath. "Mr. Fitzpatrick, are you *trying* to infuriate me?"

"Not at all, Your Honor. But I don't see what the commotion is all about. District Attorney Harry Dirkson is the one who brought up the matter of the defendant being nude. He mentioned it several times. He took great pains to emphasize the point."

"Which he has every right to do," Judge Wallingsford snapped. "And you have every right to emphasize the points you wish to emphasize in *your* opening argument. But you went beyond that. You asked the defendant to stand up and take her clothes off."

"Only to make a point, Your Honor."

"You're not supposed to be making points. At least, not in that manner. You're supposed to be stating what you intend to prove.

This is a courtroom, not a sideshow. I won't put up with such theatrics."

Dirkson, who had been fuming on the sidelines, could control himself no longer. "It's not him, Your Honor," he said irritably. He pointed to Steve Winslow. "He put him up to it. It's a typical Steve Winslow stunt. This whole thing is pure Winslow."

Judge Wallingsford turned to Steve Winslow. "And what do you have to say for yourself?"

"I resent Mr. Dirkson's remarks, Your Honor," Steve said. "Fitzpatrick and I are co-counsel, and naturally we have conferred on strategy. I find the phrase 'put him up to it' offensive, and I'm sure Mr. Fitzpatrick does too."

Judge Wallingsford frowned. "That is not the point. I must say, I find your attitude irritating at best. At worst, it borders on contempt of court. I hope I make myself clear. I do not intend to put up with this sort of nonsense in my courtroom."

"Begging Your Honor's pardon," Steve said, "but I don't think you ever ruled on the objection."

"What?"

"Mr. Dirkson's objection. Mr. Fitzpatrick was making his opening statement, Dirkson objected, you cut him off and ordered us in here. You never ruled on the objection. In fact, I don't believe Mr. Dirkson ever finished making it. So I'm not clear what the grounds for his objection are."

"Son of a bitch!" Dirkson snapped.

"Mr. Dirkson, that will do," Judge Wallingsford said. "Mr. Winslow, your attitude is insolent and borders on contempt of court. You know perfectly well what's going on here. Mr. Dirkson has objected to outrageous behavior which has no place in the courtroom. His objection will be sustained. And I hereby serve notice that if you persist along these lines, I *will* find you in contempt of court."

"Noted, Your Honor. But if we could please clarify this one point. I assume this applies only to the suggestion that our client take her clothes off, and not to anything else. Specifically, not to any remarks Mr. Fitzpatrick made conceding that the defendant did indeed type nude. Especially since those remarks were only replying to allegations made by District Attorney Harry Dirkson in his opening statement."

"Certainly," Judge Wallingsford said. "As offensive as those remarks might be, the door was certainly open for them and they may stand. But I would hope this will be the end of that particular issue."

"So would I, Your Honor," Steve said. "Then the only bone of contention here is the suggestion the defendant take her clothes off?"

"That's right."

"Fine," Steve said. "Then if Mr. Fitzpatrick agrees, we will withdraw that suggestion, rendering the matter moot. Is that acceptable to you, Fitzpatrick?"

"Absolutely. Your Honor, I hereby withdraw that remark and tender my apologies to the court."

"Very well," Judge Wallingsford said. "Then, gentlemen, if we could proceed."

"I trust Your Honor will explain the situation to the jury," Steve said.

"Naturally," Judge Wallingsford said.

"Will you explain to them that the defendant is not going to take her clothes off because District Attorney Harry Dirkson doesn't want them to see that?"

Judge Wallingsford opened his mouth. His lip quivered. He attempted to fight back a smile but was unsuccessful. He chuckled, then shook his head angrily. "Damn it," he said. "Mr. Dirkson, I apologize. There is nothing funny about this. It is a murder trial. Let's try to get on with it." He glared at Fitzpatrick. "And I warn you, any more theatrics will be considered contempt of court."

With that he turned and stalked out of his chambers.

Dirkson glared at Winslow and Fitzpatrick, then turned and followed him.

In front of Judge Wallingsford, Fitzpatrick had looked positively contrite. But as they followed the judge and the D.A. out of chambers, Fitzpatrick nudged Steve Winslow in the ribs, leaned over and whispered, "Most fun I've had in years."

28

THE *NEW YORK POST* AND the *Daily News* both had the headline, "TAKE HER CLOTHES OFF!" The *New York Times* had a small paragraph in section two.

Steve Winslow, Mark Taylor and Tracy Garvin read the papers the next morning in a small coffee shop near the courthouse.

"Not bad," Taylor said.

"The coffee or the coverage?" Steve asked.

"The coverage, of course. The coffee sucks."

Steve took a sip, grimaced. "No argument here. What do you think of the press?"

"Obnoxiously sexist," Tracy said.

"No argument on that either. That's what it is."

"It may be sexist, but it sure is funny," Taylor said.

"No it isn't," Tracy said. "Here's a young woman on trial for murder, and everyone's making fun of her."

"That's true," Steve said.

"So what's the point?"

"Overkill."

"What?"

"The press knows she typed nude, the public knows she typed nude, the jurors know she typed nude. Everyone knows she typed nude. There's nothing we can do about that. The only thing to do is overplay it until it becomes boring and everyone forgets about it."

"Fat chance on that," Taylor said.

"You know what I mean," Steve said. "The fact is, if we sat on this and tried to fight it, it would titillate the jury and drag out through the whole trial. So we have a big splash now, get it out of our system and get on to other things."

"Such as?" Taylor said.

Steve frowned. "That's the problem. The prosecution has a case. We don't."

"Any more surprises planned?"

Steve shook his head. "Nope. That was it. From here on in it will depend on what Dirkson throws at us." He jerked his thumb at the headlines. "I knew this was coming, so I had it in the bag."

"How come Fitzpatrick did it and not you?" Tracy asked.

"That was the whole point," Steve said. "Dirkson would expect this from me. It's the sort of thing I'd pull. From Fitzpatrick he wouldn't have a clue. Besides, coming from me it wouldn't have meant anything. Typical Winslow trick—of course I'd say that. But respectable, dignified Fitzpatrick standing out there in his three-piece suit—well, from him it really made a splash."

"I'll say."

"Well, eat up," Steve said. "I wouldn't want to be late for court. I can't wait to see what Dirkson throws at us next."

29

FOR HIS FIRST WITNESS Dirkson called Joyce Wilkens, David Castleton's cleaning lady, who testified to coming to work at nine o'clock, letting herself in with a key as was her custom and finding him lying dead on the floor. She then called the police and waited for them to arrive.

Fitzpatrick held a whispered conference with Steve Winslow, then took her on cross-examination.

"Miss Wilkens, you say you called the police?"

"That's right."

"How?"

"I beg your pardon?"

"Where did you call them from? What phone did you use?"

"From there. The phone in the apartment."

"So you handled the phone in the apartment?"

"Yes. Why?"

"Did you touch anything else in the apartment?"

"No."

"While you waited for the police to arrive, where were you?"

"There."

"In the apartment?"

"Yes."

"And while you were waiting for them to arrive, are you sure you didn't do anything? Start straightening up from force of habit?"

"No, I did not."

Fitzpatrick nodded. "I see. Now, you say the body was that of David Castleton?"

"Yes."

"How did you know?"

The witness stared at Fitzpatrick. "I saw him. I saw the body."

"Yes, Miss Wilkens," Fitzpatrick said. "But the point I'm making is, how did you know who the body was?"

"He's the man I work for."

"I see. Tell me, how long have you worked for David Castleton?"

"Oh, must be two years now."

"How often did you work for him?"

"Once a week."

"You came in once a week to clean for the past two years?"

"That's right."

"I see," Fitzpatrick said. "And on that particular morning you arrived at nine o'clock and let yourself in with a key, is that right?"

"Yes."

"Was that unusual, or do you always do that?"

"I always do that."

"Why?"

"Why? Because I have to get in. By nine o'clock David Castleton has left for work."

"I see. So you get there at nine o'clock. And what time do you go home?"

"Four o'clock."

"Is David Castleton home then?"

"No."

"Then how do you get paid?"

"He leaves money in the foyer for me."

"I see. So when you're finished, you take your money, lock up and go home, is that right?"

"That's right."

"I see," Fitzpatrick said. "Miss Wilkens, I ask you again, how did you know the body was that of David Castleton?"

"I told you. I recognized him."

"How? According to your testimony, you've never seen him.

You arrive after he leaves for work and leave before he gets
home. When did you ever see him?"

"I saw him when he hired me."

"When he hired you?"

"Yes."

"That was two years ago?"

"That's right."

"Have you ever seen him since?"

The witness hesitated. "I think there was once when he was
home sick."

"You think?"

"No. I remember. There was a time he was home sick."

"You saw him then?"

"Yes. I remember, he was sick in bed. He told me to skip his
bedroom, he wasn't feeling well, he just wanted to be left alone."

"I see. So you left him alone?"

"That's right."

"And that's the only occasion you can recall seeing him since he
hired you?"

"Yes."

"Thank you. That's all."

For his next witness, Dirkson called Walter Burke, a radio
patrol officer who testified to responding to a report of a possible
homicide at 190 East 74th Street.

"And what did you find?" Dirkson asked.

"I found the body of a white male, some twenty-five to thirty
years of age, lying facedown in a pool of blood. There was a gun
lying next to the body."

"What did you do?"

"Checked for signs of life."

"Where there any?"

"There were none."

"So what did you do?"

"Radioed for EMS and a Crime Scene Unit."

"That's all."

The defense did not cross-examine.

Next up was Detective Oswald of the Crime Scene Unit. He
testified to arriving at the apartment and photographing the de-

ceased, and a series of eight-by-ten photographs was duly marked for identification, shown to the witness, and received into evidence.

Dirkson next called Harold Kessington, who proved to be the medical examiner. Dr. Kessington was a tall, thin man with no chin and a lot of Adam's apple. He had a rather cheerful disposition for someone who dealt so often with death, and seemed quite comfortable on the witness stand.

"And what time did you arrive at the apartment, Doctor?" Dirkson asked.

"Approximately nine-forty-five."

"Can you be more precise?"

Kessington shook his head. "No. I can tell you it was after nine-forty, and I can tell you it was before nine-fifty—that I know for sure. But the exact minute I can't give you. But it was approximately nine-forty-five."

"And what did you find?"

"I found the body of the decedent lying facedown on the floor."

"Did you examine him at the time?"

"Of course."

"Was he alive?"

"He was dead."

"And what examination did you make at that time?"

Dr. Kessington smiled. "Only a very preliminary one. I determined the man was dead, and determined he had been dead for some time."

"How could you tell that?"

"The body had cooled considerably, and the blood on the floor had coagulated."

"I see. Did those factors tell you the time of death?"

"Oh, absolutely not. I told you this was very preliminary."

"Did you later determine the time of death?"

"Yes, of course."

"When was that?"

"After the body had been removed to the morgue. When I did my autopsy."

"When was that?"

"At ten-thirty that morning."

"Which was approximately forty-five minutes after you initially saw the body?"

"That's right."

"And what did you determine in your autopsy?"

"The decedent met his death due to a bullet wound to the heart."

"A bullet wound?"

"That is correct. The bullet had entered the body through the decedent's chest and had penetrated the left ventricle."

"That was the sole cause of death?"

"Yes, it was."

"I see. And was the bullet still in the body when you performed your autopsy?"

"Yes, it was."

"Did you remove that bullet from the body?"

"Yes, I did."

Dirkson took a small plastic bag from the prosecution table, had it marked for identification, and handed it to the witness. "Doctor, I hand you a plastic bag marked People's Exhibit Two, and ask you if you recognize it?"

"Yes, I do."

"What do you recognize it to be?"

"This is a plastic bag containing the bullet that I removed from the body of the decedent. I scratched the initial K for Kessington, on the base of the bullet. You can see the scratches right here."

"Thank you, Doctor. This is the bullet that you extracted from the body, the bullet that was the sole cause of death of the decedent, David Castleton?"

"Objection, Your Honor," Steve Winslow said.

Judge Wallingsford frowned. "Objection? Very well. Let's have a sidebar."

Fitzpatrick flashed Steve Winslow a glance of inquiry. Steve shook his head slightly, indicating let's not discuss it here, and motioned toward the sidebar. Fitzpatrick got up, and he and Steve Winslow walked over to meet Judge Wallingsford, who had come down from his bench.

Dirkson bustled up, looking miffed. "What are you objecting to?" he demanded.

"The question is leading and suggestive," Steve said. "And assumes facts not in evidence."

"What?" Dirkson said, incredulously.

Judge Wallingsford held up his hand. "One moment," he said. "Let me handle this. Mr. Winslow, I have to agree with the district attorney. The question might technically be considered leading, but all the facts he summarized were already testified to by the witness. So the objection is hardly valid."

"I beg Your Honor's pardon," Steve said. "but the question *is* leading and suggestive, and some of the points summarized are *not* in evidence."

"Nonsense," Dirkson said. "He already identified that bullet as being the one he extracted from the body, and he already testified that it was the sole cause of death."

"No problem there," Steve said. "But you also referred to the decedent, David Castleton."

"Of course," Dirkson said.

Steve shook his head. "That's what's leading and suggestive and assuming facts not in evidence. To date, we have had no testimony that the body is indeed David Castleton."

Dirkson stared at him. "But that's absurd."

"Not at all."

"And we *have* testimony." Dirkson said. "The testimony of the maid who found the body."

"Who admitted on cross-examination that she comes to work after he's left for the office and leaves before he gets home in the afternoon. A witness who saw him once two years ago when he hired her. Who saw a facedown corpse on the living-room floor. I do not consider such testimony sufficient to make a positive identification."

Judge Wallingsford. "Are you questioning the matter of identity, Mr. Winslow?"

"No, Your Honor. I'm merely asking for orderly proof. So far, there's been no conclusive proof that the body was that of David Castleton, and I object to the prosecutor leading the witness by stating the fact that it was."

Judge Wallingsford took a breath. "Mr. Winslow. You are perhaps within your rights, but don't you think you're being a little overtechnical?"

"Perhaps, Your Honor. But if I'm going to err at all, I'm going to err on the side of the defendant. I stand on my objection."

"In which case, the objection will be sustained. Gentlemen, this is a rather minor matter. Mr. Dirkson, do you think you could save us some trouble by rephrasing your question?"

"Very well," Dirkson said shortly. He glared at Steve Winslow and stomped off.

As Steve sat back down, Kelly Wilder grabbed his arm. "What was that all about?"

"Not important," Steve said.

"Yes, but—"

"Shhh."

Judge Wallingsford had returned to the bench. "Mr. Dirkson, would you please rephrase your question?"

"Yes, Your Honor," Dirkson said. "Doctor, referring to the bullet, People's Exhibit Two, is that the bullet that you removed from the body during your autopsy, the bullet that you referred to as the sole cause of death of the decedent?"

"That's right."

Steve Winslow grinned as he watched the faces of the jurors during that question and answer. Of course the jurors couldn't hear what was going on during the sidebar, so Steve knew, human nature being what it was, the jurors were all listening to how the question was rephrased to try to figure out just what the objection had been. From the puzzled frowns on their faces, he was sure none of them could tell the slightest difference.

"Thank you, Doctor," Dirkson said. "Tell me this. Did you determine the time of death?"

"Yes, I did."

"And what time was that?"

"To the best I could determine, the decedent met his death some time between the hours of eleven o'clock and twelve midnight on the night of June twenty-eighth."

"And your autopsy was performed on the morning of June twenty-ninth?"

"That is correct."

"Thank you, Doctor. Your witness."

Fitzpatrick flashed a glance of inquiry at Steve Winslow. Steve leaned across Kelly Wilder and whispered, "Take him on the time element."

Fitzpatrick nodded. He stood up and approached the witness. "Between eleven o'clock and midnight, Doctor?"

"That's right."

"How did you arrive at that figure?"

"Primarily from the body temperature."

"Could you elaborate on that, Doctor?" Fitzpatrick smiled. "In as nontechnical terms as possible?"

Doctor Kessington smiled back. "Certainly. As you know, a person's normal body temperature is ninety-eight point six degrees Fahrenheit. When a person dies, the body begins to cool and the temperature begins to drop. Since the rate of cooling is a constant, approximately one and a half degrees Fahrenheit per hour, by taking the body temperature of the corpse it is possible to determine when the person died."

"I see. And that is what you did in this case?"

"Exactly. If I might consult my notes?"

"Please do."

Doctor Kessington pulled a notebook from his jacket pocket and paged through it. "Here we are. In this instance, I took the body temperature at ten-thirty A.M. on June twenty-ninth. The body temperature was eighty-two degrees Fahrenheit. A drop of sixteen and a half degrees from ninety-eight point six. Dividing by one and a half degrees per hour, I can compute that the man died approximately eleven hours prior to the time I took the temperature."

"I see," Fitzpatrick said. "Tell me, Doctor. Was that the *only* means you used to determine the time of death?"

Doctor Kessington shook his head. "Certainly not. That was the primary means, but I verified my findings by checking the stomach contents."

"The stomach contents, Doctor?"

"Yes. Since digestion ceases after death, by checking the stomach contents and seeing how far digestion has progressed, it is possible to determine when a person died relative to when they ingested their last meal."

"I see. And in this particular case?"

"In this case, the stomach contents included a partially digested meat that proved to be veal. The extent to which digestion had progressed indicated the decedent had died approximately three hours after ingesting the veal."

"Three hours, Doctor?"

"That's right."

"Tell me, Doctor, how does that verify your finding that the decedent died between eleven and twelve that night?"

Doctor Kessington smiled. "In and of itself, it doesn't. It does not tell us the time of death. As I stated, it only pinpoints the time of death relative to his last meal. I don't personally know when the decedent ate his last meal. But I understand that fact *is* known and will be brought out in evidence in this trial. And that fact *was* communicated to me, and based on that hearsay evidence, which I can't testify to, I was able to use the stomach contents to verify my own personal findings based on the body temperature that the decedent died between eleven and twelve."

"I see. But in verifying those findings, you are relying on what people told you regarding when the decedent ate his last meal?"

"That is correct."

"And if those people were mistaken, then you could be mistaken?"

Dr. Kessington frowned.

"Can't you answer that, Doctor?"

"Yes, I can. I wish to phrase my answer so as to be absolutely fair. The figure I gave you—three hours from the time the decedent ate the veal till the time he died—that is a constant. That would not change, regardless of the accuracy of what anyone told me. As to the exact time of the day the victim died, that of course would be affected."

"I see. Now you say he died three hours after he ate his last meal. You also say he died between the hours of eleven and twelve. The median time would be eleven-thirty. Three hours prior to that would be eight-thirty. Working backward, from your personal medical findings, and *not* based on anything anyone told you, is it your personal opinion that the decedent ate his last meal at eight-thirty on the night that he died?"

Dr. Kessington nodded. "That is correct."

"Fine, Doctor. Then let me ask you this hypothetical question. From District Attorney Harry Dirkson's opening statement, there is reason to believe that we will hear testimony that the decedent ate a long and leisurely meal. If it should turn out that the decedent was not actually served his veal until nine o'clock, would that change your findings any? You say three hours is a constant. Would you then say, the decedent probably died at midnight, midnight is the median time, he could have died between eleven-thirty and twelve-thirty?"

Dr. Kessington shook his head. "No, I would not."

"Why not, Doctor?"

"As I said, digestion is merely a secondary factor in verifying the time of death. The primary method, body temperature, is the more precise method, and the one on which I would rely. It indicated death between eleven and twelve, and that is the finding I would rely on. If the stomach contents indicated the time of death to be around midnight, I would take that as a confirmation rather than a contradiction of that finding."

Fitzpatrick nodded. "Very well put, Doctor. And you say the body temperature indicated that the time of death was between eleven and twelve o'clock?"

"Yes. As I've stated several times."

"It could have occurred at midnight, Doctor?"

"It could. But that is an outside limit. The optimum time would be around eleven-thirty. Eleven and twelve are outside limits."

"But death *could* have occurred at twelve o'clock?"

"It could."

"Could it have occurred at twelve-oh-one?"

For the first time, Doctor Kessington appeared annoyed. "Now you're splitting hairs, Counselor."

"Maybe I am, but I'd still like the question answered. Are you telling me death *could* have occurred at twelve o'clock, but could *not* have occurred at twelve-oh-one?"

"No, I'm not," Dr. Kessington said irritably. "I'm a reasonable man attempting to make a rational answer. My expert findings indicate death occurred between eleven and twelve. If you want to stretch that by one minute, obviously there is no argument I can make against it that will not sound ridiculous."

"I appreciate your dilemma, but I would still like a yes or no answer. *Could* death have occurred at twelve-oh-one?"

Dr. Kessington took a breath. He glared at Fitzpatrick. "It is stretching the bounds of likelihood," he said. "But the answer is yes."

Fitzpatrick nodded. "Thank you, Doctor. So," he said breezily, "if I understand you correctly, you are now testifying that your expert medical findings indicate the decedent met his death sometime on June twenty-eighth or sometime on June twenty-ninth. Thank you. That's all."

Dirkson roared an objection, and Judge Wallingsford admonished Fitzpatrick for the comment.

As Fitzpatrick sat down, Steve Winslow leaned across Kelly Wilder and nodded approvingly. "Not bad."

30

FITZPATRICK SPENT the lunch hour on the phone to his office, catching up on his law practice.

Steve Winslow, who had no law practice to catch up on, had lunch with Mark Taylor and Tracy Garvin at a small deli near the courthouse. They ordered at the counter, carried their food to a small table in the back.

Mark Taylor sat down, took a huge bite of pastrami sandwich and washed it down with coffee. "So," he said. "Tell me about the time element."

"What about it?" Steve said.

"You always make a big deal of the time element. Last case it was bullshit. What about this time? Does it mean anything?"

"Yes and no."

"What does that mean?"

Steve shrugged. "For the most part, it's just bullshit. Give the jury a show. Mess the facts up, create reasonable doubt. Besides, it's standard practice to pick on the doctor. Why? Because the jurors like that. Doctors make big bucks. Doctors don't make house calls. Doctors are professional men who are apt to come off pompous and arrogant, and jurors love to see 'em taken down a peg." Stave shrugged again. "It ain't fair, but that's just the way it is.

"But in this case, it actually does mean something. The doctor puts the time of death at eleven-thirty. We happen to know eleven-thirty was the time Kelly Wilder left the apartment.

172

That's pretty damning. You don't stick around after you kill someone. You kill 'em, and you leave. She shot him at eleven-thirty and got the hell out of there."

Taylor grimaced. "Christ, Steve," he said with a mouthful of pastrami. "You're torturing me."

"Yeah, well at least I'm not spoiling your appetite," Steve said dryly. "I'm sorry, Mark, but that's the fact. She left at eleven-thirty. We know it, the prosecution doesn't.

"But think what that means. If the time element gets screwed up, if the waiter from that restaurant gets on the stand, says he didn't serve the veal until after nine—well, we got the doctor saying he died three hours after that. Which would be midnight. And in that case, when he was shot Kelly Wilder was long gone."

"Right," Taylor said irritably. "You know it and I know it. But how the hell are we gonna prove it? Call the detectives to the stand? For one thing, we can't even find 'em. For another thing, if you did, you'd put me on the hook for withholding evidence."

"I know that, Mark."

"I know you do, but so what? I know you. You'll do anything for your client and the hell with anybody else. If you manage to prove David Castleton was killed at midnight, it's gonna be 'Sorry, Mark, I know it's gonna cost you your license, but I gotta put your detectives on the stand.' "

"No, it isn't."

"Oh yeah? Tell me why not."

"For one thing, there's no way we can prove he was killed at midnight. We can raise the inference, I can create reasonable doubt, and it could be the time he ate his last meal will bear me out. But that's all it is, reasonable doubt. You get what I saying? It doesn't matter if I prove he *could* have been killed at midnight. The only thing that would make any difference would be if I could prove he *couldn't* have been killed at eleven-thirty. And there's no way I can do that."

"So the time element thing is basically bullshit?"

"Basically, yes."

"That's a relief. That's what I figured, but when I heard Fitzpatrick pushin' so hard for midnight I wasn't sure. Tell me something."

"What?"

"Did you *tell* Fitzpatrick to push for midnight?"

Steve shook his head. "No. I just told him to take the guy on the time element. I didn't tell him how to do it. That cross-examination was all Fitzpatrick. I must say, for a guy who isn't in court that much, he's pretty damn good."

Taylor shook his head. "That's not what I mean."

"What do you mean?"

"You *know* what I mean. Does Fitzpatrick know Kelly Wilder's got a cold alibi for eleven-thirty on? By two witnesses who can place her at the scene of the crime at the time of the murder, but who haven't surfaced yet?"

Steve frowned. "You think he'd be on the case if he did?"

"Not a prayer."

"There's your answer."

"I'd hate to be in your shoes when he finds out."

Steve took a breath. "Mark, it's a mess, I know it's a mess. I don't ever want to go through this again either. You don't have to rub it in."

"Could I change the subject?" Tracy said.

"Love you for it," Steve said. "Jump right in."

"The sidebar. And your objection. What was that all about?"

"Yeah," Taylor said. "That made absolutely no sense. The jury was looking around like 'what's going on?' and the judge says, 'Rephrase the question,' and Dirkson does, and I can't tell if your objection's been sustained or overruled or what the hell it was to begin with."

Steve grinned. "Yeah, that was kind of weird. I objected to him referring to the decedent as David Castleton on the grounds they hadn't proved identity yet."

Taylor frowned. "What?"

"Why did you do that?" Tracy asked.

"To force them to identify the body."

"But there's no question about it," Taylor said.

"Exactly," Steve said. "But I still want them to go through the motions."

"Why?"

"Because I'm groping in the dark and I need all the shots I can get. So I'm going to be very technical about procedure. Proper procedure is, Dirkson must show the corpus delicti before he can introduce any evidence connecting Kelly Wilder to the crime. Part of the corpus delicti is proving the identity of the corpse."

"So what?" Taylor asked. "It is David Castleton, isn't it?"

"Of course it is. But I'm not going to take the word of a cleaning lady for it. I want to make Dirkson put someone on the stand to identify the body."

"Why?"

"So I get a shot at him. The way I see it, it will be either Milton or Stanley Castleton. They're both bound to be witnesses later on. Whichever it is, Ill get two cracks at him on the cross-examination. It can only help."

"Yeah," Tracy said. "But if Dirkson only calls them to identify the body, isn't that all you can cross-examine them on?"

"Yeah, but it's always relevant to show bias. And I can bring out a lot of stuff to show these guys have every reason to be biased against Kelly Wilder on account of her brother. I can drag in the embezzlement bit."

"I thought Dirkson was gonna drag it in anyway." Taylor said.

"Yeah, but you want to bet I can make it sound different than he can?"

"No takers."

"I still say what's the point?" Tracy said.

Steve sighed and ran his hand over his head. "The point is, sooner or later Dirkson's gonna rest his case. When he does, we got a big problem. For one thing, we already shot our opening argument. That was a judgment call, and I still think it was worth it, but it's done. Which means we open our case cold. I can't stand up and tell the jury what we expect to prove. I gotta call witnesses and build our case from them. Well, that being the case, I wanna lay as big a foundation as I can before Dirkson rests and we take over. In other words, I want the jury to hear as much corroboration as possible before they hear Kelly Wilder's story."

"You gonna put her on the stand?" Tracy said.

Steve grimaced. "That's the problem. At this point, frankly, I just don't know."

31

When court reconvened Dirkson stood up and said, "Call Stanley Castleton."

Steve Winslow watched with some interest as Stanley Castleton made his way to the stand. He was tall and thin, but his slumped shoulders and lowered head greatly diminished his height. Steve wondered if it was due to the loss of his son or if it was his standard posture.

As Stanley Castleton came forward and took the stand his movements were tentative and hesitant. Steve figured Mark Taylor's description had been right on the money—weak and ineffectual.

When Stanley Castleton had been sworn in, Dirkson rose and crossed to him.

Naturally Dirkson made a big show of being solicitous and sympathetic. "Mr. Castleton," Dirkson said, "I know how hard this is for you and I'll try to be as brief as possible. Please tell me, what is your relationship to David Castleton?"

Stanley Castleton blinked twice. His lip trembled, and when he spoke, his voice quivered. "He is my son."

Dirkson nodded. "Thank you, Mr. Castleton. Now, I ask you, on June twenty-ninth were you asked to go to the morgue to identify a body?"

"Yes, I was."

"And did you identify it?"

"Yes, I did."

"Whose body was it?"

This time his whole face seemed to quiver. Tears brimmed in his eyes. He opened his mouth to speak, choked back a sob. He exhaled, took a breath, then croaked, "It was my son. David."

Stanley Castleton dissolved into sobs.

Dirkson paused a moment before saying softly, "Thank you. That's all."

Judge Wallingsford said, "Does the defense wish to cross-examine?"

Fitzpatrick looked a question at Steve.

Steve looked over at Stanley Castleton weeping on the witness stand. There was no way he could cross-examine him without alienating the jury. Hell, some things worked and some didn't. Steve took a breath. He shook his head. "No questions, Your Honor."

"The witness is excused," Judge Wallingsford said.

Stanley Castleton might not have heard him. He just sat there, sobbing. Dirkson had to come forward, put his hand on his shoulder, lead him from the witness stand.

Steve Winslow gritted his teeth. It was a hell of a moment, guaranteed to prejudice the jury against the defendant. But there wasn't a damn thing he could do about it.

When Stanley Castleton had finally been escorted from the courtroom, Dirkson recalled Detective Oswald from the Crime Scene Unit, who testified to finding a gun next to the decedent. The gun was produced, identified and marked for identification as People's Exhibit 3.

He also testified to finding a folded piece of paper in the decedent's pants pocket. The paper was produced, identified and introduced into evidence. Oswald then read what was written on it into the record. The paper proved to be a note, written in ink, of an address and apartment number. Oswald was able to testify that he had personally gone to that address and could verify that it had turned out to be the apartment of the defendant, Kelly Clay Wilder.

That caused some raised eyebrows in the courtroom. Dirkson hadn't even mentioned the note in his opening statement. Obviously this was a case where the prosecution had more evidence against the defendant than it could ever possibly need.

Finally Oswald testified to developing and photographing latent fingerprints in the decedent's apartment, and photos and fingerprint lifts were received into evidence.

Steve Winslow took him on cross-examination, which created a stir of interest among the jurors. Up till now they seen only Fitzpatrick. And Fitzpatrick looked like a lawyer. But what was this young man with long hair and sloppy clothes up to?

Naturally, the jurors expected Steve to cross-examine Oswald on the gun and the note.

He did neither.

"Officer Oswald," Steve said. "You testified to taking photographs in the decedent's apartment, did you not?"

"Yes, I did."

"Now, in addition to taking the photographs, you were a witness to what you photographed, were you not?"

"Yes, of course."

"You examined the apartment for evidence, did you not?"

"Yes, I did."

"Was there a computer in the apartment?"

"Yes, there was."

"Does it show in the photographs you took?"

Detective Oswald frowned. "I'm not sure."

Steve picked up the stack of photographs from the court reporter's desk and handed them to the witness. "Well, take a look and see."

Detective Oswald thumbed through the photographs. "Yes, here it is," he said. He held up the photograph and pointed. "You can see it here, in the upper left-hand corner."

"Which photograph is that?"

Oswald turned it over and looked at the back. "That is People's Exhibit Five-N."

"I see," Steve said. "And does the computer show in any of the other photographs?"

Oswald riffled through them. "No, it does not."

"I see," Steve said. He took the photographs back from the witness. "And since you weren't sure if the computer was in the photographs at all, and since it only appears in one of them and only in the background, and since these are photographs of the objects from which you obtained latent fingerprints, am I correct in assuming you got no fingerprints from the computer?"

"That is correct."

"Is that unusual?"

Oswald shook his head. "Not at all. A computer keyboard is like a typewriter. The keys are struck many times. There's no hope of getting a clear latent print. Only indecipherable smudges."

"Which is what you got in this case?"

"That is correct."

"Then let me ask you this. Is there any chance those indecipherable smudges might contain enough whorls and arches, no matter how fragmented, to be able to attempt a comparison with the prints of any known person?"

"I would say no."

"But that is just your opinion?"

"It is an expert opinion."

Steve smiled. "Yes, it is. But the manner in which you just expressed it was, 'I would say no.' You didn't *say* no. You told me that's what you *would* say. Which is not exactly the same thing, and which indicates a certain degree of doubt."

Oswald shook his head. "There is no doubt in my mind. If I misspoke myself, I apologize. What I said was a figure of speech. If you want to build on it, I can't stop you. But the fact is, I would say no, because the answer is no, so that's what I would say."

That sally brought smiles to the faces of some of the jurors. Dirkson grinned approvingly.

Steve Winslow took no notice. "That may well be," he said. "But I'd rather let the evidence speak for itself. Tell me, did you photograph the keyboard of the computer?"

"No, I did not."

"Why not?"

"I told you. Because there were no legible prints."

"Which you have no way of proving, since you didn't take the photograph of the keyboard."

"Objected to as argumentative," Dirkson said.

"Sustained."

"*Did* you photograph the keyboard?" Steve asked.

"Objected to as already asked and answered."

"Sustained."

Steve Winslow frowned. "No further questions."

In the back of the courtroom, Mark Taylor nudged Tracy Garvin. "What's he up to now?"

Tracy leaned over to whisper. "Giving the impression the prosecution's hampering his investigation by being overly technical."

Taylor grinned. "You're gettin' good at this."

Next, Dirkson called Phillip Riker from the police crime lab, who testified to examining the fingerprints that had been received in evidence.

"Mr. Riker," Dirkson said. "Did you compare those prints with the known prints of any person or persons?"

"Yes, I did."

"And who would that be?"

"Well, I first compared the prints with the prints taken from the decedent, David Castleton."

"With what results?"

"The majority of the prints were his. May I consult my records?"

"Please do."

Riker took a notebook from his jacket pocket. "Yes, here we are. There were thirty-one prints in all. Twenty-six of them proved to be prints of the decedent, David Castleton."

"The remaining five—did you compare those with the known prints of any person?"

"Yes, I did."

"With what results?"

"Four of those prints matched absolutely with the known prints taken from David Castleton's cleaning lady, Joyce Wilkens."

"I see," Dirkson said. "And the one remaining print—did you compare that with the known prints of any person?"

"Yes, I did."

"With what result?"

"That print matched absolutely with the right thumb print taken from the defendant, Kelly Clay Wilder."

There was a murmur in the courtroom. Judge Wallingsford silenced it quickly with the gavel.

"Thank you, Mr. Riker," Dirkson said. "To which print are you now referring?"

"May I see the exhibits?"

"Certainly," Dirkson said. He handed the fingerprint lifts to the witness.

Riker riffled through them, compared them to the list in his notebook. "Here we are," he said. "I'm referring to the lift marked for identification as People's Exhibit Six-J. It is the print I compared to the right thumbprint taken from the defendant, Kelly Clay Wilder."

"And where was that print found?"

"It was taken from the doorknob of David Castleton's apartment."

"The front doorknob?"

"That is correct."

"The outside doorknob?" Dirkson asked.

"No, sir. The inside doorknob."

Dirkson let the jury see his smile of satisfaction. "Thank you, Mr. Riker," he said. "That's all."

Steve Winslow rose to cross-examine. "Mr. Riker," he said. "Were you present at the scent of the crime?"

"No, I was not."

"You compared prints furnished to you by the Crime Scene Unit?"

"That is correct."

"Then when you state that the thumbprint of the defendant, Kelly Clay Wilder was taken from the inside doorknob of David Castleton's apartment, you are not testifying to what you personally observed. You are going by the information furnished you on the fingerprint lift. Is that right?"

"No, it is not."

"It is not? How can that be if you were never at the scene of the crime?"

"I'm willing to explain if you'll allow me."

"Please do."

"Certainly I rely on the information on the lift as a guideline, but I am not basing my testimony on it. In addition to comparing the defendant's fingerprints with the fingerprint found on the lift, People's Exhibit Six-J, I also compared it to the photograph of that fingerprint taken in place on the doorknob. I believe that photograph has also been introduced into evidence. Now I can't swear to you that's the doorknob of David Castleton's apartment, since I've never been there—you'll have to go by the testimony of other witnesses for that. But as to where that one particular fingerprint came from with regard to the set of fingerprints— well, I'm not taking the word of what anyone told me. It is my own personal observation that the fingerprint came specifically from the doorknob in the photograph."

Winslow nodded, as if conceding the point. "Well answered, Mr. Riker. You yourself didn't gather any fingerprints from the scene of the crime, did you?"

"I've already stated I was never there."

"That's right, you did. So in comparing the fingerprints found at the scene of the crime, you were only able to compare those fingerprints furnished to you, is that right?"

"Of course."

Steve Winslow leafed through the photographs on the evidence table. "I call your attention to the photograph People's Exhibit Five-N. Would you please take a look at it?"

The witness took the photograph.

"Do you see a computer in the upper left-hand corner?"

"Yes, I do."

"Did you examine any fingerprints taken from that computer?"

"No, I did not."

"So, if there were any legible fingerprints on the keyboard of that computer, you would have had no way to compare them, would you?"

"Objection. Argumentative."

"Sustained."

"*Were* there any legible fingerprints on the keyboard of that computer?"

"Objection. Not proper cross-examination."

Judge Wallingsford frowned. "Overruled."

"Were there any fingerprints on that computer."

Riker shook his head. "I can't answer that."

"Yes, you can," Steve said. "You can say yes, you can say no, or you can say you don't know."

"Objection."

"Sustained."

"Do you know for a fact, of your own knowledge, if there were legible prints on the keyboard of that computer, yes or no?"

"Objection."

"Overruled."

Riker took a breath. "No."

Steve smiled. "Thank you, Mr. Riker. So you don't know. I didn't think you did. That's all."

"Oh, Your Honor," Dirkson said.

"Exactly," Judge Wallingsford snapped. "Mr. Winslow, you will avoid such side remarks."

"Yes, Your Honor."

Dirkson next called a handwriting expert who testified that he had examined the note of the defendant's address that had been found in the decedent's pocket, and determined that it had definitely been written by David Castleton.

When the defense did not cross-examine, Judge Wallingsford took note of the time and adjourned court until ten o'clock the next morning.

32

"DID YOU TYPE on the computer?"

Kelly Wilder frowned at Steve Winslow through the wire mesh screen of the lockup. "Yes, I did. Why?"

"Because if you didn't, there's no use my pushing the point."

"That's what I mean. Why are you? What's the big deal?"

"If there's any chance at all, I want to be able to show you typed on the keyboard of David Castleton's machine."

"Why? What's the point?"

Steve took a breath. "Sooner or later we gotta make a big decision. The decision is whether you tell your story. If you do, we need all the corroboration we can get."

"What do you mean, *if* I tell my story?"

"Just that. A murder trial's a funny thing. There're no set rules. You can play it any way you want."

Kelly's eye's blazed. "Damnit. Don't give me half-assed rhetoric. Talk about me."

"I'm talking about you."

"No, you're not. You're talking bullshit. Now cut it out and give me a straight answer. Are you gonna let me tell my story? If not, why not? What the hell is going on?"

Steve took a breath. "Okay," he said. "Am I gonna let you tell your story? Right now I don't know. I know that's no answer, but it's the way things stand. It depends on what the prosecution does. But the way things look, yes, I am going to put you on the stand. You're gonna have to tell your story and you're gonna have to tell it straight, and then you're gonna take the biggest beating you ever took in your life. Dirkson may not look like much, but so far you're only seen his good side. He's puttin' on his case, those are his witnesses, he's bein' nice to 'em. You get on the stand, you're in for a jolt, 'cause that sarcastic son of a bitch is gonna tear you apart."

"I can take it."

"Great, wonderful, I'm proud of you," Steve said dryly. "But that's not the point. Dirkson's gonna make you look like a scheming, lying slut. If you can take that, bully for you, but in the eyes of the jury you're still gonna look like a scheming, lying slut."

Steve paused and ran his hand over his dead. "I'm sorry. I don't mean to be rough on you, but I gotta make you understand. The thing is, you're so wrapped up in this you only see it from your point of view. *You* know you went up to David Castleton's apartment to show him the disk on the computer. But you're the only one who knows that. When you tell your story, the jury will be hearing that for the first time. They're not gonna believe it unless it checks out.

"Now, the disk that you left with David Castleton disappeared. And the disk you left in your apartment disappeared. Which leaves nothing. A big fat zero. You're telling your story with nothing to back it up.

"Now you see why I want to be able to show you typed on that keyboard?"

"I see that, but—"

"But what?"

"You say I got nothing to back it up. You're wrong. I got Herbert."

"Yeah," Steve said flatly.

Kelly's eyes blazed. "Damnit—"

Steve held up his hand. "Hey, let's not get into it. Herbert's your brother, you love him, you trust him, you believe him. Fine. I'm not going to say a word against him. But the fact is, in the eyes of the jury he's a convicted embezzler and he's your brother and his testimony ain't worth a damn. Now that may not be fair, but that's the way it is. The bottom line is, I need something to corroborate your story, and Herbert's testimony doesn't count."

Kelly glared at him but said nothing.

"Okay," Steve said. "Now, if you go on the stand and tell your story, you got one shot and that's it. So it better be the truth. Every bit of it. You let Dirkson catch you in one lie, any lie, no matter how small, and you're through. If we can't prove everything you say, well, that's all right. But if Dirkson can *disprove* any of it, that's the ball game. You understand that?"

"Yes."

"So I gotta know you're telling me the truth."

"I've told you the truth."

"You did find a memo in the backup file?"

"Yes, I did."

"And copied it?"

"Yes."

"And gave a copy to David Castleton?"

"Yes, I did."

"That's the truth?"

"Yes, that's the truth."

Steve Winslow stared at her a few moments. He sighed. "It better be."

33

WHEN COURT RECONVENED the next morning Dirkson recalled Detective Oswald of the Crime Scene Unit.

After Oswald had taken the stand and Judge Wallingsford had reminded him he was still under oath, Dirkson walked up to the witness, smiled and said, "Detective Oswald. You recall yesterday you were asked if you had ever photographed the keyboard of the computer in David Castleton's apartment?"

"Yes, I do."

"And what answer did you make at that time?"

"I said I had not."

"I ask you again if you have ever photographed the keyboard of the computer in David Castleton's apartment?"

Oswald smiled. "Yes, I have."

Dirkson raised his eyebrows. "Oh? And when did you do that?"

"Last night after court was adjourned. I went to David Castleton's apartment and took photographs of the computer in general and the keyboard in particular."

"I see," Dirkson said. "And what was the condition of the computer and keyboard last night when you went to the apartment to take those photographs?"

"They had already been processed for prints."

"What do you mean by that?"

"Fingerprint powder had already been dusted on the computer and keyboard in order to bring out any latent prints."

"Do you know who did that and when?"

187

"Yes. I did it myself on June twenty-ninth when I originally processed the apartment."

"The powder was still there?"

"Yes, it was."

"Did it show any latent prints?"

"No, it did not. There were several smudges on the keyboard, but not even remotely clear enough to classify."

"But you photographed them anyway?"

"Yes, I did."

"Do you have those photographs with you?"

"Yes, I do."

When the photographs had been produced and marked for identification, Dirkson said, "That's all."

"No questions," Steve said.

Dirkson then recalled Phillip Riker of the crime lab.

"Mr. Riker, I hand you these photographs marked People's Exhibits Seven A–F and ask you if you have ever seen them before."

"Yes, I have."

"And just when and where was that?"

"They were delivered to me at eleven o'clock last night at the crime lab."

"And what do these photographs show?"

"They are photographs of a computer and keyboard that have been processed for fingerprints."

"Do they show any legible fingerprints?"

"No, they do not. There are smudges, but none of them clear enough to classify."

"That is your expert opinion?"

"It is."

"I see," Dirkson said. "Now, despite the fact you say none of these smudges are clear enough to classify, let me ask you this. Did you make any attempt to compare the smudges in these photographs with the known prints of the defendant, Kelly Wilder?"

"Yes, I did. I was up all last night attempting to do so."

"And could you tell us your results?"

"Certainly. I found a total of seven points of similarity."

Dirkson narrowed his eyes. "Seven points of similarity?"

"That is correct."

"Tell me, in comparing a fingerprint, how many points of similarity are necessary to make a positive identification?"

"There is no set number that is universally demanded. But it is generally held to be ten to twelve."

"Ten to twelve?"

"That is the accepted standard. I consider it low, and always make an effort to find more points of similarity than that."

"But it is an accepted standard?"

"Yes, it is."

"Ten to twelve points of similarity are sufficient to make a positive identification? To say that one fingerprint compares exactly with the known fingerprint of another person?"

"That is correct."

"Now, in this instance you say you found seven points of similarity?"

"That is correct."

"Now, according to your testimony, that is not sufficient to make a positive identification."

"No, it isn't."

"Fine. But let me ask you this. Is it enough to indicate a likelihood? Can you say, well, seven is more than half the points required, if the fingerprint hadn't been smudged there's a good chance I could have found the other three to five points?"

"Not at all."

"And why is that?"

Riker smiled. "Because ten to twelve points of similarity is the number required for identification in matching a single fingerprint."

Dirkson raised his eyebrows. "You're saying that is not the case here?"

Riker shook his head. "Not at all. When I say I found seven points of similarity, I mean I found a *total* of seven points of similarity among *all* the smudged fingerprints and the fingerprints of the defendant, Kelly Clay Wilder."

"A total of seven?"

"That's right. And no two were within the same smudge. I found seven in seven separate smudges. Moreover, these seven points of similarity did not match up with one of the defendant's fingerprints, they actually matched up with five." Riker took a notebook from his jacket pocket and flipped it open. "To be precise, two of the points of similarity matched up with the defendant's right index finger. Two other points of similarity matched up with her left middle finger. One matched up with her right middle finger. One matched up with her right ring finger. One matched up with her left ring finger. And one matched up with her left thumb."

"I see," Dirkson said. "Now let me clarify this. When you say matched up with her finger, you mean matched up with *one point of similarity* in her finger?"

"Absolutely," Riker said. "I hope I didn't give the wrong impression. What I mean is there was one, and only one, point of similarity between, for instance, one of the smudges and Kelly Wilder's left ring finger."

Dirkson nodded. "I understand, Mr. Riker. Speaking as an expert, what significance does this evidence have? Being able to match one characteristic between a single smudge and a single finger?"

Riker shook his head. "None, whatsoever. In terms of making an identification it is absolutely meaningless."

Dirkson nodded. "Thank you. That's all."

"Does the defense wish to cross-examine?" Judge Wallingsford said.

Steve Winslow stood up. "Yes, Your Honor." He crossed in to the witness. "Mr. Riker, you are rather quick to say this has no scientific significance whatsoever."

"I say it because it's a fact."

"That may well be, but don't you think it's a fact we should judge for ourselves?"

"I'm an expert delivering an expert opinion. I doubt if the jurors have studied the science of fingerprinting."

"Maybe not, but that's still all it is—an opinion. It's your opinion the similarities between the prints on the computer and the prints of the defendant are meaningless. Is that right?"

"Yes, it is."

"But there *are* similarities."

"There are seven points of similarity, as I have already stated."

"Seven points where the prints on the computer correspond with the prints of the defendant?"

"That is correct."

"Then let me ask you this: did you find any thing to indicate those prints were *not* those of the defendant?"

The witness hesitated.

"Objection," Dirkson said. "Argumentative."

Judge Wallingsford frowned. "Overruled."

"Can you answer that, Mr. Riker?"

Riker frowned. "The answer to that question would be totally meaningless."

Steve smiled. "Yes, but Judge Wallingsford says I can have it."

Riker took a breath. "No, there was nothing to indicate they weren't the prints of the defendant."

Steve smiled again. "Thank you. That's all."

"Redirect, Mr. Dirkson?"

"Yes, Your Honor. Mr. Riker, you stated you found seven points of similarity between those prints and the prints of the defendant?"

"That's correct."

"Let me ask you this. Did you compare those prints with the prints of any other known person?"

"Yes, I did."

"With what results?"

"I found *eight* points of similarity."

"Eight points?"

"That's correct."

"One more point of similarity than you found with the defendant?"

"That is correct."

Dirkson nodded gravely. "I see," he said. "Tell me, Mr. Riker—with whose prints did you compare the smudges on the keyboard and get eight points of similarity?"

Riker smiled. "With my own."

There was a murmur in the courtroom. Judge Wallingsford banged the gavel.

"With your own, Mr. Riker?"

"That is correct. After I compared the smudges with the defendant's fingerprints and found seven points of similarity, I compared them to my own fingerprints and found eight."

"You found eight points of similarity between the smudges on the keyboard and your own fingerprints?"

"That is correct."

"Mr. Riker, have you ever been in David Castleton's apartment?"

"No, I have not."

"Ever type on that keyboard?"

"No, I have not."

"And you found eight points of similarity between your fingerprints and the smudges on that keyboard?"

"Yes, I did."

Dirkson's smile was rather a smirk. "Thank you. That's all."

34

AFTER THAT, Dirkson picked up speed. He seemed to draw strength from his strategic victory on the fingerprint evidence, and forged ahead with a vengeance, becoming even more of a showman and playing to the jury.

The jurors, of course, had no idea what the fingerprint evidence was all about, what Winslow had been hoping to prove. For that matter, neither did Dirkson. But it didn't matter. All the jurors knew was there had been a pitched battle and Dirkson had won. Dirkson used that as a springboard and played it for all it was worth.

First he called the ballistics expert, who testified conclusively that the bullet, People's Exhibit 2, had been fired by the gun, People's Exhibit 3.

Dirkson then called the manager of a sporting goods store to introduce records of the fact that the gun, People's Exhibit 3, had been duly purchased by and registered to Herbert Clay.

Steve Winslow did not cross-examine either of those witnesses. He knew nothing he could do would shake their testimony, and after the fingerprint fiasco he couldn't afford another fruitless argument.

After the witness had been excused, Dirkson said, "Call Herbert Clay."

There was an excited buzz in the courtroom.

Kelly Wilder squeezed Steve's arm. "Why are they calling Herb?"

"To identify the gun."

"Oh."

"And to show your brother's a convicted felon."

"Oh." She grimaced. "Why can't they leave him alone?"

"Shhh."

Two court officers escorted Herbert Clay in through the side door.

Steve took one look and sighed. They'd allowed Herbert Clay to dress for court, but even so, the impression he made was terrible. There was a certain arrogance about him, a sullen punk insolence that nothing was going to hide. He looked exactly like what he was—a convicted felon.

Herbert Clay took the oath and sat on the witness stand, glaring hostilely around the courtroom. Seeing this, Dirkson paused a few moments before starting his questioning, to let the jurors get a good look at him.

"What is your name?" Dirkson said.

The witness raised his eyes to glare sullenly at him. "Herbert Clay."

"What is your relationship to the defendant, Kelly Clay Wilder?"

"She is my sister."

"I submit, Your Honor, that this is a hostile witness and I should be allowed to use leading questions."

"Granted," Judge Wallingsford said.

Dirkson picked up the gun and crossed to the witness. "Mr. Clay, I show you a gun marked People's Exhibit 3 and ask if you have seen it before?"

Clay glared at Dirkson defiantly. "I don't know."

"You haven't looked at it."

"I've looked at it."

"And you don't know?"

"No."

"The serial number on this gun is nine three two four seven six two. Does that refresh your memory any?"

"No, it does not."

"Mr. Clay, I show you a gun register marked People's Exhibit Eight and ask if you have ever seen it before?"

"I don't know."

"I ask you to look at it more closely, and I ask you if this is not your signature right here on this page?"

Reluctantly, Herbert Clay looked where Dirkson was pointing.

"Is that your signature?"

"Yeah. So?"

"That is your signature here on this page of the gun register, indicating you purchased the gun with the serial number nine three two four seven six two?"

"Yeah. I guess so."

"Mr. Clay, once again I show you the gun marked for identification as People's Exhibit Three and ask you if you have ever seen it before?"

"I don't know."

"But you've seen a gun like it?"

"Yeah."

"You purchased a gun like it, did you not?"

"What if I did?"

"Is that the gun you purchased at that time?"

"I don't know."

"But you did purchase a gun similar to this one?"

"Yeah, I did."

"Why did you purchase that gun?"

"Because I wanted one."

Dirkson took a breath. "Mr. Clay. According to the gun register, you purchased this gun three years ago on September seventeenth. Is that right?"

"I guess so."

"Where were you employed at that time?"

Clay took a breath. There was an edge in his voice. "At Castleton Industries."

"Castleton Industries. Was that the company owned by Milton Castleton?"

"Yes."

"You were the bookkeeper there, were you not?"

"Yes, I was."

"Who was your immediate supervisor?"

Clay took a breath. "David Castleton."

"David Castleton, the decedent in this case?"

"Yeah."

"Mr. Clay, as bookkeeper, was it sometimes your job to deposit large sums of money for the corporation?"

"Yes, it was."

"Was that why you had the gun?"

"Yeah. That's why I had it."

"Where did you keep the gun?"

"In my office."

"In your office?"

"Yes. In my desk."

"You kept it in your desk so you would have it for those cash transactions?"

"That's right."

"Did you take the gun home with you?"

Clay shook his head. "Never."

"Never?"

"That's right. I kept it in the office."

"These cash transactions—these deposits you made—were they in the evening after work?"

"Sometimes."

"After you made a deposit, you'd go home, wouldn't you?"

Clay shook his head. "No."

"No?"

"No, I'd go back to the office and put away my gun."

"Even if it was late at night?"

"Sure."

"You could get into the office then?"

"Absolutely. There's a night watchman. Twenty-four hours. I could always get in."

"You always returned the gun to your office and never took it home?"

"That's right."

"And if your roommate, the man with whom you shared your apartment, should testify that he had seen the gun lying on your bureau, he would be mistaken, is that right?"

"Objection. Argumentative."

"Sustained."

"You say you never took the gun home?"

"Never."

Dirkson stood staring at the witness a moment. "Mr. Clay, have you ever been convicted of a felony?"

Clay's eyes blazed. He said nothing.

"Your Honor, would you instruct the witness to answer the question."

"Mr. Clay," Judge Wallingsford said. "You are required to answer."

"Have you ever been convicted of a felony?" Dirkson repeated.

"Yes," Clay snapped.

"What was the charge?"

"Embezzlement."

"You were convicted of embezzling over a hundred thousand dollars from Castleton Industries, were you not?"

Clay glared at the prosecutor. He took a breath, let it out slowly. "Yes."

"Mr. Clay, where do you currently reside?"

"Rikers Island."

"You are in jail?"

"Yes."

"For the embezzlement?"

"Yes."

"How long have you been there?"

"Two years."

"Mr. Clay, where were you on the night of June twenty-eighth?"

"There."

"In jail?"

"Yes."

"Mr. Clay, did you kill David Castleton?"

"No."

"Thank you. That's all."

"Does the defense wish to cross-examine?" Judge Wallingsford asked.

Not on your life, Steve thought. But he merely smiled and said, "No questions, Your Honor."

"Call Jeff Bowers," Dirkson said.

Jeff Bowers took the stand and testified that he knew Herbert Clay and had shared an apartment with him up until the time that he'd been sent to prison.

"Mr. Bowers," Dirkson said, "during the time that Herbert Clay shared your apartment, did you ever see him with a gun?"

"Yes, I did."

"I show you a gun marked People's Exhibit Three and ask you if that is the gun you saw in the possession of Herbert Clay?"

"It looks like it. I don't know if it's the same gun."

"Thank you, Mr. Bowers. Now when you say Herbert Clay had the gun in his possession, what do you mean?"

"I mean he had it on him. He was wearing it, in a holster on his belt."

"In your apartment?"

"That's right."

"On more than one occasion?"

"Oh yeah. Several times."

"Did you ever see the gun when he was *not* wearing it in a holster on his belt?"

"Oh, sure."

"When was that?"

Bowers shrugged. "I can't remember exactly. Again, it was several times. When he came home with the gun, he wouldn't walk around wearing it all evening. He'd take it off and leave it on his dresser."

"His dresser?"

"Yeah. Or he'd stick it in one of the dresser drawers."

"You saw him do that?"

"Yes, I did."

"On more than one occasion?"

"Several."

"Did he ever *leave* the gun in the apartment? When he went back to work, I mean."

"Yes, he did."

"On more than one occasion?"

"That's right."

"How many times?"

Bowers shrugged. "I don't know. Several times."

"It was common practice, then, for him to leave his gun at home?"

"Objection."

"Sustained."

"You say he left the gun at home several times?"

"Yes, he did."

"For how long? Just one day, or longer?"

"Longer."

"Are you sure?"

"Absolutely."

"How can you be sure?"

"He talked about it. He bragged about it, you know. About the gun and how much money he was carrying on him. He'd take out the gun, say, 'Guess what secret agent just smuggled ten thousand dollars through enemy lines.' "

"That's when he *brought* it home. How are you so sure he *left* it home?"

"I remember another time he came home and told me he just made a fifteen-thousand-dollar deposit totally unarmed because he'd forgotten to take his gun."

"Where was his gun?"

"In his dresser drawer."

"How do you know?"

"After he said that, he went in and checked to make sure it was there. He looked for it in the office, couldn't find it, then he came home and found it at home."

"I see," Dirkson said. "Now let me ask you this. Are you familiar with Herbert Clay's sister, the defendant, Kelly Clay Wilder?"

"Yes, I am."

"How do you know her?"

"She came to the apartment once. About four months ago."

"How did that happen?"

"When Herbert went to jail, I lost a roommate. That left me stuck for the rent. For a while it was all right. I'd been getting pretty steady work, and it was nice having my own apartment.

"Then money got tight, I got hit with a rent increase, and I decided I couldn't go it alone anymore. Herbert wasn't paying anything and Herbert wasn't coming back. So I wrote him a letter, told him I was gonna have to put his stuff in storage and rent the room.

"Then she called me. His sister. Kelly Clay Wilder. Said Herbert told her about it and wanted her to come pack his stuff for him."

"And she did?"

"Yes, she did. She came over with a bunch of boxes and tape and stickers, packed all his stuff and labeled it. A storage company came and carted it away."

"She packed up Herbert Clay's things?"

"That's right. All of it."

"Did you help her with it?"

He shook his head. "She wouldn't let me. Kicked me out of there. Said she'd do it alone. Very possessive, she was."

"Did you watch while she packed?"

"No. I offered to help her and she said no. Frankly, she was a nice-looking girl and I tried to make conversation with her, but she obviously wasn't having any of it, so I left her alone."

"So you didn't see her pack the boxes?"

"No, I did not."

"And there was nothing to prevent her from taking— Withdrawn. Mr. Bowers, do you recall if the defendant, Kelly Clay Wilder, brought anything with her to the apartment?"

"Like I said, cartons and tape."

"Aside from that?"

"Yeah. Her purse."

"What kind of a purse was it?"

"A drawstring purse. More of a bag, you know."

"Was it a large purse?"

"Yes."

"Big enough to hold a gun?"

Fitzpatrick was on his feet. "Objection, Your Honor. The question is viciously leading and suggestive. I ask that the prosecutor be admonished."

Judge Wallingsford banged the gavel. "Mr. Fitzpatrick, that will do. I will thank you to state such objections at the sidebar, out of the presence of the jury."

Fitzpatrick stood his ground. "The question was asked in the presence of the jury, Your Honor."

"I said that will do. The objection is sustained. Jurors, you are instructed to disregard that question. Is that clear? Proceed, Mr. Dirkson."

"Yes, sir. Mr. Bowers, did the defendant take those cartons with her when she left?"

"No. They were left for the storage van."

"Did she take *anything* with her when she left?"

"Yes. She took her purse."

Dirkson smiled. "Thank you." He paused a moment, then, "Mr. Bowers, did you kill David Castleton?"

Bowers frowned, then smiled and shook his head. "No, I did not."

"Did you know David Castleton?"

"No. I never met him."

"Do you know anyone from Castleton Industries?"

"No one. Except for Herbert Clay."

"Mr. Bowers, where were you on the night of June twenty-eighth between the hours of eleven and twelve?"

Bowers smiled. "I'm an actor. I was onstage in an off-Broadway production."

"At eleven o'clock at night? Isn't that long for a play to run?"

"It's a cabaret piece. It runs an hour and fifteen minutes. We do two shows a night, one at nine and one at eleven."

"So you were onstage that night from eleven o'clock until twelve-fifteen?"

"That's right."

"Thank you. That's all."

Fitzpatrick looked over at Winslow.

"Take him," Steve said.

Fitzpatrick rose, crossed to the witness. He frowned and said, "Mr. Bowers, I'm not sure what you and Mr. Dirkson were getting at in the latter part of your testimony. Perhaps you could clarify it for me. Is it your contention that you could not have taken Herbert Clay's gun and killed David Castleton because at the time of the murder you were onstage performing in cabaret theater?"

Bowers smiled and shrugged. "Isn't that obvious?"

"Yes and no, Mr. Bowers. If what you say is true, you couldn't have fired the fatal shot. But you certainly could have taken the gun. Isn't that right?"

Bowers frowned. "No. I didn't take it."

"But you had the opportunity to, didn't you?"

"I suppose so."

"There's no supposing about it. How long was it from the time Herbert Clay went to jail to the time the defendant, Kelly Clay Wilder showed up to pack up his room?"

"I don't know exactly."

"Was it over a year?"

"Yes, it was."

"And during that time Herbert Clay was in prison?"

"Yes, he was."

"And during that time you were the sole occupant of that apartment?"

"That's right."

"Then when you say you suppose you had an opportunity to take the gun, that's a pretty fair supposition, isn't it?"

"Objection." Dirkson said.

"Sustained."

"Did you have the opportunity to take the gun?"

Bowers took a breath. "Yes, I did. But I didn't take it."

"I'm not saying you did, Mr. Bowers. I'm just saying you had the opportunity. That's true, isn't it?"

"Yes."

"Thank you. Now, Mr. Bowers, during that time over a year when you were the only occupant of the apartment, the time during which you admit you had an opportunity to take the gun, did you ever search Herbert Clay's room?"

Bowers hesitated. "No, I did not."

"Perhaps you object to the word search. Did you ever *look* in Herbert Clay's room?"

"I looked in a couple of times."

"Did you? Good. Maybe you can help us here. You've testified that when Herbert Clay came home he sometimes left his gun on top of his dresser, is that right?"

"That's right."

"Now, on these occasions when you happened to look into Herbert Clay's room—referring now to the time when you were the sole occupant of the apartment after he'd been sent to prison—on those occasions did you happen to see the gun on the dresser?"

"I don't recall."

"Are you testifying that the gun was not on the dresser?"

"No, just that I don't recall seeing it."

"If the gun had been on the dresser, you'd have seen it, wouldn't you?"

"Objection. Argumentative."

"Sustained."

"Was the gun on the dresser?"

"I don't know."

"Do you recall specifically looking at the dresser?"

"No, I do not."

"Is there anything you *do* recall specifically looking at?"

"No. I tell you I just looked in the room. I wasn't looking for anything in particular."

"Did you look in the dresser drawers?"

"No, I did not."

"Never opened them?"

"No."

"After Herbert Clay went to jail, you never saw the gun again?"

"No, I did not."

"Then you have no knowledge whatsoever whether that gun was in your apartment?"

Bowers frowned. "No. I do not."

Fitzpatrick smiled. "Thank you. That's all."

Judge Wallingsford glanced at the clock. "It is approaching the hour of noon recess. I'm going to break now, and we'll resume at two o'clock."

35

WHEN COURT RECONVENED, Dirkson called Phil Danby to the stand.

"Mr. Danby," Dirkson began, "are you connected with Castleton Industries?"

"Yes. I've been employed by them for the past fifteen years."

"In what capacity?"

"My title is business manager, but I serve in several capacities. Chief among them is being personal assistant to Milton Castleton."

"You are referring to Milton Castleton, retired head of Castleton Industries, the grandfather of the decedent, David Castleton?"

"That's right. Up until his retirement, I served as his personal assistant at the company. Since his retirement, I have served as his liaison to the company."

"Am I to assume that, though retired, Mr. Castleton still has an active role in the business?"

Danby smiled. "I think that would be a safe assumption."

"Mr. Danby, where do you work?"

"I divide my time between Mr. Castleton's office, which is in his apartment, and the company itself. I am, as I said, his liaison."

"And you still have an active role in the company?"

Danby smiled. "Very much so."

"Mr. Danby, are you familiar with the defendant, Kelly Clay Wilder?"

"Yes, I am."

"How did you happen to meet her?"

"Mr. Castleton is currently writing his memoirs and employing secretaries to type them. He advertised in the *Times* and she answered the ad."

"She came to apply for the job?"

"That's right."

"Tell me, did she give you the name Kelly Wilder?"

"No."

"Or Kelly Clay?"

"No."

"What name *did* she give you?"

"Kelly Blaine."

"Kelly Blaine?"

"That's right."

"Tell me, did she get the job?"

"Yes, she did."

"She went to work for Castleton Industries?"

"No, for Milton Castleton. The writing of his memoirs he considered a personal matter, not a function of the company."

"Then he was employing her and paying her salary, rather than the company?"

"That's right."

"So where was she working?"

"In an office in his apartment."

"How long did she work for Milton Castleton?"

"About two weeks."

"And during that time did she ever meet Milton Castleton?"

"No, she did not. Her dealings were entirely with me."

"Tell me, Mr. Danby, at the time of David Castleton's death, was Kelly Clay Wilder still working for Milton Castleton?"

"No, she was not."

"How did that employment come to be terminated?"

Danby took a breath. "It was on the afternoon of June twenty-first. Milton Castleton was not there. He was off at a doctor's appointment. Kelly Wilder was in her office, typing at her word processor."

"She had her own office?"

"Yes, she did."

"Go on."

"I was in Milton Castleton's office next door. Looking up some facts on his computer. And I happened to notice Miss Wilder through the window."

"The window?"

"Yes. Mr. Castleton's office and Miss Wilder's office were side by side. There was a window between them."

"You saw her through the window?"

"Yes."

"Could she see you?"

"No. It's a one-way glass."

"What caught your attention at the time?"

"The screen of her word processor."

"What about it?"

"I have to explain. She was supposed to be typing memoirs. In other words, prose. But that wasn't what was on the screen of her terminal. From that distance, I could tell exactly what it was, but I could tell it wasn't prose. Screens were coming on, one after another, with symbols and instructions on them. That doesn't happen when you're typing. That happens when you're working in the Direct Operating System of the computer."

"Had Kelly Wilder any reason to be working in the Direct Operating System?"

"Absolutely none. Her job was simply to use a word processor that was functioning as a typewriter."

"I see. And from this, what conclusion did you draw?"

"Objection," Fitzpatrick said.

"Sustained.

Steve Winslow leaned across Kelly Wilder, tugged Fitzpatrick's arm. "Let this go in," he whispered.

Dirkson thought a moment. "Tell me, at that time, in your own mind, did you form any opinion about the defendant, Kelly Clay Wilder?"

"Yes, I did."

"And what was that?"

"She was an industrial spy."

"That was your evaluation of her?"

"Yes, it was."

"Can you tell me why you formed that opinion?"

"I could think of no other reason why she would be playing with the computer terminal."

"That terminal was hooked into the main computer?"

"Yes, it was."

"It would have access to the records of Castleton Industries?"

"Absolutely. The computer in Milton Castleton's office carried all the data of the entire company."

"Does Castleton Industries have industrial secrets worth stealing?"

Fitzpatrick looked at Winslow. Steve shook his head. "Let it go in."

Danby smiled. "I would imagine a competitor would pay a small fortune to get the inside track on Castleton Industries."

"I see," Dirkson said. "So how did you feel when you saw this?"

"I was outraged, of course. You have to understand. I have a great sense of loyalty to Castleton Industries and Milton Castleton."

"So what did you do?"

"I tried to stop her."

"How?"

"I ran out of the office to her office door. I took out a key and unlocked it."

"The door was locked?"

"Yes."

"Why?"

"That was one of the specifications of the employment. That she would work alone in an office with the door locked."

Dirkson nodded, as if that arrangement were perfectly reasonable, and did not follow up on the subject. "I see," he said. "So you unlocked the door and opened it?"

"Yes, I did."

"What did you find?"

"Miss Wilder was sitting at the word processor. When she saw me, she leapt up."

"What did you do?"

"I made for the machine."

"What did she do?"

"When she saw what I was doing she lunged for the machine, pressed a button on the keyboard."

"What happened?"

"Whatever had been on the screen disappeared and was re-placed by the page she'd been typing."

"Did you get a look at what had been on the screen before?"

"No, I did not."

"What did you do then?"

"I confronted her, demanded to know what she'd been doing."

"Did she answer?"

"No, she didn't. She kept backing away from me, around the desk."

"What did you do?"

"I followed her."

"What happened then?"

"When the desk was between me and the door, she turned and ran."

"Out the door?"

"Yes."

"What did you do?"

"I chased her."

"What did she do?"

"Ran down the hall and out the front door of the apartment."

"What did you do then?"

"I ran to the front door. By the time I got there, she was gone."

"I see," Dirkson said. "Tell me, Mr. Danby. What was the defendant wearing at that time?"

"Nothing."

"Nothing?"

"She was naked."

"Naked? And why was that?"

"That was one of the requirements of the job. Mr. Castleton's secretaries typed nude. That was why it was specified they would work alone in their own office with the door locked."

"I see," Dirkson said. "So for the two weeks the defendant had been working there, she had been working naked?"

"That is right.'

"She was naked when you confronted her and accused her of being an industrial spy?"

"That's right."

"She was naked when she ran out of her office and out the front door?"

"Yes, she was."

"I see," Dirkson said. "Tell me, Mr. Danby. From the time she ran out the front door of Milton Castleton's apartment, did you ever see the defendant again?"

Danby shook his head. "Not until today."

"Let me ask you this. Did you ever *talk* to her again?"

"Yes, I did."

"And when was that?"

"The first time was on June twenty-seventh."

"The day before David Castleton was killed?"

"That's right."

"And how did that happen?"

"She called the office."

"Mr. Castleton's office?"

"Yes."

"Who answered the phone?"

"I did."

"And it was the defendant, Kelly Clay Wilder?"

"Yes, it was."

"Did she identify herself?"

"Not as Kelly Wilder. She identified herself as Kelly Blaine."

"Which was the name you'd known her by?"

"Yes."

"What did she want?"

"She wanted to talk to Mr. Castleton."

"*Did* she talk to Mr. Castleton?"

"No. I told her she couldn't talk to him, she'd have to talk to me."

"What did she do?"

"She said, 'Too bad,' and hung up."

"What happened then?"

"She called back an hour later."

"What did she want?"

"The same thing. To talk to Mr. Castleton."

"What did you tell her?"

"That if she'd come to the apartment, Mr. Castleton would be willing to talk to her."

"I assume you'd conferred with Mr. Castleton in the mean-time?"

"Yes, I had."

"What did she say to that?"

"She wouldn't do it. She said she wanted to meet Mr. Castleton alone in a public place. I told her that was out of the question. Mr. Castleton was in poor health, he wasn't going to meet her in a public place and certainly not alone."

"What happened then?"

"She said 'Too bad," and hung up."

"Did she call back again?"

"Yes, she did."

"What happened in that conversation?"

"She repeated her demands. I told her they were out of the question. Then I suggested a compromise."

"What was that?"

"While Mr. Castleton couldn't go and meet her, he would send his grandson, David, in his place."

"What did she say to that?"

"We talked about it some, and the end result was she agreed to the arrangement."

"She agreed to meet David Castleton?"

"That's right."

"And this was on June twenty-eighth, the day he was killed?"

"That's right."

"And that was the last time you talked to the defendant?"

"Yes, it was."

"Then let me ask you this. Did you speak to David Castleton on June twenty-eighth?"

"Yes, I did."

"At what point did you speak to him?"

"After the last phone call from the defendant, I conferred with Milton Castleton, then I called David Castleton on the phone."

"Called him where?"

"At work. At his office. At Castleton Industries."

"What did you tell him at that time?"

"I told him it had been arranged for him to meet the defendant that evening, and immediately after work he should come by his grandfather's apartment to confer with me and Milton Castleton and then go meet the defendant."

"Did he agree to this?"

"Of course."

"Did he come to Milton Castleton's apartment?"

"Yes, he did."

"What time was that?"

"Around five-fifteen."

"He met with Milton Castleton at that time?"

"Yes, he did."

"Were you present at that meeting?"

"Yes, I was."

Dirkson turned to Judge Wallingsford. "Your Honor, I maintain that the conference between David Castleton and his grandfather, Milton Castleton, on the evening of David Castleton's death is part of the *res gestae* and therefore admissible in evidence."

Judge Wallingsford frowned. "So far, there's been no objection from the defense. Let's proceed, and deal with this if and when there is one."

"Very well," Dirkson said. He turned back to the witness. "Now, Mr. Danby, what was the substance of that meeting between David Castleton, Milton Castleton and yourself?"

"It was in the nature of a briefing."

"A briefing?"

"Yes. We told him what was going to happen and what we expected him to do."

"Which was?"

"Primarily, to find out who she was and what she wanted."

"And why was that?"

"Well, you have to understand. At this time, we had no idea who the defendant was. We knew her only as Kelly Blaine. And we knew that name was bogus."

"How did you know that?"

"Because we'd tried to get in touch with her and failed. The name she gave us was obviously bogus. The address she gave us did not exist."

"Why were you trying to get in touch with her?"

"To find out what her game was. At first it seemed obvious. On the afternoon of the incident, when she left work, her attorney, Steve Winslow, showed up, charging us with sexual harassment and unjust termination and demanding a settlement on the part of the defendant."

"And how was that situation handled?"

"We paid him off. Milton Castleton wrote him a check for fifty thousand dollars."

"Fifty thousand dollars?"

"Yes. At the time it seemed dirt cheap. We were glad to pay and be rid of her. Because this seemed to indicate she was not an industrial spy after all, just an unscrupulous woman pulling a shakedown."

"If that's true, why did you want to get in touch with her?"

"Because we weren't entirely convinced. There was still that business about her playing with the computer. We'd talked to her attorney, but we wanted to talk to her personally to make sure the matter was absolutely settled."

"And did you?"

"No. That was when I tried to contact her and learned that the name, address and telephone number she had given us were bogus."

"What did you do then?"

"Well, that confirmed our worst fears. Despite the settlement, we were afraid of what this woman might do next. So we made every effort to find out who she was."

"How did you do that?"

"We sent David Castleton to her attorney's office. We primed him to tell a story indicating that he was attracted to the defendant and wanted to date her."

"And did that approach work?"

"No, it did not."

"He was not put in touch with the defendant?"

"No, he was not."

"So David Castleton knew all about the situation before you called him in on the night that he was murdered?"

"That's right."

"Getting back to that night, he met with you and Milton Castleton after work, then went out, presumably to meet the defendant?"

"That's right."

"And where was he going to meet her?"

"At the Cove, a singles bar on Third Avenue."

"Who chose that as the meeting place?"

"We did. It was a place near the office where David was used to going. I suggested that location in my last phone call with the defendant."

"And she agreed to it?"

"Yes, she did."

"She agreed to meet him there?"

"Yes."

"At what time?"

"Seven o'clock."

"What time did David Castleton leave his grandfather's apartment that night?"

"I'm not exactly sure. About six-fifteen or six-thirty."

"And that was the last time you saw David Castleton alive?"

"Yes, it was."

"And the instructions you gave him at that time were to meet with the defendant, try to find out what she wanted and in particular to try to find out her real name and address?"

"That's right."

"Thank you. That's all."

Judge Wallingsford had just turned toward the defense table when Dirkson said, "Excuse me, Your Honor, that's not all. I'm sorry, Your Honor, there's one more matter I forgot to bring up. Mr. Danby, are you familiar with the defendant's brother, Herbert Clay?"

"Yes, I am."

"How do you happen to know him?"

"He was an employee of Castleton Industries."

"Who was his immediate superior in the firm?"

"David Castleton."

"Do you happen to know if Herbert Clay owned a gun?"

"Yes, I do."

"Did you ever see that gun?"

"Yes, I did."

"How did you happen to see it?"

"He had the gun for his work. As bookkeeper, it was sometimes his job to deposit large sums of cash. He carried the gun for
his protection."

"You saw him on some of those occasions?"

"Oh, yes. In many instances I actually gave him the money."

"So you were familiar with his gun?"

"I wouldn't say I'm familiar with it, but I've certainly seen it."

"I show you a gun marked for identification People's Exhibit
Three, and ask you if that is the gun Herbert Clay had?"

Danby took the gun, looked it over. "I can't identify positively,
but it certainly looks like it."

"Thank you," Dirkson said. He took the gun back from the
witness. "Now, did there come a time when Herbert Clay left the
employ of Castleton Industries?

"Yes, there did."

"Can you tell us what happened at that time?"

"Yes. When it became clear that Herbert Clay was not going to
be returning to he firm, and we were going to have to replace
him, we naturally cleaned out his office to make way for the new
bookkeeper."

"Did you clean out the office yourself?"

"No. I ordered it done."

"Where you present when the office was cleaned out?"

"Yes, I was."

"What was done with Herbert Clay's belongings?"

"They were packed in boxes."

"Including the things in his desk?"

"Yes."

"Were you present when his desk drawers were cleaned out?"

"Yes, I was."

"Why?"

"While the employees were packing, I was sorting."

"What for?"

"To differentiate between Herbert Clay's personal possessions
and those belonging to the company. Naturally, all company papers and files needed to be turned over to the new bookkeeper."

"I see. So you did the sorting yourself?"

"Yes, I did."

"And in cleaning out his desk, did you happen to find his gun?"

"No, I did not."

"The gun was not in his desk at the time?"

"No, it was not."

"Thank you," Dirkson said. "That's all."

Steve Winslow stood up. "Mr. Danby, you mentioned me in your testimony, did you not?"

"Yes, I did."

"You said on the afternoon of the incident when Kelly Wilder left Milton Castleton's employ, I came to Milton Castleton's apartment, accused you of sexual harassment and improper termination, and effected a settlement. Is that right?"

"Yes, it is."

"Fine," Steve said. "On that occasion, when I came there and made those accusations, what explanation did *you* give for the defendant leaving her job?"

"Objection, Your Honor. Incompetent, irrelevant and immaterial."

Judge Wallingsford frowned. "Let's have a sidebar."

When the attorneys had gathered at the sidebar, Judge Wallingsford said, "Mr. Winslow, I tend to agree with Mr. Dirkson. This is certainly a side issue and hardly relevant."

"It relates to his bias," Steve said.

"We freely admit his bias, Your Honor," Dirkson said. "The witness is fiercely loyal to Castleton Industries and is biased against the defendant because he believes that she killed David Castleton. Any remarks he may have made about her leaving her employment are certainly a side issue."

"I suppose that would depend upon the answer given," Judge Wallingsford said. "Mr. Winslow, are you assuring me his answer *will* show bias?"

"The point is actually moot, Your Honor," Steve said. "The question is admissible for another reason."

"What is that?"

"It's an elemental rule of law that when the prosecution introduces part of a conversation on direct examination, the defense is entitled to the entire conversation on cross."

"But I didn't ask for any conversation," Dirkson said.

Steve smiled. "Come, come. Didn't the witness testify that I came to Milton Castleton's apartment, accused him of sexual harassment and demanded a settlement?"

"But that's not asking for a conversation."

"Do you contend that I came there and handed them my demand in writing, or perhaps conveyed it to them by mental telepathy?"

Dirkson frowned.

Judge Wallingsford said, "I think that's conclusive, Mr. Dirkson. As far as the court is concerned, the door is open. The objection is overruled."

After the judge and the lawyers had resumed their positions, Steve Winslow said, "I'll repeat the question, Mr. Danby. On the occasion when I came to Milton Castleton's apartment, accused you of sexual harassment and demanded a settlement, what explanation did you give for the defendant leaving her employment?"

Danby shifted position on the witness stand. "I believe I said that she had made improper advances toward me."

"You *believe* you said that?"

"No, I said that."

"That is what you said, Mr. Danby?"

"Yes, it is."

"That's mighty strange. You just got on the witness stand under oath and told us the defendant left Milton Castleton's employ because you caught her playing with the computer terminal and thought she was an industrial spy. Did you not so testify?"

"Yes, I did."

"Well, gee, which is correct, Mr. Danby? The story you told on the witness stand, or the story you told me that day in Milton Castleton's apartment?"

"I have testified to the truth."

"Then the story you told me in Milton Castleton's apartment was a lie?"

Danby took a breath. "It was not the entire truth."

"The *entire* truth? It wasn't true at all, was it?"

"Well . . ."

"Was it true or wasn't it?"

"No, it was not."

"It was a lie, was it not, Mr. Danby?"

"Objection. Already asked and answered."

"Overruled."

"Yes, it was."

"The story you told me that afternoon in Milton Castleton's apartment about how the defendant left her job was a lie, is that right?"

"Objection. Already asked and answered."

"Sustained."

"Mr. Danby, why did you lie to me that afternoon in Milton Castleton's apartment?"

"Objection."

"Overruled."

Danby hesitated. He seemed to be choosing his words very carefully. "You were the defendant's attorney. We didn't know what you knew. Since we were dealing at arm's length, we didn't want to give you any information you didn't already have. We didn't know what the situation was, we were playing it very cautiously."

"When you say we, you mean you and Milton Castleton?"

"That's right."

"Tell me, Mr. Danby. Did you just lie to me, or did you lie to Milton Castleton as well."

"Objection."

"Sustained."

"Did Milton Castleton know the story you were telling me was a lie?"

"Objection."

"Sustained."

"Mr. Danby, getting back to your explanation of *why* you lied to me, you say it was because you didn't know what was going on and you didn't know what I knew. Is that right?"

"Yes it is."

"So you were trying to protect yourself?"

"That's right."

"By yourself, you mean you and Milton Castleton?"

"That's right'.'

"Mr. Danby, I take it that you are fiercely loyal to your employer?"

"It is no secret that I am loyal to Milton Castleton."

"And you would do anything to protect him? Even lie?"

"Objection."

"Sustained."

"Thank you. That's all."

36

After Phil Danby's testimony, the next witnesses were somewhat of an anticlimax. Dirkson couldn't help that, but he was sharp enough to know it and to compensate for it. He simply shifted gears, quickly, coolly and methodically tracing David Castleton's last moments on the night of his death.

First he called the bartender from the singles bar on Third Avenue, who testified that David Castleton had showed up sometime in the vicinity of six-thirty to seven o'clock. David Castleton was a regular there, the bartender knew him well, and there was no doubt about it. He'd been at the bar, drinking and talking with a young woman who was not the defendant. But he had not left with her. He had left her at the bar to go talk to another woman who had just arrived. The bartender could not identify that woman as the defendant, Kelly Clay Wilder, and was forced to admit he had not been paying that much attention. Nor could he testify that David Castleton had left with this woman. All he knew was that from that point on he didn't recall seeing him again.

Next up was the cabdriver who testified to picking up a young man and woman outside the singles bar and taking them to Gino's, a small Italian restaurant on the upper East Side. The cabdriver could not identify the man, but testified that he thought the woman was the defendant. His identification of her was shaky at best, and on cross-examination Fitzpatrick all but made him retract it.

That turned out to be a moot point, because next up were the waiter and maitre d' from Gino's, both of whom knew David Castleton well and identified him absolutely, and both of whom were equally positive the woman he had dined with was Kelly Clay Wilder. The waiter also testified that he had served the veal no later than nine o'clock, and would not budge, despite a grueling cross-examination by Fitzpatrick.

Next came the cabdriver who had picked up a young man and woman and driven them from the restaurant to David Castleton's apartment. He introduced his trip sheet, which showed the time of the pickup, ten-twenty, and the exact address of the apartment, 190 East 74th Street. He could not identify the man as David Castleton, but his identification of Kelly Clay Wilder as the woman carried conviction. The cabdriver was young, cocky, slightly arrogant and obviously fancied himself as something of a stud. The jury had no trouble believing he would take particular notice of a woman as attractive as Kelly Wilder.

On cross-examination Fitzpatrick did a good job in forcing him to admit that he had not seen these two people enter the building where he had taken them and that for all he knew the defendant could have said good-night to the young man and walked off down the street.

But that didn't faze Dirkson. When Fitzpatrick was done, Dirkson simply stood up on redirect and said, "And what time was it when you dropped off these two people, one of whom was the defendant, Kelly Clay Wilder?"

"Ten-thirty."

"And once again, what address did you take them to?"

"One ninety East 74th Street."

Dirkson smiled and said, "That's all."

And when the defense had no further questions of the witness, Dirkson smiled again and rested his case.

37

"WE'RE GONNA put you on the stand."

Kelly Wilder blinked at Steve Winslow and Harold Fitzpatrick through the wire mesh. "I thought you weren't sure," she said.

"Yeah, well we are now," Steve said. "We have no choice. Dirkson's built up a strong case of circumstantial evidence, and frankly we haven't been able to shake it. Our only hope now is to tell your story and sell it to the jury."

"Good."

Steve shook his head. "It's *not* good."

"But I *want* to tell my story."

"I know," Steve said. "It's been bottled up inside you, it's been frustrating as hell, you want to tell the whole world. That's natural. But you don't know what you're in for. Because it's your story and you know it's true, so you think that's all there is to it. But no one else knows it's true, and no one else has even heard it. The jury will be getting this stuff for the first time. Believe me, they're gonna be skeptical. 'Cause you're gonna be contradicting things the prosecution's already sold them on. I'm not saying it's impossible, but I'm telling you it's no cakewalk."

"I know that. What do I have to do?"

"Just tell the truth. Simple, straight, the way it happened. Don't worry. Fitzpatrick will lead you through it."

"Fitzpatrick? Why not you?"

"Fitzpatrick will carry more weight with the jury. He'll be kind, sympathetic, a father figure."

Fitzpatrick grinned. "Thanks a lot."

"Now," Steve said, "we're not gonna rehearse your story—we don't want you to sound coached. Just tell it in your own words the way it happened. Just try not to get carried away."

"You mean don't get emotional?"

Steve frowned. "Yes and no. I don't want you to seem cold and detached—juries peg a person like that as a methodical killer. No, the whole thing's been a horrible experience, of course you're upset about it, and it's terribly frustrating to be on trial for a murder you didn't commit. That's only natural

"But try not to be bitter. Try not to come across as vindictive, because that's the picture that Dirkson's been trying to paint. See what I mean?"

"Yeah. Anything else?"

"Yeah. Tell the truth."

"Of course I'm gonna tell the truth."

"Yeah, but tell the *whole* truth. Don't leave anything out. And don't say anything that isn't so. Just let Dirkson catch you in one lie, however small, and you're through. Even if it's something as stupid as the color of the purse you were carrying, you either get it right or you say you don't know.

"This may seem stupid, but you haven't seen Dirkson in action. He'll get you confused on what you had for breakfast that day. And if he can get you to contradict yourself on anything, even once, there goes your whole testimony and there goes the case. It'll be 'How sure are you David Castleton was alive when you left? As certain as you were you had Rice Crispies that morning?' "

"That's stupid."

"It's stupid when I say it, but wait till you hear Dirkson."

"Won't you object to questions like that?"

"We'll protect you all we can, but it's a two-edged sword. If we're objecting all the time, the jury starts to think you need protection, that you can't handle yourself. They think, if her lawyers are afraid to let her answer questions, then she must be guilty."

Kelly bit her lip.

"So you see what you're up against," Steve said. "We're taking a gamble on you. We're gambling that your story about the computer disk is true. If it is, then telling your story is the only way to play it. But if it's not, god help you."

Kelly took a breath. "It's true. Every word of it."

"You left the computer disk with David Castleton?"

"Yes, I did.

"And you never told him your right name?"

"No."

"And you never told him your address?"

"No." Kelly frowned. "Would it be better if I said I did?"

"What?" Steve said.

"They found my address written down in his pocket. So if I say I didn't give it to him, they'll think I'm lying. So should I say I did?"

"*Did* you give him your address?"

"No."

Steve took a breath. There was an edge in his voice. "Do you understand what I just told you? If they catch you in the smallest lie, you're through. Now you ask me if you should tell a lie because it would sound better. And I have to wonder how much of the story you told us is really true."

"It's all true. I swear it."

"Then get that stupid idea out of your head. If you say you gave him your address, you'll have to answer a million questions about why you did it. And you don't have the answers, so you can't do it, and Dirkson will eat you alive. You tell the truth, you tell the *whole* truth, or you don't tell it at all.

"You got that?"

Kelly exhaled. "Yes," she said.

But she didn't look happy.

38

It WENT well.

When Fitzpatrick stood up and called the defendant, Kelly Clay Wilder, to the stand, it caused a buzz of excitement in the courtroom. This was going to be good. The defendant had never told her story to the police, to the press, to the public. Now they were finally going to get to hear it. The mystery woman, the beautiful young defendant, the woman whose name had been on the front page of the papers for days, the woman who had held down the bizarre job of typing nude for a multimillionaire, was finally going to speak. As she took the stand, the jurors were actually leaning forward in their chairs in anticipation.

And she was good. She told her story simply and directly in a clear, calm voice. And for the most part, she kept the bitterness out. As a result, her story came through.

Her brother had gone to jail for a crime he didn't commit. It was up to her to get him out. These were the steps she had taken to do that.

She told of meeting her brother in jail, of trying to jog his memory to find anything that might help to clear his name.

The mention of the memo caused quite a stir. It was the first the jurors had ever heard of it. It sparked their interest. The defendant's actions, almost incomprehensible up till now, suddenly took focus. Perhaps there *was* a reason for what she did.

Fitzpatrick led her skillfully through the next part of her testimony. How she tried to figure out a way to get inside Castleton

Industries. How she learned Milton Castleton was having his memoirs typed. How she saw the ad in the *Times*, applied for the job, and her subsequent interview with Phil Danby. And how she learned the job would require her typing nude.

She was good here too. She didn't duck the issue, she met it head on. She didn't want to work nude, she found it distasteful and demeaning, but she felt she had to do it to help her brother.

Fitzpatrick, conservative, kind, sympathetic, set just the right tone. And that difficult phase of her testimony came off without a hitch.

She told of using her terminal to tap into the main computer. Of searching Fax-log for the memo and finding it had been erased. Of searching the backup system and finding it.

That made quite a sensation. Some of the jurors were actually listening openmouthed to the rest of it. Of her copying the memo onto a floppy disk and hiding it in her purse. Of Danby surprising her and chasing her from the apartment. Of her attorney retrieving the purse and her finding the floppy disk still there.

And finally, her meeting with David Castleton.

"Now let me make no mistake about this," Fitzpatrick said. "You met with David Castleton, just as the prosecution said you did?"

"Yes, I did," Kelly said.

"You met at a singles bar on Third Avenue, you went by taxi to a restaurant called Gino's and proceeded to have dinner?"

"That's right."

"Over dinner you told him what you actually wanted?"

"Yes, I did."

"Did you tell him who you were?"

"No, I didn't."

"He had no idea you were Herbert Clay's sister?"

"No, he didn't."

"But he knew you were interested in the case?"

"Yes, of course."

"Then why did you go to his apartment?"

"To show him the memo."

"The memo you found in the Fax-log backup file in Milton Castleton's computer?"

"That's right."

"The memo you claim was sent to Milton Castleton by your brother, Herbert Clay?"

"Yes."

"How were you going to show it to him?"

"I had the floppy disk with me."

"You had it with you?"

"Yes. It was in my purse."

"Did you tell him that?"

"No, I did not. I only asked him if he had a computer. When he said he did, I asked him questions to find out if it was IBM compatible."

"What do you mean by that?"

"There are different kinds of computers. The floppy disk I had was for an IBM-compatible machine. It would only play on one of those."

"I see. And was his IBM-compatible?"

"Yes. I figured it would be. He would naturally want to have a computer that was compatible with his grandfather's, so he could transfer data back and forth."

"I see. And when you learned he had an IBM-compatible computer, what did you do?"

"I told him I wanted to go to his apartment."

"Did you tell him why?"

"No."

"Did you go?"

"Yes, we did."

"What time was that?"

"It was about ten-fifteen when we left the restaurant."

"How did you get to his apartment?"

"In a cab."

"Did the cab take you right to the door?"

"Yes, it did. David gave the cabdriver his address."

"What time did the cab let you out?"

"Around ten-thirty."

"You went up to David Castleton's apartment around ten-thirty?"

"Yes, I did."

"And what happened then?"

"I asked him to show me his computer."

"Did he?"

"Yes, he did."

"Then what?"

"He switched it on. I put the floppy disk in and I called up the memo."

"You showed the memo to David Castleton?"

"Yes, I did."

"Did he read it?"

"Yes, he did."

"What was his reaction?"

"Objection," Dirkson said, then seeing the looks of exasperation on the jurors' faces at this unwelcome interruption, said "Withdrawn."

"What was his reaction?" Fitzpatrick repeated.

"He was floored," Kelly said. "He couldn't believe it."

"Did he tell you that?"

"Yes. In exactly those words. He said, 'I can't believe it.' "

Fitzpatrick frowned. " 'I can't believe it' is a colloquial phrase expressing surprise. Did you understand David Castleton to mean that he actually didn't believe that this was a memo—"

"Objection," Dirkson said.

"Sustained."

"Miss Wilder, did David Castleton make any other comments about the memo?"

"Yes, he did."

"What did he say?"

"He was shocked."

"Objection. Not responsive to the question."

"Overruled. You can cross-examine on it. Go on, Miss Wilder."

Kelly took a breath. "Well, he was shocked. He said he couldn't believe that this had happened. He said his grandfather couldn't possibly have known about this, because his grandfather wouldn't have allowed it. And he couldn't imagine how this could have happened *without* his grandfather knowing about it. Because his grandfather was on top of everything. That's why he was shocked."

"I see," Fitzpatrick said. "Tell me, Miss Wilder, did he express any doubt about the memo?"

"Doubt?"

"Yes. Regarding it's authenticity. Was he skeptical? About what it was and where it had come from?"

Kelly hesitated. "Well, actually he did. In fact, he was quite skeptical at first. He asked me a lot of questions about the memo. About how I found it, about how I knew it was there, how I knew where to look for it."

"How did you answer those questions?"

"Well, you have to understand. David Castleton didn't know what you know. He didn't know I was Herbert Clay's sister. He didn't know I'd spoken to him in jail."

"What *did* he know? What did you tell him?"

"I told him he'd have to take me on faith. I told him that I had access to this information and had reason to believe it to be true."

"Did that satisfy him?"

"No, it didn't"

"What did?"

"Objection. There's no testimony that David Castleton *was* satisfied."

"Sustained."

"Were you able to satisfy him?"

"Not entirely. But I gave him an argument that he didn't have an answer to."

"What was that?"

"If what I told him wasn't true, why else would I have taken that despicable job?"

"What did he say to that?"

"He had no answer. I think he believed me."

"Objection. Move to strike."

"Overruled."

"What did he do then?"

"Well, he was very upset."

"Why?"

"Because of he implications. If Herbert hadn't embezzled that money, then someone else had."

"Who would that be?"

"Objection."

"Sustained."

"Did he *say* who that might be?"

"No."

"What *did* he say?"

"He said the whole thing made no sense to him. That Herbert Clay was the most likely suspect. That there was evidence Herbert liked to play the ponies, and for him to take the money was only logical. If he hadn't, it opened up disturbing possibilities."

"Why were they disturbing?"

"Objection."

"Sustained."

"Did he *say* why they were disturbing?"

"Yes, he did. He said he was Herbert's immediate superior. If Herbert hadn't taken the money, the most likely person would be himself."

"Did he say he had?"

"No, he most emphatically said he had not."

"Did you believe him?"

"Yes, I did. I didn't want to believe him, but I did."

"Why didn't you want to believe him?"

"Because he *was* the most likely person. He was the one I had suspected from the beginning. I knew it wasn't Herbert, so I thought it had to be him. But he said it wasn't him and I believe him. Particularly in light of what happened next."

"What was that?"

"He was murdered."

"I see. Tell me, did you discuss with him who it might have been? The embezzler, I mean?"

"Not in so many words."

"Well, what did you say?"

" I asked him who his immediate superior was in the company."

"And did he tell you?"

"Yes, he did."

"And who did he tell you his immediate superior was?"

"His father, Stanley Castleton."

This produced a reaction in the courtroom. Judge Wallingsford banged the gavel.

"What did you do then?" Fitzpatrick asked.

"We talked about it some more. David promised me he'd get to the bottom of this. He told me he'd take it to Milton Castleton first thing in the morning."

"When you say 'take it,' what do you mean?"

"The whole thing. What I just told you. Oh, I see. And the floppy disk. The one with the memo."

"You left that with him?"

"Yes, I did."

"You trusted him with it?"

"It was a copy. I still had the original."

"You left a copy with him?"

"That's right."

"How was the copy marked?"

"It was marked X dash one in gold pen on the top of the disk."

"You left that disk with David Castleton?"

"That's right."

"What time was it when you left his apartment?"

"Eleven-thirty."

When she said that, there was an air of anticipation in the courtroom. Her testimony was obviously winding down. The moment everyone had been waiting for was about to arrive. This beautiful, young defendant was about to be cross-examined by Harry Dirkson.

No one was looking forward to that moment more than Harry Dirkson himself. This marked the first time he had ever had a chance to cross-examine one of Steve Winslow's clients on the witness stand. Always before, Winslow had managed to maneuver things to prevent him from doing so. But not this time. The defendant was on the stand, she was Dirkson's meat, and nothing was going to save her.

Dirkson shifted restlessly in his chair. He couldn't wait to get a crack at her.

"Now," Fitzpatrick said, "when you left David Castleton's apartment at eleven-thirty that night, was he alive?"

"He most certainly was."

"And you left with him a floppy disk marked X dash one containing the memo you claim was written to Milton Castleton by your brother, Herbert Clay?"

"Yes, I did."

"And where was the original floppy disk? The one you used to copy the memo from Milton Castleton's computer?"

"In a box of floppy disks in my apartment."

"And was it marked?"

"Yes."

"How?"

"With a gold X."

"Do you know where that floppy disk is now?"

"No, I do not. I asked my attorney, Steve Winslow, to get it for me, and he informed me it is not there."

"Objection. Hearsay."

"Sustained. That remark will go out."

"I see," Fitzpatrick said. "But to the best of your knowledge, the original memo from which you copied the floppy disk still exists in the backup file in Milton Castleton's computer?"

"As far as I know."

"Thank you. That's all."

With the announcement, spectators burst out talking. Judge Wallingsford banged for quiet.

Dirkson rose to his feet.

But before Dirkson could cross over to the defendant, Steve Winslow stood up and said, "Your Honor, at this point I have a motion which must be made outside the presence of the jury."

Dirkson stopped in midstride. His face darkened. "Your Honor, I object. This is completely out of order. The defendant is on the stand, and I am about to cross-examine. The defense has no right to make a motion now."

"Your Honor, I ask to be heard," Steve said. "Not only is my motion in order, but by it's very nature it is a motion that can *only* be made now."

"Nonsense," Dirkson said. "Your Honor, this is a stalling tactic. To keep me from cross-examining the defendant. I insist that—"

Judge Wallingsford's gavel cut him off. "Mr. Dirkson, that will do. Whatever the actual case, this will not be argued in the presence of the jury. Bailiff, will you please show the jury to the jury room."

Dirkson fumed in silence while the jurors were led out. As soon as the door closed, he wheeled around. "Your Honor," he said angrily "this is exactly what I object to. Just by arguing this motion, counsel is accomplishing his purpose. Which is to prevent me from cross-examining the defendant. Which it is both my right and duty to do. I ask that you cite Mr. Winslow for misconduct."

Judge Wallingsford took a breath. "Mr. Dirkson, I understand your impatience, but you're getting ahead of yourself. You're arguing against a motion we have not yet heard. Let's find out what this is all about, and then I'll be able to tell if your argument has any validity. Mr. Winslow, what is your motion?"

"Your Honor, at this time I must ask that the defendant be temporarily excused from the stand so that the defense may put on some evidence out of order."

Dirkson's face purpled. "There, Your Honor. It's exactly as I told you. To get the defendant off the stand before I can cross-examine her. It's absolutely outrageous. The motion should be denied, and the attorney should be censured."

Judge Wallingsford nodded. "Mr. Winslow. Mr. Dirkson has a point. What possible reason can you give for removing the defendant from the stand at this time to put on additional evidence?"

"Because, Your Honor," Steve said, "the evidence I am referring to is by its very nature perishable. If I were not to introduce it now, there is a clear and present danger that this evidence might cease to exist."

"Perishable, Mr. Winslow?"

"Yes, Your Honor."

"Then I beg your pardon. Mr. Dirkson, if the evidence Mr. Winslow is referring to is indeed perishable, then his motion *would* have validity and I would have to consider it. But it is now necessary for us to go into the nature of the evidence." He turned back to Steve Winslow. "But I must warn you, Mr. Winslow. If it should turn out that this is *not* the case, if the evidence you are referring to is *not* pertinent, *not* perishable, in fact has no bearing on these proceedings whatsoever, if you indeed have made this motion merely as a stalling technique to prevent Mr. Dirkson from his right and just cross-examination, then you would indeed be in danger of being cited for misconduct. So be fairly warned, and think before you answer. Do you wish to continue with this motion?"

"I do, Your Honor."

"Very well. You are aware of what the consequences might be. Tell me. What is this evidence you wish to introduce?"

Steve Winslow turned and looked out over the courtroom to the man who was sitting in the back next to Mark Taylor and Tracy Garvin. "Mr. Pennington, would you please stand up?"

Pennington, a tall man with a thin face, a shock of untidy brown hair and horn-rimmed glasses, stood up.

Steve Winslow pointed. "Your Honor, this is Mr. Arthur Pennington. He is a senior technician with IBM. He is prepared to testify that what the defendant just told you about the backup system of the IBM computer is true, that it is possible to erase a document from the main files, and have that document still exist in the computer's backup system."

"So what?" Dirkson said. "The prosecution will stipulate that."

Steve went on as if he hadn't heard the interruption. "He is further prepared to testify that it's also possible for a person who knows computers to erase that same document from the backup file itself so that no trace of it could ever be found in the computer by any technique whatsoever.

"Now, Your Honor," Steve said, "Miss Wilder has testified that the memo existed in Fax-log and was subsequently erased from there. According to her testimony, that memo still exists in the backup file. And Your Honor will note that up until the time she gave her testimony, she was the only one who knew this. So if she is telling the truth, there is every reason to believe the memo still exists.

"But now that she has said so in open court, now that people know that it is there, Mr. Pennington will testify that anyone who didn't want that memo to be found could erase it just like that."

Judge Wallingsford frowned.

Steve pressed his advantage. "Your Honor must take judicial cognizance of the importance of that memo. The prosecution claims Kelly Clay Wilder killed David Castleton as part of a vindictive campaign against Castleton Industries. The defendant's testimony contradicts that. The crux of the defendant's testimony is the piece of evidence that she went there to retrieve. The piece of evidence that she found and gave to David Castleton. If that piece of evidence exists, it corroborates her story and demolishes the prosecution's theory, because why would she have killed

David Castleton after making him privy to information that could only persuade him to join her side?"

"Your Honor, Your Honor," Dirkson said. "This is the sheerest nonsense. The defense attorney has no right to make a speech. If that memo exists or not, it doesn't prove anything like he just said. How do we know she ever showed that memo to David Castleton? How do we know it turned him into an ally? We have only the defendant's word for that. She could have shown him the memo, he could have reacted in such a way as to lead her to believe *he* was the embezzler, she could have become angry and shot him over that."

A high-pitched, inarticulate grunt caused every head in the courtroom to turn.

Dirkson looked around to see Milton Castleton, his eyes flaming, attempting to pull himself out of his chair in the second row.

Dirkson's face flushed. He realized he'd gone too far. "I withdraw that, Your Honor." Dirkson said. "It was the wildest fantasy. I was just trying to show you how ridiculous the defense attorney's contentions are. We know nothing like that happened. What I am saying is, the existence of this memo, which I personally do not believe exists, wouldn't prove a thing he says it would. I ask that the motion be denied."

Steve opened his mouth to say something, but Judge Wallingsford held up his hand. "That will not be necessary, Mr. Winslow. The court is now going to rule. The court rules that once this matter has been brought up, it cannot be dropped. That in view of the defendant's testimony, in view of Mr. Winslow's assurances that Mr. Pennington would testify that if this memo does indeed exist that it could be erased, the court rules that the evidence *is* perishable and that steps will be taken to preserve it.

"The court makes the following directive. The court orders court officers to proceed immediately to Milton Castleton's apartment and seal up the premises until the evidence can be seen. The court further instructs that any attempt on the part of any of the parties involved to communicate with any of the occupants of the apartment shall be considered contempt of court. And that includes Mr. Castleton himself.

"The court further directs that Mr. Pennington, Mr. Fitzpatrick, Mr. Winslow, Mr. Dirkson and myself shall proceed immediately to Milton Castleton's apartment, and in our presence Mr. Pennington will examine that computer and see if that memo does indeed exist in the backup file. Mr. Castleton and his associates will, of course, be present.

"As this will effectively take up the afternoon, we will then adjourn for the day. The defendant is hereby remanded to custody, and the jurors may be sent home. The rest of us will proceed immediately to Milton Castleton's apartment to examine the evidence, and we will reconvene tomorrow morning at ten o'clock.

39

THE PROCESSION OF CARS made its way up Madison Avenue. Only three of the cars were official: the limousine carrying Milton Castleton, Stanley Castleton and Phil Danby; the car carrying Judge Wallingsford, Harry Dirkson and Arthur Pennington; and the car carrying Steve Winslow and Harold Fitzpatarick. The rest of the cars carried the hordes of reporters who, while they had no right to be there, weren't going to miss it.

The cars went across 72nd Street, down Fifth Avenue and pulled up in front of Milton Castleton's building. Winslow and Fitzpatrick got out in time to see Phil Danby and Stanley Castleton assisting Milton Castleton out of the limo. Judge Wallingsford, Dirkson and Pennington walked up and they all met in front of the apartment, where Milton Castleton was demonstrating that he was still very much in charge.

Castleton pointed a bony finger at Judge Wallingsford. "All right," he said. "You've ordered this, so I, of course, will allow it. If such a memo exists, I want to know it. But I have to tell you I don't believe a word of it, and I personally resent the intrusion."

"I understand, Mr. Castleton," Judge Wallingsford said. "And I hope you understand why it must be done."

Milton Castleton did not even acknowledge that. "Well, let's get on with it," he said irritably.

Dirkson cast an exasperated glance at the taxis full of reporters that had just pulled up. "Yeah, let's do it," he said.

The two court officers already stationed at the front door let them in, then moved with a degree of satisfaction to keep the reporters out.

Inside, an elevator large enough for all whisked them up to the eighth floor where they emerged in the spacious foyer of the floor-through apartment. Milton Castleton, with his son's and Phil Danby's assistance, led the way to the office. Danby opened the door and they went in.

Of the lawyers, judge and witness, only Steve Winslow had been in the office before. The others were slightly overawed, first, by its size, and second, by a sight that they all observed but no one pointed out or even alluded to—the curtained window in the office wall.

The huge computer was on the opposite wall. Pennington spotted it, rubbed his hands together happily, made for it and sat down. The others formed a semicircle around him. Pennington switched the computer on.

As the computer began to whir, Dirkson said, "At this time I'd like to renew my objection to this entire proceeding. I'd like to point out that even if the memo does exist, it proves nothing. The defendant admits fiddling with the workings of this computer. If Mr. Pennington should find a memo in the backup system, there is nothing to prove that the defendant didn't type it there herself."

"You pointed that out in the car, Mr. Dirkson," Judge Wallingsford said.

"I want to point it out in front of opposing counsel. I want to point out that Mr. Pennington, your own witness, bears out that contention. According to him a memo could be inserted in the backup system just as well as one could be deleted."

"You'll have a chance to make those points in court, Mr. Dirkson," Judge Wallingsford said. "Right now we are concerned with whether that memo exists at all. Is there anything you need, Mr. Pennington?"

Pennington was already beating out a rhythm on the keyboard. Letters and symbols were flashing on the screen. "I'll let you know," he said, and went on typing.

The words *Fax-log* appeared on the screen.

"Got it," Pennington said.

He continued to hit function keys. Documents went whizzing by.

"All right," Pennington said. "Here's the date in question. We have one, two, three memos on that day. One from a salesman in Austin, Texas." He hit a key. Another document appeared. "One from Stanley Castleton at the main office." He hit another key. "And one from a company in Palm Springs."

"Anything relevant in the Stanley Castleton memo?" Judge Wallingsford asked.

Pennington backed up a screen. The others leaned in and looked. The memo concerned the purchase of packing cartons.

"Nothing in that," Judge Wallingsford said. "And that's all for that date?"

Pennington pressed some keys. "That's right," he said. "Next memo you're into the next day."

"Those memos are recorded in chronological order?"

Pennington smiled, the smug smile of an expert at a layman's ignorance. "Of course," he said. "That's the purpose of the log."

"The defendant certain of the date?" Judge Wallingsford asked.

"Yes, she is," Steve said.

"All right, can you get into the backup file?"

Pennington seemed pained by the question. "Of course," he said. He began pressing keys at seemingly lightning speed, as if to show up Judge Wallingsford for doubting his competence. Symbols appeared and disappeared on the screen too fast for anyone to even read them.

Moments later, Pennington said, "Here we are. In the backup system. Now to get to Fax-log." More symbols flashed. "Here we go. Now the date."

Pennington hit more keys. Everyone leaned in to look, and one of the previous memos appeared.

"Here we are. The memo from the buyer in Texas."

He pressed a key.

"The memo from Stanley Castleton."

Another key.

"The memo from Palm Springs."
Another key.
And another memo they had seen before appeared.
The memo from the next day.
The memo from Herbert Clay was not there.

40

THE *DAILY NEWS* HEADLINE was "DEFENSE GAMBLE LOSES." The *New York Post* had "NAKED TYPIST STRIKES OUT!". Even the *Times* had a column on the front page.

It was hot stuff. The murder trial was sensational enough in itself. But to have the defense pull a grandstand play, a regular Perry Mason stunt, only to have it backfire—well, that was more than any newsman could have wished for. It not only made the papers, it was the lead story on the morning news on every radio and TV station in the city.

As a result, the courtroom was packed. Seating had been at a premium before, but now it was ridiculous. People were standing four-deep in the back of the courtroom and jostling for position.

Judge Wallingsford looked out over the courtroom and banged the gavel three times. "Order in the court. Ladies and gentlemen, somewhat against my better judgment, I have allowed spectators for whom there are no seats. Please understand that you are here at my tolerance, so do not abuse the privilege. If I cannot have quiet, I will order everyone who is not seated out. Is that clear?"

It was. The rumbling subsided. No one wanted to leave.

"Now then," Judge Wallingsford said. "Before we bring the jury in, let me explain the situation. The defendant was on the stand, but was removed from the stand so the defense could attempt to introduce some new evidence.

"Now, Mr. Winslow, you made a motion that you be allowed to

introduce new evidence at this time. I ask you now if you have any new evidence that you wish to introduce?"

Steve Winslow stood up. He took a breath. "I do not, Your Honor."

That announcement, though totally expected after all the publicity, still drew murmurs from the back of the courtroom.

Judge Wallingsford banged the gavel. "I will not warn the spectators again. Now then. The defense has withdrawn its motion to introduce new evidence. When that motion was made the defendant was on the stand, and the defense had concluded its direct examination. It is now time for the prosecution to cross-examine. So, will you bring in the jury and return the defendant to the stand—"

Judge Wallingsford broke off as he realized Harry Dirkson was paying no attention to him, but was instead conferring excitedly with an associate. "Mr, Dirkson?" he said.

Dirkson stood up and turned around. His face was such a confusion of emotions it was almost comical. He ran his hand over his head. "Your Honor, Your Honor," he said. "If I could have your indulgence for a moment."

"Yes, Mr. Dirkson. We are all waiting on you."

"I'm sorry, Your Honor. But before we proceed, a matter has arisen that requires my immediate attention."

Judge Wallingsford frowned. "You're asking for an adjournment, Mr. Dirkson?"

"No, no, Your Honor. Not a matter connected with my office. A matter connected with this case."

"The defendant was on the stand, Mr. Dirkson. And you were about to cross-examine."

"I know, Your Honor. But a matter has come up of which I was totally unaware. At least until a few moments ago. And it is a matter that is so grave, I feel I may be forced to take action. At this time, I must ask to reopen my case."

Judge Wallingsford stared at Dirkson. "Mr. Dirkson, you rested your case. If you have new evidence, you can bring it out on rebuttal. That is the proper way to do so. But I can think of no reason to allow you to reopen your case now."

"But I have new evidence, Your Honor, which should be introduced before I cross-examine the defendant. Evidence which will definitely link her with the commission of the crime."

"Then it should have been introduced as part of your case."

"I wasn't privy to the information, Your Honor. It has only come into my hands now. I have a witness who will definitely put the defendant at the scene of the crime."

Judge Wallingsford shook his head. "That is not proper procedure, Mr. Dirkson. If the defense raises an objection, as I am sure they will, I would have to sustain it."

Dirkson's face was grim. "The defense can *have* no objection, Your Honor. Because I am prepared to prove that the only reason this witness was unavailable in the first place was because this witness was carefully and deliberately concealed from us by the defense."

Judge Wallingsford's eyes widened. "That is a most serious charge, Mr. Dirkson. You mean the defense had full knowledge of the existence of this witness?"

"They did, and I can prove it," Dirkson said.

"They deliberately concealed this witness from you?"

"That is correct, Your Honor."

Judge Wallingsford took a breath. "And where is this witness now?"

There was a commotion in the back of the courtroom as the doors behind the spectators were thrown open.

"I believe she's here now," Dirkson said.

Everyone turned to look as two court officers pushed through the crowd leading in a defiant but rather harried-looking Marcie Keller.

41

MARCIE KELLER LOOKED like a beast at bay. She tossed her head, shaking the long, curly hair off her face, gripped the arms of the witness stand and glared defiantly down at Harry Dirkson.

She had been installed on the witness stand after a long, brawling argument between Harry Dirkson and Steve Winslow, at the end of which Judge Wallingsford had ruled that Dirkson be allowed to reopen his case.

The jurors, of course, had heard none of this. In fact, they had not been in court since early the previous day. So they had no idea what was going on, only that it was taking an unusually long time. The last they heard, the defense attorney was about to make a motion, so those jurors who had been responsible enough to heed Judge Wallingsford's admonition about not reading the papers had to figure the delay was on account of that. So they were absolutely bewildered when Judge Wallingsford informed them that it was the District Attorney who would be putting on new evidence and that Harry Dirkson had been allowed to reopen his case.

Which made the attractive young woman on the witness stand even more fascinating. She was not a surprise defense witness, she was a surprise prosecution witness.

And obviously a reluctant one.

What the hell was going on?

Dirkson, showman that he was, prolonged the suspense by pausing dramatically for several seconds and just standing there looking at the witness before crossing in to question her. When he did, he began slowly, gently, even conversationally, a slight smile on his lips but a hard glint in his eye. It was a good tactic, implying the easy assurance of a man who has every ace in the deck, and it created the desired effect. The witness is mine, Dirkson's attitude seemed to say. There is nothing to worry about. She won't get away.

"What's your name?" he asked.

Marcie took a breath. "Marcie Keller."

"And what is your occupation, Miss Keller."

Marcie's chin came up. "I'm an actress."

"An actress?" Dirkson said. "Now that's interesting. There are thousands of actresses in New York City. Competition for jobs is rather fierce. Tell me, are you presently employed?"

Marcie glared at him. "I am presently on the witness stand," she said dryly.

That sally drew a laugh from the spectators. Judge Wallingsford frowned and banged the gavel.

Dirkson was too shrewd to appear annoyed. He smiled, as if in appreciation of the answer. "Well said, Miss Keller. But I mean, are you working?"

"I did a *Kojack* last week."

"*Kojack?* The TV show?"

"Yes."

"Did you have a part in that, or was it extra work?"

"It was extra work."

"That's usually for a day, isn't it?"

"Yes."

"You worked one day on that show?"

"Yes, I did."

"Then that job is over. Tell me, Miss Keller, do you have a job today?"

There was an edge in Marcie's voice. "I *had* an audition today. Obviously I'm not going to make it."

"I'm sorry about that, Miss Keller, but some things take precedence. Then you don't have a job today?"

"No."

"Have you had an acting job since last week's *Kojack?*"

"No, I have not."

Dirkson nodded. "I see. Miss Keller, actors and actresses often don't have steady work. Many of them do other jobs—wait tables, drive taxis. Apart from your acting, do you have another job?"

"No, I do not."

"You are not employed elsewhere at the present time?"

"No."

Dirkson nodded. "Very well. Miss Keller, referring now to June twenty-eighth—did you have another job then?"

Marcie took a breath. "Yes, I did."

"Oh really? And who was that job with?"

"The Taylor Detective Agency."

"You were employed by the Taylor Detective Agency?"

"Yes, I was."

"In what capacity?"

"As an investigator."

Dirkson raised his eyebrows. "As a private detective?"

"If that's what you want to call it."

Dirkson smiled. "It's not what *I* want to call it, Miss Keller. It's what *you* want to call it. How would you describe your employment?"

"I was an operative of the agency."

"An operative?"

"Yes."

"What did you do as an operative?"

"Whatever I was told."

"Very commendable, Miss Keller. And who was your employer at the agency?"

"Mark Taylor."

"Mark Taylor? The head of the Taylor Detective Agency?"

"That's right."

"You took your orders from him?"

"Yes, I did."

"Very good, Miss Keller. Now, referring once again to the date June twenty-eighth—did Mark Taylor give you any instructions on that date."

"Objection to anything this witness was told to do by a third party," Steve said.

"Sustained."

In the back of the courtroom Tracy Garvin squeezed Mark
Taylor's arm. Mark Taylor looked positively sick. Tracy Garvin
had been keeping up a good front, but Steve Winslow's objection
cut through her like a knife. This wasn't the Steve Winslow she
knew, the heroic figure, standing up, battling insurmountable
odds and letting the chips fall where they may. No, the objection
was that of a desperate man fending off body blows, trying to
keep the damning evidence out. Tracy's stomach felt hollow.

"Very well," Dirkson said, unruffled at having the objection
sustained. "Never mind what you were *told*. Let's talk about
what you *did*. First off, are you familiar with the decedent, David
Castleton?"

Marcie took a breath. "Yes, I am."

"Did you see the decedent, David Castleton, on June twenty-
eighth?"

"Yes, I did."

"Where did you see him?"

"Outside Castleton Industries."

"On the street?"

"Yes."

"What was he doing?"

"Walking."

Dirkson frowned. "I'd like a little better answer than that, Miss
Keller. Do you mean to say you were standing outside Castleton
Industries and you saw David Castleton come out the front door?"

"Objection. Leading."

"The witness is obviously hostile, Your Honor," Dirkson said.
"Leading questions should be permitted."

"So ruled," Judge Wallingsford snapped. "Objection overruled.
Witness will answer."

"Is that right, Miss Keller? You were there and saw David
Castleton come out the door?"

"Yes, that's right."

"Had you ever seen him before, Miss Keller?"

"No, I had not."

"That was the first time you had ever seen David Castleton?"

"That's right."

"Then tell me, how did you recognize him, Miss Keller?"

Marcie hesitated. "I had seen his picture."

"His picture?"

"Yes. His photograph."

"Oh? And what kind of photograph was that?"

"It was a newspaper photo."

"I see," Dirkson said. "Tell me, who gave you that photo?"

"Mark Taylor."

"Mark Taylor? The head of the Taylor Detective Agency?"

"Objection. Already asked and answered."

"Overruled."

"Yes."

"Mark Taylor gave you a photograph of the decedent, David Castleton?"

"Yes, he did."

"And did you have that photograph with you when you were standing on the street outside Castleton Industries when you saw David Castleton come out?"

"Yes, I did."

"Did you look at the photograph at that time?"

"Yes, I did."

"And what time was that?"

"Five o'clock."

"Five o'clock in the afternoon?"

"That's right."

"I see," Dirkson said. "And what did David Castleton do?"

"He walked up the street."

"Up Third Avenue?"

"That's right."

"And what did you do?"

"I followed him."

"You followed David Castleton?"

"That's right."

"Was that as a result of instructions you received for your job?"

"Objection. Hearsay."

Judge Wallingsford frowned. "Sustained."

"Where did David Castleton go?"

"Up Third Avenue, over to Fifth Avenue and into a building."

"David Castleton went into a building on Fifth Avenue?"

"Yes, he did."

"Did you follow him in?"

"No, I did not."

"What was the address of that building?"

"I don't recall."

"You can't recall the address?"

"No."

"Then let me ask you this. Did the address of that building mean anything to you at the time? In other words, had you been told the address of that building and been told anyone lived there?"

"Objection."

"Sustained."

Dirkson frowned. Thought a moment. "Let's do it another way. Miss Keller, at the time you were following David Castleton, did you have a pocket notebook with you?"

"Yes, I did."

"Was the address of the building David Castleton went into written in your pocket notebook *before* you followed him to that address?"

"Objection."

"Overruled."

Marcie took a breath. "Yes, it was."

"Then that address *had* special significance for you?"

"Objection. Argumentative. Calls for a conclusion."

"Overruled."

"I was familiar with the address."

"Had you ever been there before?"

"No."

"But you had it written in your notebook?"

"Yes."

"Then answer me this. Did you have the *name* of anyone who lived there written in your notebook?"

"Yes, I did."

"And who was that?"

"Milton Castleton."

"Milton Castleton? The grandfather of David Castleton?"

"That's right."

"So," Dirkson said. "You followed David Castleton from Castleton Industries to his grandfather's address?"

"That's right."

Dirkson turned and smiled at the jury, as if to show what an ordeal it had been to establish that one simple fact. "Well, Miss Keller. That wasn't so hard now, was it?"

"Objection."

"Sustained."

"What time was it when David Castleton reached his grandfather's apartment building?"

"About five-thirty."

"When he went inside, what did you do?"

"I waited on the sidewalk."

"Until he came out?"

"Yes."

"What time was that?"

"About six-thirty."

"Where did he go?"

"He walked back across town to Third Avenue and down to a singles bar."

"You followed him?"

"Yes, I did."

"Did you go into the bar?"

"Yes, I did."

"What did David Castleton do in the singles bar?"

"He sat at the bar and ordered a drink."

"I see. And did you order a drink?"

"Yes, I did."

Dirkson smiled. "I see. Now tell me, Miss Keller, did there come a time when you spoke to David Castleton?"

"Yes, I did."

"Tell me. How did that happen?"

"I was standing next to him at the bar."

"What were you doing?"

"Ordering a drink."

"Another drink?"

"Yes."

"When you ordered your first drink, were you standing next to him?"

"No, I was at the other end of the bar."

"I see. You drank that, then moved down the bar and stood next to David Castleton to order another?"

"That's right."

"That's when you spoke to him?"

"Yes, it was."

"Tell me, who started the conversation, you or him?"

"I did."

"Tell me, Miss Keller, why did you speak to David Castleton?"

"To find out what he was doing."

"That was your job?"

"Objection to what the witness was instructed to do."

Judge Wallingsford took a breath. "Mr. Dirkson, there's a fine line here. Let's not cross it. The objection is sustained."

"Very well, Your Honor. What did you and the decedent talk about?"

"About his job."

"His job at Castleton Industries?"

"Yes."

"Did you talk about your job?"

"Yes, I did."

"What did you tell him your job was?"

"I told him I was an actress."

Dirkson smiled. "Which is the same thing you told the court."

"Objection."

"Sustained."

"Now, let me ask you this. Are you familiar with the defendant, Kelly Clay Wilder?"

"Yes, I am."

"Did you see the defendant Kelly Clay Wilder on June twenty-eighth?"

"Yes, I did."

"Where did you see her?"

"She came into the singles bar."

"The one where you were talking to David Castleton?"

"That's right."

"Were you talking to David Castleton at the time?"

"Yes, I was."

"What happened then?"

"He saw her come in, and got up and met her at the door."

"What did you do?"

"I went to the telephone."

"The telephone?"

"Yes."

"Did you make a telephone call?"

"Yes, I did."

"Who did you call?"

"The agency."

"The Taylor Detective Agency?"

"That's right."

"Who did you talk to?"

"No one. Well, actually, just the receptionist. Then I hung up."

"Why?"

Marcie took a breath. "Because I saw them start to leave."

"David Castleton and Kelly Clay Wilder?"

"That's right."

"So what did you do?"

"I followed them."

"Out of the bar?"

"That's right."

"What happened then?"

"By the time I got outside they were gone."

"I see," Dirkson said. "Tell me. You say you saw the defendant, Kelly Clay Wilder, come into the bar?"

"That's right."

"Had you ever seen her before?"

"No, I hadn't."

"Had you seen a picture of her?"

"No."

"Then how did you recognize her?"

"I didn't recognize her."

"Then how did you know it was her?"

"I didn't know it at the time. I know it now because I see her here in court."

Dirkson frowned. "You didn't know the woman who came into the bar was Kelly Clay Wilder?"

"No, I did not."

"Did you *suspect* it was Kelly Clay Wilder?"

"Objection."

"Sustained."

"Now, when you got outside the bar and discovered David

Castleton and Kelly Clay Wilder weren't there, what did you do?"

"I returned to the Taylor Detective Agency."

"Did you see anyone there?"

"Yes. Mark Taylor."

"Did you see anyone else?"

"Yes."

"Who was that?"

"Steve Winslow."

"Steve Winslow? The defendant's attorney?"

"That's right."

"You spoke with them?"

"That's right."

"After you spoke with them what did you do?"

Marcie raised her voice. "Well, Mark Taylor had instructed me to go home, but—"

"Objection," Dirkson said. "You already ruled this witness can't testify as to what she was instructed to do."

Judge Wallingsford smiled. "She can't be compelled to, but if she wants to volunteer it, that's another matter. Are you asking that the remark be stricken?"

"No, let's get on with it. Miss Keller, regardless of what you were instructed to do, when you left the Taylor Detective Agency, what *did* you do?"

"I went to an address on East Seventy-fourth Street."

"What address was that?"

"I can't recall exactly."

"Was *this* an address you had written in your notebook?"

"Yes, it was."

"Whose address was it?"

"The address of David Castleton."

"You went to that address and what did you do?"

"I waited outside the building."

"What were you waiting for?"

"To see if David Castleton would show up."

"I see. Tell me. Was there anyone else waiting with you?"

"Yes, there was."

"And who was that?"

"Dan Fuller."

"Oh? And did you know this person?"

"Yes, I did."

"How did you know him?"

"We worked together."

"For the Taylor Detective Agency?"

"That's right."

"I see. So the two of you waited there together?"

"That's right."

"You were waiting to see if David Castleton would show up?"

"That's right."

"Did he?"

"Yes, he did."

"What time was that?"

"Approximately ten-thirty."

"How did he arrive?"

"By taxi."

"Was anyone with him?"

"Yes."

"Who was that?"

"The defendant."

"You saw them get out of the taxi together?"

"Yes."

"What happened then?"

"They went into the building."

"You saw them go in?"

"Yes, I did."

"Could you see what happened after they went into the build-ing?"

"Yes, I could."

"And what was that?"

"They went into the elevator."

"The doors closed?"

"Yes."

"Tell me, did you see David Castleton again that night?"

"No, I did not."

"Did you see the defendant, Kelly Clay Wilder again that night?"

"Yes, I did."

"And what time was that?"

"It was eleven-thirty."

"And where did you see her?"

"She came out of the elevator and walked out of the building."

"Out of David Castleton's building?"

"That's right."

"Where did she go?"

"She walked across town to an address on Eighty-eighth Street."

"You followed her?"

"Yes, I did."

"The other detective—Dan Fuller—did he follow her too?"

"Yes, he did."

"You both followed the defendant?"

"That's right."

"To this address on Eighty-eighth Street?"

"Yes."

"What happened then?"

"The defendant went in."

"What did you do?"

"I stayed and watched the building."

"For how long?"

"All night."

Dirkson's surprise was genuine. "All night?"

"Yes."

"Till when?"

"Nine thirty the next morning."

"And how did you happen to leave?"

"Dan Fuller came, told me to go home."

"He hadn't stayed all night?"

"No, he'd gone home about one."

"And he came back at nine-thirty?"

"That's right."

"And that's when you went home?"

"Yes."

"All right. Tell me this. After you went home that morning—on the day of June twenty-ninth—did you meet with Mark Taylor of the Taylor Detective Agency and Steve Winslow, the attorney for Kelly Clay Wilder?"

"Objection," Steve said. "Incompetent, irrelevant, and immaterial. The prosecutor is now inquiring into matters that happened well after the decedent met his death, matters that happened outside the knowledge of the defendant and that can have no bearing on these proceedings."

"It goes to the bias of the witness, Your Honor."

"Overruled."

"Did you meet with Mark Taylor and Steve Winslow?"

"Yes, I did."

"I'm not going to ask you what was said in that meeting, but I am going to ask you this. Since that meeting have you ever communicated what you saw on the night of June twenty-eighth to the police?"

"No, I have not."

"Are you still in the employ of the Taylor Detective Agency?"

"No, I am not."

"When did you leave the Taylor Detective Agency?"

"June twenty-ninth."

"*Why* did you leave the Taylor Detective Agency?"

Marcie raised her chin defiantly. "I wanted to pursue my acting career."

Dirkson's eyes widened. "Oh," he said with elaborate sarcasm. "Your acting career. You chose this precise moment to pursue your acting career?"

"I thought I'd been neglecting it."

"Your detective work taking up too much of your time?"

"That's right."

"You left the Taylor Detective Agency to devote full time to your acting?"

"Yes, I did."

"So much so that you never heard of the murder of David Castleton or the arrest of Kelly Clay Wilder?"

Steve Winslow stood up. "Your Honor," he said. "Let the record show that I am appearing as the attorney for Marcie Keller. It now appears from his questions that the district attorney has reason to suspect this young woman of a crime. Therefore, at this time I am advising Marcie Keller not to answer that question on the grounds that an answer might tend to incriminate her."

That was the moment Dirkson had been waiting for. He turned to look at Steve Winslow and as their eyes locked, Dirkson's face broke into a triumphant grin.

Dirkson turned, shared his satisfaction with the rest of the court. "In that case, Your Honor," he said, "I have no further questions of this witness."

With that, the courtroom burst into an uproar.

42

Fitzpatrick's face was hard. "You should have told me."

Steve Winslow was slumped back in his desk chair. He ran his hand over his head. "I know," he said.

Fitzpatrick was sitting in the clients' chair. Mark Taylor, too agitated to sit, was pacing back and forth. Tracy Garvin stood in the background, looking on. Her eyes were sad.

"If you'd told me, this wouldn't have happened."

"If I'd told you, you wouldn't have taken the case."

"This is true."

"You have every right to be angry."

"I know."

"I let you down. I let Mark down. The whole thing's a mess."

"No argument here," Fitzpatrick said.

Steve straightened up in his chair, pointed his finger at Fitzpatrick. "But you're not on the hook, and you don't have to be," he said. "That's the saving grace. If I'd told you, you'd be in the soup. But I didn't. You didn't know any of this. You can testify to that, and Mark and I will back you up."

"Fat lot of good that will do."

Steve shook his head. "You're wrong. You don't have to take the fall for this, Fitzpatrick. You stand up in court tomorrow, you tell the judge all this comes as a complete surprise to you. You were caught flat-footed, taken aback and feel you cannot continue with the proceedings. You ask permission to withdraw from the case."

Fitzpatrick shook his head. "No, I don't."

"Why not?"

"I'm mad as hell, but I'm not a quitter. That would be unfair to our client and unfair to you." He pointed his finger at Steve. "Don't make any mistake, I'm pissed as hell. If you think I'd ever handle another case with you, you're out of your mind. But as far as this case goes, I'm sticking it out, sink or swim. So get your shit together and figure out what the hell you're gonna do. On the off chance you should happen to, do me the favor of letting me know."

Fitzpatrick stood up. "If you'll excuse me, I have to get back to my firm and see if I'm still senior partner or if the other partners got together and voted me out."

Fitzpatrick pushed past Tracy Garvin and went out, slamming the door.

"Can't blame him a bit," Steve said.

Taylor sighed. "That's a fact. Oh, Jesus Christ, what the hell are we going to do?"

"It's bad, Mark, but it ain't over yet."

Taylor collapsed into the chair. "That's easy for you to say. You know the law. I don't know shit. The way I see it, they got me dead to rights, I lost my license, and I'm up shit creek."

"You haven't lost anything yet."

"So what's my defense? The devil made me do it? My attorney made me do it? That ain't gonna cut no ice."

"I know how you feel."

Taylor looked at him. "Do you? You're an actor all your life. You're used to losing one job after another, bouncing from place to place. Me, what do I know? Football and this. If it weren't for the injury, if I'd played pro a year or two, I could have had a name, maybe opened a small restaurant. Or got a job on the radio doin' play-by-play. As it is, this is all I know. Fifteen years now. I'm not trained for anything else." He shook his head. "I just don't know what the hell I'd do."

"It ain't over till it's over."

"Great. Thanks, Yogi. Sorry to piss and moan. You got your own problems. But, Jesus Christ."

Taylor stood up. "I'm gonna get back to the office. See if anything's come in that will help. Like a plane ticket out of the country."

"It's not that bad, Mark."

"No," Taylor said flatly. "Of course not."

Mark Taylor went out. Steve leaned back in his chair, closed his eyes.

He felt a hand on his shoulder. He looked up to see Tracy standing next to him. Her eyes were misted over. "I'm sorry," she said.

"I know," Steve said. He sighed. "It's my own damn fault. I shouldn't have done it."

"No. You should. You did right."

Steve looked at her. "I did?"

"Of course you did. You have to fight for your client. That comes first."

Steve looked at her for a moment. Chuckled. Shook his head.

"What's so funny?" Tracy said.

"You. That's the thing about you. You think I did right because you like our client. That's the bottom line. You like her, so anything I did for her is okay in your book. If you didn't like her, you'd think I was a total schmuck. Remember how you felt in the Jeremy Dawson case?"

"You didn't do anything like this in the Jeremy Dawson case."

"That's for damn sure. If I had, you'd have pinned my ears back but good." Steve exhaled heavily. "Jesus, what a fucking mess."

"So what can you do?" Tracy said.

"Do?"

"Yeah," Tracy said. "We've been kicked in the teeth and we all feel bad. But it's not like you to just quit. So tell me, what the hell can you do?"

Steve shook his head. "I don't know. Believe me, I really don't know." He rubbed his head, then looked back up at her. Managed a small smile. "The way I see it, there's only one saving grace in the whole thing."

Tracy frowned. "What's that?"

"Dirkson reopened his case."

43

JUDGE WALLINGSFORD LOOKED down from his bench at the packed courtroom. He frowned, cleared his throat. "All right," he said. "Before we bring in the jury and proceed, let's attempt to determine where we are. Mr. Dirkson, when we left off yesterday you had just completed your direct examination of the witness, Marcie Keller."

"Yes, Your Honor."

"Where is the witness now?"

"She is in police custody, Your Honor."

"Has she been charged?"

"She is being held as a material witness."

"But she's already *been* a witness."

"It's entirely possible we may recall her, Your Honor. It's also entirely possible she may be charged."

"With what?"

"Withholding evidence. Obstruction of justice. Aiding and abetting. Possibly even as an accessory to the crime."

"But she has not been charged as yet?"

"No, Your Honor. Nor have any of the other principals in this matter. Mark Taylor, Steve Winslow or Harold Fitzpatrick."

Judge Wallingsford frowned. Steve Winslow rose to his feet. Judge Wallingsford held up his hand. "Hold on, Mr. Winslow. I'll handle this." Judge Wallingsford turned back to Dirkson. His face was stern. "Mr. Dirkson, this is neither the proper time nor the proper place for such remarks. Remarks that have no bearing

260

on the present proceedings and were in my opinion intended solely for the benefit of the public and the press. What you have alluded to may be a matter for the Bar Association, but it has no place here. And I warn you, if you make any remarks of that kind in the presence of the jury, any allegations of misconduct about the defense attorneys, any allusions to the fact that they might possibly be charged with a crime, you would be in serious danger of forcing me to declare a mistrial. You are the district attorney, and I should not have to point this out to you. Is that clear?"

"Yes, Your Honor."

"Now, if you were informing me that charges *had* been brought, that is something I might need to know. But alluding to the fact that charges *might* be brought is the type of insinuation and innuendo that is associated with the tabloid press and has no place in my courtroom. Is *that* clear?"

"Yes, Your Honor."

"Fine," Judge Wallingsford said. "Let's see if we can proceed. Two days ago the defendant was on the stand and had concluded her direct examination. Due to the peculiar turns this case has taken, she has yet to be cross-examined by the prosecution. I would hope that could be accomplished this morning, once these other matters have been set aside.

"When we left off yesterday, the witness Marcie Keller was on the stand, and had concluded her direct examination. You say she is in police custody, Mr. Dirkson?"

"That's right, Your Honor."

"I trust she is available to us?"

"Certainly, Your Honor. The officers are just awaiting your order to bring her in."

"Fine. Before we do so—Mr. Winslow, Mr. Fitzpatrick, may I ask if you intend to cross-examine this witness?"

Steve Winslow stood up. "We do not, Your Honor."

"That simplifies things," Judge Wallingsford said. "Then there is no need to have her in. Bring in the jury, and return the defendant to the stand."

Steve Winslow was still on his feet. "Before you do, Your Honor, while I have no questions of Miss Keller, at this time I would like to recall one of the other prosecution witnesses for cross-examination."

Dirkson jumped up. "Objection, Your Honor. That's out of order. The prosecution has rested its case."

"You reopened your case to put Marcie Keller on the stand, and you've not yet rested it again. I think the court reporter will bear me out on that."

"Well, I'm resting it now."

"You can't do that. I've already made my request to recall one of your witnesses."

"Your Honor, he's out of order," Dirkson said. "I insist you rule I've rested my case, and return the defendant to the stand. There is no precedent for him recalling another prosecution witness now."

"The order of proof is at the discretion of the court, Your Honor," Steve Winslow said. "The prosecutor interrupted the defendant's testimony to put on this witness out of order. To do so, he reopened his case. I must say that the unusual and unorthodox production of this testimony has caught me completely by surprise and forced me to reevaluate my case."

"Nonsense," Dirkson said. "How can he stand up here and say that when he knew about this witness all along, and *he* was the one who concealed her from me?"

"That's not at issue, Your Honor," Steve said. "As Your Honor has said, that is a matter for the Bar Association. What *is* at issue is that the prosecutor rested his case, and on the basis of that I decided to put the defendant on the stand. Now, before cross-examining her, the prosecutor has chosen to reopen his case. I submit, Your Honor, that for all the district attorney's bluster, this was done for no practical purpose except to embarrass the defense in general and me in particular."

"Nonsense," Dirkson said. "This is a material witness with pertinent information that had previously been withheld."

Steve smiled. "Perhaps," he said. "But Your Honor will note, there was actually no new information elicited from this witness. There is nothing in Marcie Keller's testimony that had not already been testified to on the witness stand by the defendant. The supposedly damaging facts she's testified to are things we've already cheerfully admitted. Therefore, I submit that the production of this witness was *not* made in good faith for the purpose of bringing out new evidence against the defendant, but was totally for the purpose of laying the groundwork for charges against the witness herself and the attorneys for the defense."

"That's ridiculous," Dirkson said. "Eyewitness testimony is always pertinent and admissible, even in the event the defendant has already admitted the crime."

"Let's try not to go off on a tangent," Judge Wallingsford said. "Mr. Winslow, *specifically*, what is it you contend?"

"I contend that the witness Marcie Keller was put on out of order. I also contend that had she been part of the prosecution's *original* case, I would have cross-examined the witnesses differently than I had, *before* I put the defendant, Kelly Clay Wilder, on the stand. It's too late to correct that now—her direct examination has already been given. But I feel at the very least I should be given an opportunity to augment my cross-examination of one of the prosecution's witnesses *before* the prosecutor uses this irregular testimony of Marcie Keller to cross-examine the defendant."

"Mr. Winslow. Do you have some definite purpose in mind?"

"Absolutely, Your Honor. It is crucial to my case to be allowed to cross-examine a witness at this time."

"I submit, Your Honor," Dirkson said, "that that is absolute nonsense, if not an out-and-out lie. The defense attorney has used every stalling tactic he can think of to keep me from cross-examining the defendant. This is merely another one of them. I submit that his only real intention here is to postpone the moment when I get to cross-examine the defendant on the stand. He is so desperate to avoid that, he is willing to try anything. If you allow him to recall one witness, he'll recall them all. And keep on recalling them until we have to adjourn and the case goes over the weekend."

Steve Winslow held up his hand and shook his head. "I give you my assurance, Your Honor, that this is not the case. I wish to recall one witness only, and my cross-examination will be brief. And as to the allegation that I am unwilling to let the prosecutor cross-examine the defendant, that simply isn't so. The defendant has told the absolute truth, and no cross-examination can hurt her. And as proof of this, let me state that if the prosecutor is willing to let me recall one of his witnesses for a brief cross-examination, I am willing to stipulate that when he cross-examines the defendant, the defense will not raise a single objection to any of his questions, whatever they may be."

Judge Wallingsford frowned. "This is entirely irregular, Mr. Winslow."

Dirkson was waving his hands. "Your Honor. Your Honor. One moment. On consideration, the prosecution is inclined to accept that stipulation."

Judge Wallingsford looked at him with exasperation. "Well, the court is not. I don't care what the prosecutor and the defense attorneys are willing to do, the court is not going to allow a defendant's rights to be stipulated away in that manner. I must say, if the defense attorney refuses to object, the court will impose objections for him. Is that clear?"

"Yes, Your Honor," Dirkson said.

"The court is now going to rule. Mr. Dirkson, since you seemed so willing to enter into that stipulation, I must conclude that you have no real objection to the defense attorney recalling one of your witnesses. Proof *is* at the discretion of the court. It is my discretion that the witness be recalled. The witness will be recalled, cross-examined, and then if *you* have no further questions, you may once again rest your case. At which time the defendant will be returned to the stand.

"Mr. Winslow, what witness do you wish to recall?"

"Phil Danby, Your Honor."

All eyes turned to the second row of the courtroom, where Phil Danby sat next to his employer, Milton Castleton.

"Very well," Judge Wallingsford said. "Bring in the jury. Phil Danby, take the stand."

While the jurors were being led in, Fitzpatrick leaned over to Winslow. "What are you doing?" he whispered.

"Gambling."

"On what?"

"Frankly, a long shot."

"Why are you doing that?"

Steve smiled grimly. "Because there's nothing else to bet on."

After the jurors had filed in and been seated, Judge Wallingsford addressed them. "Ladies and gentlemen of the jury. Yesterday, the witness Marcie Keller, completed her direct examination. The defense has no cross-examination of her and that witness has been excused. At this point, the witness Phil Danby has been re-called for further cross-examination.

"Mr. Danby, I remind you you are still under oath."

"Mr. Winslow. Mr. Fitzpatrick. Let us proceed."

Steve Winslow stood up, crossed in to the witness. He began his cross-examination almost conversationally, as Dirkson had done with Marcie Keller. "Mr. Danby, you testified, did you not, that you saw the defendant, Kelly Clay Wilder, on the afternoon when she left her employment with Milton Castleton, is that right?"

"Yes, it is."

"You further testified that while you spoke to her on the phone several times, you had not seen her since that day until you saw her here in court. Is that right?"

"Yes, it is."

"Is it, Mr. Danby? I don't think that's true. I put it to you that you saw the defendant, Kelly Clay Wilder, on June twenty-eighth, the day David Castleton met his death. Is that not a fact?"

"No, it is not."

"You didn't see the defendant on that day?"

"No, I did not."

"Really, Mr. Danby? Didn't you testify that on June twenty-eighth you were present at a meeting between David Castleton and his grandfather in Milton Castleton's apartment?"

"Yes, I did."

"I believe you referred to it as a strategy session, program-ming him for his meeting with Kelly Wilder?"

"Yes. That's right."

"What time did David Castleton leave the apartment?"

"Six-thirty. As I've already testified."

"And after David Castleton left for his appointment with the defendant, what did you and Milton Castleton do then?"

"Mr. Castleton was tired from the meeting and went off to bed. I went home to my apartment."

"You live alone, Mr. Danby?"

"Yes, I do."

"Then you can't verify that, can you?"

Danby shrugged. "I see no reason why I should."

"You know, Mr. Danby, I personally find that rather strange.

Your going home, I mean. You knew David Castleton was going to be meeting with the defendant. You were eager to find out the defendant's name, address, what she was up to. There was no reason to assume David Castleton would be able to get that out of her. I wonder why you would choose to go home and leave that entirely up to him."

"There's nothing strange about that," Danby said. "It simply wasn't that important. We wanted to know what the defendant was up to, yes. But you have to remember, a settlement had already been made. This woman obviously intended to cause trouble of some kind or another, but as far as we were concerned, we'd taken care of it. We'd primed David to handle it. There was no reason to assume it was so important it couldn't be entrusted to him. Now, if you don't want to take my word for it, ask Milton Castleton and he'll tell you the same thing. I did not involve myself personally at that point because it simply wasn't that important."

Steve smiled. "It may not have been that important to Milton Castleton, but I submit, for reasons unknown to him, it may have been that important to you. You testified that you left Milton Castleton's apartment and went straight home that evening?"

"Yes, I did."

"I put it to you that you didn't. Is it not a fact that after you left Milton Castleton's apartment you went straight to the singles bar on Third Avenue and staked it out from across the street?"

"No, it is not."

"I think it is. I think you arrived there shortly after David Castleton did. I think you looked through the window and saw him at the bar engaged in conversation with Marcie Keller, the woman who testified yesterday on the witness stand.

"Which of course puzzled you. David Castleton was there for a particular purpose, and he wouldn't be paying attention to any young woman unless she was the one coming on to him. Be that as it may, I think you then retreated from the window and continued to watch the bar from across the street. I think you were there when the defendant, Kelly Clay Wilder, showed up. You saw her go in, and you saw her and David Castleton come out.

"I think you tailed them to the restaurant Gino's, waited outside while they had their dinner and then tailed them back to his apartment.

"Where you ran into a strange situation. Two detectives were staking out the place. They didn't see you because you saw them first and took pains to see that they didn't.

"And how did you spot them before they spotted you? For that matter, how did you spot them at all? Very simple. Because one of the detectives happened to be the young woman you had already seen talking to David Castleton in the bar. So you knew what they were, and you knew who they were there for. So you stayed out of sight, watched and waited.

"And what happened? An hour later the defendant came out alone and walked back to her apartment. The detectives followed. You followed right behind. The defendant walked back to a brownstone apartment house and went inside. The detectives took up positions, staking it out. Minutes later, a light on the second-floor front window came on. You figured that was the best you could do. With the detectives watching, you couldn't get close enough to read the bell. Not without being seen. But you noted down the address.

"What did you do then? You went straight to David Castleton's apartment. He was surprised to see you, of course. He hadn't known you would be tagging along, because that wasn't part of the plan. I don't know what you told him, but probably something like his grandfataher had sent you as an afterthought. At any rate, you told him you'd been there, tailed the defendant to her home and found out where she lived. You still didn't have her name, but now at least you had her address.

"You gave him that address. You told it to him and had him write it down. That was the address on the folded piece of paper in his pants pocket. That's why he had only her address and not her name.

"Then you questioned him. How did it go? What had he found out? What did she want?

"What he said floored you. It was the worst of all. Exactly what you had feared. This woman had proof that Herbert Clay wasn't guilty of the embezzlement. The proof was a computer disk of a memo, which you thought had long since been erased from the files. But here it was, come back to haunt you.

"David Castleton showed it to you. Put the disk in and called it up on the computer. And there it was. The missing memo from Herbert Clay.

"David Castleton was very excited about it. He was glad you were there. He couldn't wait to tell everyone. He was going to tell his grandfather first thing in the morning.

"Which was something you simply couldn't allow."

Steve paused, looked up at the witness. "And that's when you shot him, isn't it, Mr. Danby?"

Phil Danby appeared completely unruffled. If anything, his face showed the trace of a faint smile. "I most certainly did not."

"Oh, yes, you did. You shot him with Herbert Clay's gun. The gun you found two years ago when you supervised the cleaning out of Herbert Clay's desk, as you have already testified. It was right there, where Herbert Clay said it was. You found it and you took it. Probably well before his trial. You'd already framed him for embezzlement, but if that didn't come off you wanted to be prepared to frame him for something else. I'm sure you never dreamed at the time it would eventually be used to frame his sister."

Steve smiled. "Which is ironic, Mr. Danby. Because you didn't *know* she was his sister, did you? That was serendipity, wasn't it? You had the gun merely because it was a weapon that could not be traced to you. The police could figure David Castleton had taken it from Herbert Clay's desk and the murderer had picked it up in his apartment and used it. What a monumental stroke of luck it must have seemed to you when you found out the defendant and Herbert Clay were actually related.

"But that's what happened, isn't it? You shot David Castleton, and you dropped the gun next to him on the floor. Then you took the computer disk and got out. As far as you were concerned, it was a perfect frame. Even if the gun couldn't be traced to the defendant, there was enough evidence against her. You and Milton Castleton knew David had left to meet the defendant. Then there were the waiters, bartenders and cab drivers who could put them together. And the private detectives who could put her at the scene of the crime.

"You killed him between a half hour to an hour after she left, but no medical determination of the time of death could be that precise. And, as expected, without actually altering the facts, the medical examiner did everything possible to slant the time element in the prosecution's favor.

"There was only one more thing, one more gap you had to plug. The original computer disk. You left David Castleton's apartment and went straight back to Kelly Clay Wilder's.

"The young woman detective was still on guard. She showed no signs of leaving. If she had, you might have broken in that night. As it was, you had to let it go. You went home, got what little sleep you could and reported to work the next morning at nine o'clock at Milton Castleton's apartment. You were there when the police called to inform Milton Castleton of his grandson's death.

"I don't know exactly what happened after that. But Milton Castleton would be demanding immediate police reports, and being Milton Castleton he would get them. So you would know almost immediately of Kelly Clay Wilder's arrest. Some time after that and before I talked to the defendant and went to her apartment, you broke away from Castleton's long enough to go there and get the computer disk. You had no problem finding it—the copy had been marked X dash one. It followed the original would be marked simply X. You found it, you took it, verified what it was and then destroyed it.

"You did one more thing. You knew from what David Castleton had told you that Kelly Clay Wilder had found that memo in the backup system of the computer. You got into the backup system yourself, found the file and deleted it.

"That's what you did, didn't you Mr. Danby?"

Danby shook his head. "No, I did not."

"Yes, you did, Mr. Danby. Because everyone has a weakness. I'm not sure what yours is, but I would guess it's the stock market. I assume you gambled with speculative stocks and got over-extended, even for a man with your income. Which is why you embezzled from your employer and subsequently framed Herbert Clay for the crime. Which is why that memo was so devastating to you. Isn't that right, Mr. Danby?"

"No, it is not."

"Well, I happen to know that it is. You know how I happen to know?" Steve smiled. "Marcie Keller. Marcie Keller proves you did."

Phil Danby said nothing. His puzzled frown seemed quite genuine.

"That surprises you, doesn't it Mr. Danby? I thought it would. No, there is nothing in her testimony that implicates you. What implicates you is the fact she gave it at all.

"See, here's what happened. You had the perfect frame and everything was going fine. The prosecution was making a case, and you thought that would be that.

"But then I put the defendant on the stand and she told her story. The story about the memo.

"Which is when you panicked, Mr. Danby. The only time in the whole affair you lost your head and made a stupid move. But the bit about the memo scared you. You knew you'd erased it from the computer, but still hearing about it struck too close to home.

"So you tried to guild the lily. To convict Kelly Clay Wilder. To give the prosecution everything they needed to clinch the case.

"You phoned in an anonymous tip. A tip to the police to check out the Taylor Detective Agency for any young operatives, one male, one female, who might have had David Castleton under surveillance on the night of June twenty-eighth. The detective Dan Fuller has yet to be found, but they got Marcie Keller all right." Steve smiled. "Probably wasn't that hard, what with her being an actress. Probably just called SAG. Anyway, they found her and they put her on the stand.

"Which is what gives you away, Mr. Danby. Because, aside from Mark Taylor and myself, no one, the defendant included, knew those detectives were there. The only way someone could have known was if he was there too. You fingered Marcie Keller, Mr. Danby. And that puts *you* at the scene of the crime."

Steve bored in. "You killed David Castleton, Mr. Danby. Deliberately, in cold blood. You did it to cover up an embezzlement for which you had framed an innocent man. You took Herbert Clay's gun and you shot David Castleton dead. Didn't you, Mr. Danby?"

Danby's look was almost amused, his smile ironic, mocking. "No, I did not," he said.

There was a moment's silence.

"You son of a bitch!"

The shrill voice cut through the courtroom like a knife. All heads turned to stare.

On the aisle in the second row, Milton Castleton had struggled to his feet. With one hand he was gripping the back of the bench in front of him for dear life to hold himself up. With the other he was pointing a long, bony, accusing finger straight at his associate, Phil Danby.

Everyone's attention shifted from the pointing finger to the witness stand, where Phil Danby sat, where a transformation was taking place.

Under Steve Winslow's cross-examination Phil Danby had been calm, unruffled, hadn't turned a hair. But under the accusing glare of his employer, Phil Danby began to wilt. He simply could not meet the eyes of that frail, old man. Danby's eyes faltered, his face went pasty white, and he began to tremble.

Then all at once he turned suddenly and vomited over the side of the witness stand.

44

FITZPATRICK COULDN'T stop laughing. Whether it was genuine amusement, relief of nervous tension or perhaps embarrassment over the harsh things he'd said to Steve Winslow—most likely a combination of all three—the man had a pretty good case of the giggles.

"It's too much," Fitzpatrick said. "It's too much. I mean, I'm not sure this has a legal precedent. I mean, is throwing up on the witness stand considered an admission of guilt?"

Steve Winslow was leaning back in his desk chair, utterly drained. Too tired to answer, he merely smiled.

Fitzpatrick didn't mind. He was hyped with nervous energy and on a roll. "And what does the court reporter write, that's what I want to know? I'd like to get a look at the transcript. I mean, you get, 'Question:' 'Answer:' 'Question:' 'Answer:' Then you get, 'Question: (from spectator): "You son of a bitch." ' 'Witness barfs.' Is that what they write? 'Witness barfs?' Or do they write it phonetically? 'Blaaaaah!' "

Steve exhaled noisily, shook his head. "What a stroke of luck."

"Luck, hell," Fitzpatrick said. "You knew it. You had him. You were right up and down the line."

"No, I didn't," Steve said. "I never could have touched him in a million years. All I had going for me was his fear of that old man."

Fitzpatrick's grin faded. His eyes narrowed. "You played for that to happen?"

"Yeah, I did. I knew I couldn't break Danby myself. So I played to Castleton. Because I believed Kelly's story, particularly what David told her. That Milton Castleton is fair, Milton Castleton is just, Milton Castleton wouldn't let that happen.

"And Milton Castleton loved his grandson. I knew if I could sell him, he'd do the rest."

Fitzpatrick shook his head. "Jesus Christ. A man like Danby, so afraid of a sick old man."

The door opened and Mark Taylor and Tracy Garvin came in. "News from the front," Taylor said. "Danby caved in. He's making a full written confession."

"You're kidding," Steve said.

Taylor shook his head. "Not at all. He's comin' clean. When his boss turned against him it broke him. The way I get it, he'd rather go to jail than have to face him."

"Son of a bitch," Fitzpatrick said.

"What about Kelly?" Steve said.

"They released her. She's probably on her way over now."

Steve sighed. "What a fucking relief."

"Tell me about it," Taylor said.

"They release Marcie too?"

"Yeah," Taylor said. "She just called. You're not going to believe this."

"What? She wants her job back?"

"Not at all. She called her answering service. With her performance on the stand and her picture in the morning papers, she's had calls from talent agents from William Morris and ICM."

Steve grinned. "You're kidding."

"No. A literal Hollywood ending. Looks like you cost me an operative."

"Or two. Any word from Dan Fuller?"

"No. But from what Marcie says, after she read him the riot act he took off on a camping trip. I expect he'll resurface after Danby's confession hits the press."

"That's good," Steve said. "He was the joker in the piece, you know."

Taylor frowned. "What do you mean?"

"What I said to Danby on the witness stand, about tipping Marcie Keller to the cops, about how that's how I knew it was him. Well, it turned out I was right. But there was one other possibility. That was Dan Fuller got cold feet and phoned in the tip."

"Holy shit," Taylor said.

"Yeah," Steve said. "Hadn't happened, but that's what I was gambling on."

"You were gambling on a lot," Taylor said.

"I know. I don't feel good about it at all."

"So what's the situation?" Taylor said. "With Marcie and me and you guys? What difference will Danby's confession make?"

"We're off the hook," Steve said.

Taylor nodded. "You'll pardon a second opinion, but, Fitzpatrick, is that right?"

"Basically, yes," Fitzpatrick said. "Aiding and abetting, accessory after that fact." He shrugged. "You can't aid and abet an innocent person. And Kelly Clay Wilder had nothing to do with the crime. You and your detectives didn't have any knowledge about *Phil Danby's* involvement in this affair, did you?"

"No."

"There you are. Technically you still withheld evidence, but in the vernacular, who gives a shit?"

"Dirkson won't go after my license?"

Fitzpatrick shook his head. "Dirkson wouldn't dream of it. Dirkson wants to get this whole thing out of the press just as fast as he can."

Fitzpatrick stood up. "Well, I'd like to stick around until Kelly gets here, but I'm two weeks behind on my work. Make my apologies for me."

"Sure," Steve said.

Fitzpatrick took a breath, looked at Steve. "I said some rough things yesterday."

"They were deserved."

"Anyway, I apologize."

"I'm the one who should apologize."

Fitzpatrick waved his hand. "Whatever. I'm not good at this, but what I said about never working with you again. Well, I don't know how to say this. I'm not saying I ever *would* work with you again. I guess what I'm saying is, don't feel you have no right to ask."

Fitzpatrick smiled, nodded and went out the door.

"Hell of a guy," Steve said. He sighed.

Tracy took off her glasses, pushed the hair out of her eyes. "Hey, snap out of it," she said. "You're the gloomiest winner I ever saw."

"I don't feel much like a winner," Steve said.

There came the sound of voices from the outer office. Tracy pushed open the door and looked. "Kelly's here. She snagged Fitzpatrick."

Steve frowned. "Do me a favor, will you Tracy?"

"What's that?"

"Go out there and stall her off a few minutes. I want to talk to Mark."

Tracy frowned and nodded. "Sure."

She went out, closing the door behind her.

"Look, Mark—" Steve said.

Mark Taylor held up his hand. "You don't have to say it."

"Yeah, I do. I let you down. I let Fitzpatrick down. I took chances I had no right to take. We won, but that doesn't excuse it."

"So?"

"So, I'm sorry. I know it's not enough, but for what it's worth, I'm sorry."

"I know."

"I wouldn't have done it if I hadn't thought I had to."

"I know that too."

Steve sighed. "This isn't just an apology."

"What is it?"

"I guess it's a warning."

Taylor grinned, shook his head. "You don't have to tell me. I already know."

"What's that?"

"You're not about to say, 'Sorry, Mark, I won't do it again.' Because you can't promise that. You get a client, you lose all sense of proportion. You lose all sense of—Hell, you lose all sense. You'll do anything at all to protect that client, and nothing and no one's gonna stand in your way."

"I'm sorry. I don't know any other way to play it."

"So you're telling me you're real sorry this happened, but the next case that comes along you'll probably go out on a limb again."

Steve nodded. "Yeah, that's it."

"Okay. I stand warned."

"And?"

Taylor looked at him. He smiled. "Shit, Steve, we're friends. You take your business elsewhere, I will be really pissed off."

Steve exhaled, rubbed his head. He smiled. "Thanks, Mark. That means a lot."

The intercom buzzed. Steve picked up the phone. "Yeah, Tracy?"

"Fitzpatrick left, and Kelly's bouncing off the walls. With Danby's confession, they're reopening her brother's case, and the word is the conviction will be overturned and he could be out as soon as tomorrow. Kelly's absolutely ecstatic, and she can't wait to thank you. What shall I tell her?"

Steve chuckled. He grinned at Mark Taylor.

"Tell her to keep her shirt on."